Darkest Siege

Book One of the Blade Chronicles

Ryan Wilshusen

To Christopher Paolini, for inspiring me all those years ago

To my family, for never stopping their support and love

To my friends, a never ending source of ideas and characters

To you, the reader who has picked up this book

CONTENTS

Acknowledgments   i

Prologue   I

Part One: The Prophet   11

Part Two: The Outcast   81

Part Three: In Foreign Lands   111

Part Four: The Invasion   143

Part Five: Exodus   207

Part Six: Revelations   273

ACKNOWLEDGMENTS

This book would have never been possible if not for a multitude of people. I would have never been able to write this book if I hadn't had so much support from my family. My father and his amazing ability to bring clarity through questioning everything and insight on characters made my protagonists so much more believable. My mother, whose love and willingness to listen allowed me to explore almost any idea or concept, many of which are in this book. My sister is undoubtedly one of the sharpest and cold-hearted editors I know, and I love her for it. Without her, this book wouldn't be near the tale it is today.

My publishing consultant Lynn Eang, for answering even the smallest question I had throughout the publishing process.

To all of my English teachers who taught me how to really appreciate a well-written book as well as how to write one. Their instruction has made such a difference in my life and will continue to do so.

And finally, to Christopher Paolini, the author of the Inheritance Cycle. I first read his work when I was ten years old. I fell in love with the genre of fantasy and reading in general because of him. I sent him a letter of thanks for inspiring me to become an author when I started writing. Not only did he respond, he gave me advice and books he used to learn about writing. I still have that letter with me today and it reminds me of the continual inspiration and determination I needed to write this novel.

Prologue

Fellix gripped his spear tighter than ever before. This was it, either they defeated Vrasta here, or the Kingdoms would be lost. There was an unusual tension among the ranks and file in the camp. Many of them were here for the first time. *And half of them will be dead by the end*, he thought mournfully. He shook his head. Now was not the time to show fear. Not in front of his men. They needed him now more than ever. He was High Commander of the king's forces by default. Even the king had fallen. His father and six brothers had all died fighting Vrasta alongside him. Now it was up to him to face the evil. The other Kingdoms had lost their rulers, but even in their grief, they still sent men. The people knew how much depended on this battle. It was all on him...

He stood before his men now, spear in hand. His limp was prominent as he struggled up the stairs to the speaking platform they had cobbled together at the last minute. "My people!" he started. "You all have probably deduced I'm not exactly what you would call 'adept' at speeches." The crowd laughed softly as they remembered his first wartime speech. It had been a disaster. He hadn't been able to finish. But a kind of invigorating fire filled him that warmed him to the very core. He knew the feeling well.

The fire of desperation, Fellix thought. This would be his fourth battle against Vrasta. Despite his limp, and maybe because of it, Fellix had become known for his genius as a strategist. He had faced almost impossible odds, and yet emerged triumphant. But this battle had the most weighing on it. This speech could be the difference between confidence and cowardice, between a triumphant victory and a crushing defeat. This battle was for the fate of all four Kingdoms. This

"We stand on these plains as the last hope for the Kingdoms of Ollou, Rhyth, Stryne, and let us not forget our island brother of Gyllithia. Four of the greatest Kingdoms have gathered here to fight the greatest evil of our time. It is now or never!" The night's moon was bright in the sky, the torches illuminating the camps and giving off the smell of smoke, steel, and leather. Fellix slammed his spear into the platform with conviction. "Today, we will win! No matter the odds. Defeat is not an option! Neither is retreat! We will fight like the men we are! There is no great commander who did not have great men. So I implore you soldiers, lend me your courage and strength once more!" The cheers and battle cries that were unleashed before him made a small glimmer of hope in Fellix's heart shine a bit brighter. "We fight at dawn!" More cheers.

The night passed far too quickly for him after the speech. It was as though the Divine wanted this battle to take place quickly. Everyone formed up like they were supposed to. The griffin riders tried to keep their mounts at ease as best they could. The dark line of Vrasta's force was before them- an assorted lot of werewolves. The spearmen began slamming the butts of their weapons on the hard ground. "Stryne, Stryne, Stryne!" they chanted, "Stryne, Stryne, Stryne!" Fellix smirked. Many of those men weren't even from his Kingdom, but they still chanted for his homeland.

The young High Commander raised his arm and brought it down swiftly. The horn signaler gave three ascending notes, and the army began rushing forward. The only remaining griffin squadron took to the skies with a cry. The other army began to rush forward as well, the howls of werewolves filling the air. Their opposing drake squadrons flew upward, their scaled bodies rattling and claws snapping. Their leathery bat-like wings snapped through the air like a whip. Fellix scowled.

So Vrasta, you're not holding back this time. Fellix raised his left arm again, waving it up and down. It was a new signal, but he prayed the horn signalers caught on.

They did. Massive siege engines shot rocks forward into the opposing army. Fellix watched as the smooth boulders rolled unopposed through their ranks. Despite the engines, the battle was still extremely difficult. The front line kept buckling under the sheer numbers of the opponent. The griffins fared much better against the drakes than they had in the past. The new griffin formations Fellix had devised were paying off ten-fold. The drakes were being slaughtered, their huge falling bodies being cast into the armies below, causing chaos in the enemy ranks.

Fellix stayed at the back of his army. He wished he could join the fight, but his subordinates pleaded with him not to. In the end, Fellix decided to give in to their pleas. He was the master of the battle. His leg wouldn't allow him to fight well anyway. Even so, he still bore a spear, to many nobles' distaste. Spears were peasant weapons. Fellix liked spears, though. They were borne by every man; simple yet elegant and just as effective as a sword.

He looked at the army again. Almost all of the drakes had been eliminated, at the cost of half the griffins. *Come on*, he pleaded in his mind. *You have to clear the skies!* Getting the griffins to aid the ground troops as soon as possible was pivotal. He looked down at his ground forces. They were holding...barely.

He then looked at the center of his line and saw bodies flying. There was a colossal figure, wielding a black and crimson blade. Fellix's eyes widened. *The Darkest Knight!* The hellish figure wore a large helmet with wicked, twisted horns. His armor was massive, pitch black, his boots causing vibrations as they fell. This figure had been at all four battles. Fellix's brothers and his father had all been slain by his hand. After he killed them, the knight had left. *I have to stop my men from being slaughtered! I may not win the battle, but damn it, I refuse to lose the War!*

Fellix let out a scream, and galloped forward on his horse. The ranks parted before him. A werewolf jumped over the ranks to rip out his throat. Fellix swung an expert stroke with his spear. The werewolf was thrown backward, dead. More of them came after him. He kept slashing, like a steady metronome that he kept cadence with. Finally, he stopped before the Darkest Knight. The warrior finished killing his opponent and held up a hand. Everyone around them stopped fighting. All of the enemies backed off. Fellix thanked the Divine that his men were disciplined enough not to give chase. The Darkest Knight planted his immense, wicked sword into the ground before Fellix. It was like the entire army had stopped. That's when Fellix realized it had. The entire enemy force had retreated. All that was left was the Darkest Knight.

"Hail, the Crippled Lord." The voice was soft, but Fellix was stunned the warrior had even spoken. The Darkest Knight continued. "I assume you know why I am here?" The voice was deep, eloquent, and somehow entirely menacing. Fellix nodded. The Darkest Knight pulled his sword out of the ground. "Then summon your Blade, and let us begin."

Fellix shook his head. "I am not a king. I do not have a Blade."

The Darkest Knight looked around for a moment before responding. "You should." The Darkest Knight swung. Fellix blocked, only to have his spear cut in half. He knew immediately that he had lost the fight. He drew his sword, dismounted, and got into his fighting stance. One of his men stepped forward and removed the horse. Fellix swung forward, his sword flashing. Despite having a limp, he was a fair swordsman. The Darkest Knight blocked the sword easily, shearing through the steel. Fellix stared at his sword in dismay. The Knight cleaved again. Fellix dodged the strike, only to have his leg give out as he landed. He was on one knee, trying to recover. The Darkest Knight approached him.

"It is a shame you do not have a Blade...You are far more worthy than your supposed kings were. This is farewell, Fellix Cielad." The Darkest Knight swung downward. Fellix closed his eyes, waiting for the end. He heard a yell, a screech and a clang.

The commander snapped his eyes open to see a warrior had stepped forward. The man had on a simple helmet. Dark brown hair just barely stuck out of his helm. He was blocking the Knight's Blade somehow. That's when Fellix realized that the man had a ghostly sword; opaque and shimmering in his hand. It was lashed to his wrist by a chain. Fellix gasped.

A Blade of some kind?! But there's no royalty left alive in any of the Kingdoms! Only royalty can claim a Blade and live! Who is this man?

The Knight disengaged his opponent and backed away a few steps. "You are no royalty I recognize...name yourself, soldier." The soldier paused for a moment and arose. Then Fellix witnessed another feat: the Blade's handle grew. The soldier clasped it with two hands before him in a fighting stance. The fighter cleared his throat and spoke in a mild, gravelly tone.

"My name is Orin. I am a soldier of the fifth regiment from the Kingdom of Gyllithia."

The Knight pointed his sword threateningly at Orin. "Tell me, Orin, which son are you from the throne of Gyllithia? I prefer to know who I kill."

"I am of no throne, Knight."

"Then how did you come to possess a Blade?"

Orin gazed at his sword for a moment, and then laughed to himself, as if he was reflecting on a joke. "I guess you could say I belong to it."

"Where are you from?" The Knight demanded. He waited for a moment for a response and was met with silence.

"Where are you from?!" he repeated, his voice growing louder and angrier.

Orin seemed to brace himself before responding. "I'm from Stryne." The Knight seemed to pause for a moment. Fellix saw from his stance that he was confused.

"Stryne? The Shining Kingdom? It is long gone, boy. Vrasta saw to it personally."

Orin seemed to tense. His sword began to shine brightly. Fellix was in a cloud of confusion. Stryne had technically perished over six years ago. The entire royal family wiped from existence. How had this boy claimed a Blade?

"Stryne has decided on her new and final king, it seems." The Knight said. "How strange... such an event hasn't occurred since the First War. Come, face me, Orin." Orin turned to Fellix quickly.

"Lord Fellix, get the army ready. We have to win, regardless. I ask for you to leave the ring, sir? Permission to engage the Knight?" Fellix looked in the man's eyes and saw fear, mixed with an iron hard determination.

Fellix nodded. "Aye soldier, on both counts." Fellix limped from the ring and mounted his horse. He had a good view of the fight from up there. By the way Orin held his sword and set his stance the man had never held a sword before. He must have been terrified inside to be facing the most powerful enemy in Vrasta's forces. But he didn't let his fear show.

The two of them met in a flash of lights as their Blades smashed into each other with an unworldly *ring*. The Knight was far superior in skill, but Orin's sword seemed to change itself; adapting to situations. It grew shorter, longer, wider, and thinner, whatever its owner needed, it did. Orin received a large gash on his torso, his blood flying around in droplets as he remained locked in combat, not daring to stop.

The Knight thrust forward. Orin let the Blade slide off of the Knight's and he brought his sword forward in a vicious stab. His blade changed, growing thinner. The thrust went through the Knight's eye slot. Orin extracted the blade. There was no blood on it.

The Knight staggered once and fell to the ground. He disappeared, slowly dissolving into dust with his sword. The men paused for a moment to watch the dust float away on the winds. Afterward, they let out the loudest cheer Fellix had ever heard. The enemy army turned around and fled back through the mountains in a confused, unorganized mess. Fellix wheeled his horse to the front, where Orin was standing. He spoke in as loud a voice as he could.

"Let this day be remembered far and wide! Hail the chosen King of Stryne! He has won us our freedom! He has won us our peace! Hail King Orin of Stryne!" The men let out a giant cheer. Orin's eyes were wide.

"King? How am I going to be a king?"

Fellix smiled at the young man. "Don't worry," he said. "I'll help you. For now, we rebuild. There's much work to be done."

Orin smiled despite himself. The Fourth War was over. It was time for peace. But right then, he had something that mattered more: A mug of ale waiting for him back in his tent, and he was going to live to drink it. His smile fell as he realized something.

Fellix noticed. "What's wrong, Majesty?" he asked.

Orin looked at Fellix, somberness in his eyes. "This isn't over, Fellix. Vrasta will come back. Maybe not right now, or while you and I are still alive...but until we kill him, and see him dead, he'll keep coming. We may have won this battle...and even the War. But what happens when he comes back?"

Fellix had no response for a long while, and it wasn't until late that night that he came up with the answer, at the victory feast being held at camp.

"When he comes back, there will be someone like you. An unexpected savior."

The new king gave his Head Commander a skeptical smile. "I've never been one for predictions or prophecy."

Fellix looked Orin straight in the eye, a serious look on his face. "It's not a prediction, my young friend. It's a fact."

Darkest Siege

Ryan Wilshusen

Part One:

The Prophet

One

One thousand and seven hundred years later

Emesos woke up from what he considered quite possibly one of the strangest dreams he had ever had. He had been a young man who was at a war camp of some kind. In the camp, a kind of bizarre celebration had been going on. He had been in full armor and carrying a spear. People had applauded and hugged him as he passed by.

Emesos looked out the small window in his room that gave him a view of the narrow street they lived on in Cielad, the capital of Stryne. He noticed a large amount of decorations on the city streets and some banners being hung. With a jolt, he remembered what day it was.

Today's the parade! He thought with a kind of childish excitement. He got dressed in his shirt and breeches, tried in vain to do something with his brown hair and went downstairs to greet his family. His mother, Merra, was waiting for him at the kitchen table.

She smiled and gave a jerk of her head toward the family's cramped kitchen. "Come on, we have to get breakfast ready." Emesos immediately went to work, cooking and slicing with an ease brought on by years of practice.

Merra's blond hair fell about her face and as breakfast neared completion, Emesos watched what many would consider magical. Within five minutes, his older brother Hane and his father, Con, appeared and ate quickly with the rest of the family.

"I hope we get to see the royal guard today," Hane stated excitedly between mouthfuls, his green eyes flashing. "I even found the perfect spot!"

"You'll have a great time, just like you did last year," Con said with a smile on his face.

He's more jovial than normal, Emesos thought, *but then again, aren't we all at festival?*

"We should get going," Hane said, leaving the table. After they said farewell, the two brothers left the house and headed to Hane's spot. Emesos took a deep breath of the fall air, a slight metallic and smoky sting filling his nose. People were milling about and when Hane and Emesos entered the city's main market, a massive wave of people had gathered around the route the parade was supposed to take place.

"We're going to wait here and get up on those crates for a good look," Hane said, pointing to a solid group of thick wooden boxes left over from the nearby produce stands. Emesos smiled as the cheering started as the stomp of feet was heard from around the corner. Then, something caught his eye.

A single, small man with black hair and green eyes was trying to purchase some fruit. The vendor said some angry words and the man walked away, a sorrowful look on his face. Emesos thought his gait looked strange, then he noticed the man had a club-foot. Emesos went over the vendor.

"Excuse me, but what was that man asking for?" Emesos asked. The vendor gave Emesos an irritated look.

"He tried to buy a bag of apples with no money," the vendor stated.

Emesos looked at the small man with the clubbed foot. He was struggling to move through the crowd of bodies, each one cheering and craning his or her head to get a good look. Emesos turned his attention to the vendor again.

"Here," Emesos said, pulling out a stack of Kigit coins. "One bag of apples please." The vendor took the money and their hands brushed. Emesos felt a strange, sudden sensation of openness that lasted for only a second. He ignored it and took the apples from the vendor and quickly found the man he had been staring at.

"Excuse me," he called. The man turned around. Emesos handed him the bag of apples. "I believe these are yours." The fellow looked at Emesos, his face one of heartfelt thanks and joy.

The stomping of feet grew louder and so did the crowd's cheering. The man slowly hobbled away.

Emesos watched him go. *I wonder what that man needed the apples for,* he thought. Hane's voice interrupted his thoughts.

"Come on, Emesos! If you don't hurry, we might miss it!" Gonra, the king of Stryne, would soon be passing by. Everyone loved him, as his rule had brought a long stretch of peace and wealth to their nation. Emesos climbed up on the nearby crates, in time to see the king's guard pass by. It was then he saw the king.

He was covered in armor from head to toe, but there was no mistaking him. Upon a white horse he sat, erect, head held high. The people in the streets cheered loudly. The king raised a hand. The crowd fell silent. Gonra summoned his Blade. It was something to witness, appearing in just a small burst of light. It was ghostly, with a chain wrapped around his arm. It was the same Blade King Orin had used to strike down the Darkest Knight and win the Fourth War.

The cheering came back louder than ever. Hane was cheering with them, until he realized that his younger brother wasn't doing the same. When he looked over, he noticed his brother was clutching his arm, his fingers white. His teeth were gritted in pain.

"Emesos!" Hane said, kneeling down to see his brother's eyes. They had changed from their normal brown to almost pure white orbs. "Emesos, what's wrong? Talk to me."

"My arm...It feels like it's pulling apart," he managed to say. Hane looked at his brother and saw that his eyes had returned to their usual brown.

"We need to get you to a healer. Come on, let's go." Hane said as he grabbed Emesos' arm and began hauling him away from the parade.

"I'm fine. I swear it."

Hane raised an eyebrow, staring at his brother who was now a light shade of green. "Right. Come on, let's go. We're getting you to a healer." This time, Emesos didn't protest. He was walked down the street with his brother's help.

It was a bright noon and the sun was shining down without interference from clouds. They finally managed to get to the healer. It was a younger, rather attractive woman with brown hair and brown eyes. Her name was Leith, and her subtle speech and mannerisms always made Emesos uncomfortable... that and her beauty.

Oh, Hane, you're a complete ferret! he thought as Hane helped him into a nearby chair.

"What's the problem today, Hane? Your brother lovesick?" Leith asked with a smirk. Emesos groaned inwardly. The awkward sentences were already starting. Hane shook his head slowly.

"No, something really odd happened. We were in the middle of watching the parade when King Gonra summoned his Blade. I looked over and saw Emesos clutching his arm like he is now. He says his arm feels like... it's pulling apart. Did I say that correctly?" He looked at his younger brother for confirmation. Emesos nodded, clenching his teeth against the pain.

Leith went over to him and knelt down. "Uncover your arm," she directed. Emesos did so, moving his hand away from his forearm. Leith looked over the arm, giving him directions to twist certain directions and bend other things. When she looked at his hand, her eyes widened.

"What?" Emesos asked. He caught a glimpse of his hand. It was giving off flashes of light. Little burst of white, pure light. He looked up at Leith expectantly. "Is that bad? Is that good?"

Leith shook her head. "I don't know. I've never seen anything like it," she said. "It's...unnatural." Emesos' insides froze.

"Unnatural? What does that mean? I didn't do anything or touch anything strange. Will it go away, you think?" Leith looked at Emesos with slight annoyance.

"I just told you I haven't seen anything like this. How am I supposed to know?"

Emesos winced at his own question.

"Right; sorry... could you bandage it at least, so others can't see it?"

Leith grabbed a roll of the white bandages she kept neatly in her cupboards. "Sure, although I don't know why you would want to bandage such a strong and healthy hand. You'd better work on a good story for your parents." She grabbed Emesos' hand to start bandaging. A small *zap* sound occurred. Leith jerked back, sucking her fingers.

"I'm so sorry!" Emesos said, horrified. *What in the three Hels is happening to me?*

Leith smiled. "Don't be. You have such a jolting personality." Hane and Emesos groaned at the terrible pun. After Emesos finished bandaging his own hand and receiving an elixir for pain, the two boys said farewell to Leith and walked down the streets toward their home. Emesos' arm felt much better after taking the elixir, and soon the brothers were joking and racing each other to street corners.

When they arrived home, they were red in the face and panting. Their parents were professional calligraphers, preserving manuscripts in neat lettering. They also peddled small wooden children's toys, carved by Hane's. Emesos had terrible handwriting, and his carpentry skills were lacking. It was for this reason that Emesos planned to become a professional cook. It was one of the few things he truly excelled at.

Their mother looked up and smiled at them. She got up from her giant desk and gave them both hugs and a kiss on the head. "Hello boys," she said in her light, singing tone. "How was the parade? Did you get to see the king?" Hane nodded.

"King Gonra even summoned his Blade for us! It was amazing! Until Emesos got hurt, that is…" Emesos held up his bandaged hand.

"What happened?" his mother asked.

"Well…you see…" Emesos was fumbling for words.

"His hand started spitting magical light," Hane blurted. Their mother's eyes widened with surprise.

"Magical light? May I see?" Emesos nodded, glared at his brother, and started to unwrap his hand. It was perfectly normal. He felt scandalized. *It was there when I saw Gonra's Blade!* With that thought, the terrible pain in his arm started again. The small flashes of light had changed into a steady glow. His mother paled. "Con, Con, come here!"

Con's slight, pale frame came down the stairs. "What is it Merra? Is something-" He stopped in mid-sentence as he saw Emesos' hand. "What's this, Emesos?" His father's tone demanded an answer. "How long has this been happening?"

"I don't know! It just started this morning!"

Con paused to think for a moment... then arrived at an answer. "Well, try to keep your hand hidden the best you can. I'll see if I can get some answers from a few medical books." The rest of the day was fairly normal, however, and while Emesos was chopping an onion for dinner, his hand finally stopped glowing.

Maybe I'm returning to normal, he thought happily. He finished slicing the onion and threw it in the stew. After a bit of simmering, it was done. He brought the pot to the table, then nearly dropped it. His family was *glowing*. All of them were surrounded by a faint, white light. He tried to ignore it as best he could. Later that night, he crawled into bed, praying that this would all be gone in the morning. After a few minutes, he fell asleep.

******

Emesos was in a well-lit room, sitting at a desk, writing something. It was something inconsequential about healing plants. A door opened behind him. It was a man he would recognize anywhere from the endless number of portraits around Cielad. It was the legendary Orin, savior of the Fourth War.

"Anazan, I need your help." The king's voice was pleading. Emesos managed to stammer out a response.

"Of course; you're the king. Anything for the legendary Orin." Emesos almost recoiled at the sound of his voice. It was deep, quiet and scratchy. The king smiled and sat down on a nearby stool. "What do you need?" Emesos asked in the voice that wasn't his. The king smiled sheepishly.

"I need to know how to court a lady, properly." Emesos couldn't help but laugh a little. The mighty Orin, savior of Daclynand, was asking for his help on how to court. It was then he realized the king wasn't much older than he was. The king was in his late teens, early twenties at most. Emesos was soon to be eighteen himself.

"I thought it would be rather easy for you, Orin," Emesos said. "You're a rather kind individual."

Orin blushed. "Thank you Anazan. She's...different, though. She makes me uneasy..."

Emesos thought for a moment. This lady made Orin feel the same as Emesos did around Leith.

"Well," he started, "my advice would be to just grin at her remarks and be yourself as much as possible. Be polite, and listen carefully. You should have no problems after that. It wouldn't be bad to acquire something from a jeweler either."

Orin seemed to have a weight lifted off his shoulders. "Thank you, Anazan. How are you managing? I haven't been able to talk to you recently, I apologize for that."

Emesos shrugged. "It's not that big of a deal. I'm fine as I can be, I guess."

Orin nodded. "I know that it must've been painful to see your homeland in such ruin."

Emesos nodded, not knowing what the king was talking about. "Yes, it was. Don't worry, it will recover someday." Orin seemed to reflect on this for a long while. A silence fell between the two of them. Finally, Orin nodded.

"I'm sure it will, maybe not while we're alive, but it will. You know...I said the same thing to Fellix about Vrasta's return. He told me that Daclynand would be saved by an 'unexpected savior'. Do you think your country will have the same thing?"

Emesos nodded. "Yes. No doubt about it." It felt like the right thing to say. Orin nodded.

"I think so, too. Thank you for the advice. Take care, friend. I still owe you, you know."

"You owe me nothing," Emesos protested.

"Come now, you saved my life and my Kingdom. I'm still trying to return the favor. That's why today, I'm declaring law that Stryne's Manipulators are officially under the King's protection. I know it pales compared to what you've done for me, but it's a start."

"Thank you," Emesos said, *still not knowing what the king was talking about. "That is an immeasurable honor to me."*

The king walked out the door, a smile on his face.

******

Emesos woke, sweating. His dream was stuck in his head. It had felt more real than any dream he had ever had. *Why am I dreaming of King Orin? Who is Anazan?* he wondered. *Is he a real person? Where does he come from? What happened to him and his home?*

He got up, got dressed, ate breakfast with his family as usual and went to work. Emesos had an apprenticeship at the *Griffin's Claw*, a local pub that was popular for its food. The woman who owned the *Griffin's Claw* was old and had no children, so she took Emesos on as an apprentice. He worked, trying to keep his mind off of the mysterious Anazan.

As soon as he finished work, he went down to the nearest scholar's guild. Scholar's guilds were places where people could learn, funded by Gorna's personal wealth. Emesos definitely had things he wanted to learn.

He approached the front desk of the huge building. A young man about his age was working there, looking rather bored until Emesos walked in. "Welcome to the scholar's guild," he said. "How might I help you today?"

Emesos cleared his throat and asked, "Do you have anything on a person named Anazan?" The man turned to a series of massive tomes. He opened one and Emesos saw that it was a log for all of the books at the guild. The man flipped through the pages until he scanned through all of the books that started with an 'A'. After a few minutes, he closed the book.

"Sorry, we only could have one thing on a person named Anazan, and it's written in Ancient. Unless you know how to read it, I'm afraid I can't help you." Emesos' heart sank. Part of him was scared that Anazan was real, but another, stronger part of him was more curious to find out who the man was and how he was connected with King Orin.

No one in modern society could read Ancient. It wasn't connected to any of the languages currently being used in Daclynand. Many academics argued it might be the language of whatever existed before the four Kingdoms, but nothing confirmed it.

"Can I at least see it?" he asked. The young man at the desk nodded and stood.

"Follow me." Emesos followed him for a few minutes as the man went in and out of the shelves with an ease that Emesos was sure came from a good amount of experience and practice. They finally came to a halt in the back of the building on the second floor. The man used a nearby ladder to pull the book down. He handed a small, very worn tome to Emesos. "Here you go. Enjoy staring at random scratches."

Emesos looked down at the faint title on the cover and he immediately knew what it was. He could read it was written by Anazan in what looked close to modern Solic, but the actual title was obscure, a mix of babbling runes . Suddenly, it made sense. He didn't know how he knew the title of the book, he just did.

"*Ana tela Fethru nin Viceni.*" The young deskman turned around.

"What did you say?" he asked.

Emesos looked at him, his face innocent. "I said, *On the Forces and Manipulation*. It's the title of the book." The deskman looked at him strangely, as if he couldn't decide if Emesos was making it up. He turned around and walked away without another word. It was that moment Emesos realized he had spoken and read a supposedly unknown language.

Emesos set the book down on a nearby table and walked away as fast as he could without jogging. He had just spoken a language he had never heard. What was wrong with him?

He turned out onto the street, only to be almost blinded. People were milling about, shining with a soft white light. Their combined glow made him squint. He finally made it back home to find his family waiting for him. They ate dinner together and joked around as usual. Emesos didn't mention a word of what had happened at the scholar's guild.

When he crawled into bed that night he had more questions than answers. He was more concerned with what had occurred today than yesterday. Strange things were happening to him; far out of his control. He was having dreams about real people, speaking forgotten languages, and seeing lights. Emesos didn't sleep that night, scared more dreams would visit him if he did.

Two

E mesos was sure he was going insane. Two more weeks had
passed by. He was seeing more glowing lights around
people than ever before. No more dreams had visited him;
only because he had barely slept. He was exhausted emotionally,
mentally, and physically. His parents noticed, but he managed to
avoid questions by throwing an assortment of excuses their
direction. But there was one person in the household he couldn't
hide things from: Hane.

Hane wouldn't be thrown off by excuse; he knew something
deeper was wrong, more than just late night shifts.

Emesos went to leave his bedroom, but Hane appeared in the
doorway, a serious look on his face. *Oh no, Hane. Not right now,
please!* He tried to move past his brother, but Hane got in his way.
Emesos tried again, only for Hane to block his way again. "What?"
he snapped.

Hane raised his eyebrows. "We need to talk about what's wrong
with you. And don't give me an excuse. You've been acting
strangely ever since we saw King Gonra in that parade. What's
going on, Emesos?"

"I need to go to-"

"You're not going anywhere until I get some answers." Hane
said. Emesos saw the determination in his brother's face and went
back to his bed and sat down with a sigh. He told his brother
about the dream, the scholar's guild incident, and the glowing
lights that surrounded people he saw.

Hane gave an impressed whistle after the description. "That's really strange, Emesos. You're not making this up?" Emesos shook his head at his brother, giving him a slight glare.

"I'm not making it up! I'm telling the truth the best I can and here you are doubting the answers I give you!"

Hane's eyebrows drew closer together. "What did you just say?" he asked. Emesos recoiled.

Impossible... he thought, his stomach flipping. *Not again... the same thing happened at the scholar's guild...* "I said that I wasn't making it up and trying to explain the best I could," Emesos said. "Did you hear something else?" Hane nodded.

"I sure did, it sounded like you were speaking a separate language. It sounded like some kind of language anyway." Hane's eyes widened as he realized what occurred. "You did the same thing you did at the scholar's guild. You just spoke Ancient to me." They were silent for a while, then Emesos finally stood, his boots making a thud noise on the upper floor of their house.

"I have to go, or I'll be late for work," he muttered.

Hane nodded and said "Okay. If anything odd happens today, and I mean *anything*, tell me."

"I will."

"Swear to it?" Hane asked.

"I swear." Emesos said.

When Emesos left the house, he felt better than he had in the past two weeks. Being able to confide in someone made it seem less difficult to deal with than he thought. Once he buried himself in work at the *Griffin's Claw*, the day went by relatively fast. He didn't see any strange symbols, but the glowing lights were still there. Emesos did his best to ignore them.

Once he had finished work, he took his day's pay and headed down to the central market to buy supplies for that night's dinner. He was at a vegetable stand and noticed someone familiar looking next to him. It was Leith.

Oh no... he hid his inner thoughts with a smile. "How are you?" He said in a light tone. Leith wasn't smiling. "What's wrong?" he asked.

She was staring at him coldly. "You look like you've visited one of the three Hels and come back." Emesos swallowed nervously. How much did she know? Her face changed to one of concern. "Why didn't you come see me? Why haven't you been sleeping?" Emesos paid for his food and said nothing.

"Come on." He said to Leith. "It's nothing. You worry too much." She gave him an angry look and started following him.

"Don't lie to me, Emesos. Something's gnawing at you." She grabbed his hand.

Emesos felt as if a jolt had moved up his arm. It was as if he could see Leith's emotions. She wasn't happy. In that instant, he felt like he truly *knew* who she was. He felt her pains, her worries, and her longings. His eyes widened and for some reason, tears spilled down his cheeks.

Leith's face immediately shed anger for concern. "Emesos? Emesos, talk to me."

Emesos managed to speak, despite the lump in his throat that tried to obscure his speech. "I...I... Leith...You love Hane, don't you?" She froze for a moment, caught off guard by the question.

"What? What are you talking about?"

"You can't hide it from me, Leith. I know. You should stop dancing around the fact. He loves you back." Emesos looked downward, away from her eyes.

How do I know? How do I know how she feels? Was it the touch? Is this another occurrence? What's happening *to me?*

"Emesos...are you alright? You look pale." Emesos looked at Leith's brown eyes and then, everything went black.

******

"He's coming," a person said. Emesos turned around and saw that it was a king of some kind. "He's coming and I know it, Fellix." The man was speaking Strynic, so Emesos assumed he was the king of Stryne. Emesos himself apparently was a man named Fellix. Emesos reeled in shock. I'm the legendary High Commander of the Forth War! *He didn't have much time to dwell on it. He had to play the part of Fellix.*

"Do you really think so, Your Majesty?" he asked. The king nodded and went over to what looked to be a map of Daclynand. He pointed to a spot that was in the Kingdom of Rhyth, the most north-eastern of all the Kingdoms.

"Vrasta has begun his assault on Rhyth. It's only a matter of time before he reaches Stryne."

"Why don't you form an alliance with the king of Rhyth?" Emesos suggested. "Combine your forces and meet Vrasta in Rhyth, before he invades any further."

Vrasta! *He thought,* Vrasta was the enemy in the Fourth War! What does this dream mean?

The king laughed. "Do you really think I would ally with someone who wants a knife in my back?"

"I suppose not," Emesos said carefully.

The king smiled. "I thought not."

"But sire..." Emesos pleaded. "You underestimate Vrasta. He's stronger than you think. Rhyth isn't strong enough to repel him."

All cheer and good nature left the king's eyes.

"You dare contradict me, Fellix?" His tone was low and serious. *"You dare insult the courage and strength of Rhyth' men?"*

Emesos grew frustrated. *"No, I don't insult Rhyth at all. But courage and strength only go so far! Rhyth will fall if you don't help!"*

The king stood. *"I see that your accident damaged your brain as well. Fellix, as king of Stryne, I now strip you of the rank Battalion Master and revoke your nobility."*

Emesos stood there dumbly. *"What?"*

"Guards!" The king called. *"Remove this man from my sight at once. He is not to enter the castle again."* Guards came in and grabbed Emesos by the arms.

Emesos couldn't resist one last statement. *"You're only getting rid of me because you don't want to face the truth."* With that, the guards dragged him away and out the castle gates.

He walked away from the castle, fuming. That king is incredibly dense! *Emesos thought to himself as he limped down the street. His left leg wasn't working correctly for some reason.* No wonder Vrasta managed to destroy so much in the Fourth War! All the leaders in the Fourth War must have been morons!

"Hello, Fellix." He heard the voice and turned that direction. An old man was there, smoking a pipe. His pure silver beard cropped short and rough, as though it had been cut with a knife. He still had his hair, and that flowed to his shoulders. His eyes were an odd deep violet. *"I hear that you're now unoccupied. Is that correct?"*

Emesos nodded. The old man was stating the obvious. The old man smiled, his teeth slightly yellow. *"Might I offer you employment?"*

Emesos narrowed his eyes. *"Who are you?"* he asked, a slight demand behind the question. The old man stepped forward, extending his hand for introductions.

"I am called by a few names, but you may call me Anazan." Emesos recalled the man's name from his previous dream. He took the extended hand and shook it, his eyes never leaving the mysterious face.

****

Emesos' eyes snapped open to see Hane's staring back at him. "He's awake." Hane said to an unseen figure. "Emesos, can you speak to me?"

"Yes," Emesos replied. "Where am I?" Hane's face lit up with joy.

"You're at Leith's. You fainted in the middle of the market place. We were worried." Emesos tried to sit up, but his head swam too much. He turned his head and saw Leith, grasping Hane's hand like a vice. He smiled.

"I'm glad you took my advice," he joked. Leith raised an eyebrow. Hane looked back and forth between the two of them, trying to figure out what had happened. He eventually gave up and refocused on Emesos.

"Are you feeling fine now?" Hane asked. Emesos shrugged, and then answered truthfully.

"I'm scared. Plus I'm seeing lights shine off people, light's coming out of my hand, and I'm getting dreams of different people that are historically important to the Fourth War. Besides that, I'm feeling great."

Hane and Leith looked at each other. They seemed to be talking with just their eyes. They both looked back at him.

Hane grabbed Emesos' shoulder. It was awkward, considering Emesos was lying down. "What's happening to you isn't something physical. At least, I hope it isn't." Hane cleared his throat and continued. "And those dreams...what if they're not dreams?"

From the second Emesos heard the statement, he knew it was true. But Emesos was now bothered by a greater question. If the dreams weren't dreams... what were they?

Three

"This is insane," Emesos muttered, waiting in line with his brother. "How are we going to accomplish anything today with this line in front of us?" The line did stretch a huge distance. It also moved forward at an agonizing pace. They kept moving forward, but just barely. That's when Emesos saw a group of soldiers walking toward them. Emesos could tell they were nursing a hangover by the way they were clutching their heads and how dirty their clothes were.

The guards walked up to the line. One of them tried to shove a man out of the way, but the man stood his ground. The soldier shoved him harder, and still the man stood his ground. Finally, the soldier struck the man with a spear. The man crumpled to the ground and the Soldiers laughed as they stepped over him. Emesos' anger rose. Instinct took over.

"Hey!" he called to the soldiers. "You're supposed to protect your people, not beat them!" The soldier group turned around, looking at Emesos with angry, smug expressions.

Hane groaned next to him. "Emesos, don't!" he pleaded. Emesos ignored his brother's obvious complaint. The soldiers laughed for a moment before one of them stepped forward and tossed Emesos a spear.

"Alright," the man said. "You want to play soldier, boy? Let's play." Emesos picked up the spear and for some reason, it felt right in his hands, like it had always been in his hands.

Suddenly, his mind was elsewhere. He was in a battlefield, facing down six soldiers. His left leg was noticeably weaker. *Fellix.*

Emesos realized. *I'm Fellix right now.* He didn't fight the feeling; he surrendered himself to it.

The soldier lunged forward in a vicious thrust. Emesos dodged it easily, returning a strike of his own. The spear seemed to move instantaneously. The soldier in front of him reacted with growing more desperation, striking wildly. Emesos kept blocking and finally gave a vicious swing with the butt of the spear. It connected with the soldier's head, dropping him to the ground. The rest of the soldiers came charging in to avenge their comrade.

Emesos promptly disarmed two of them in one swing and broke another's nose. The three remaining soldiers surrounded him. They came in at different directions and heights. Emesos let his instincts take him one last time.

He blocked two spears and ducked to avoid the third one. He gave a sweeping blow with his spear to knock one of them off their feet, dodged an overhead attack, thrust his spear butt into the man's shin and smacked the other man upside the head with the shaft of his spear.

The soldiers quickly broke off their assault, gathered their friends, and beat a hasty and undignified retreat. Emesos took another breath, holding the spear. The sensation of him being Fellix was gone. He was himself again. *I didn't know that Fellix was so good with a spear.* Suddenly, he realized that the people in the line were staring at him. Even his brother. One person broke into applause. Soon, the entire line was cheering for him.

Emesos quickly dropped the spear and rejoined his brother in line. Hane looked at his brother. "When were you going to tell me you knew how to use a spear?" he asked. Emesos shook his head.

"I don't know how to use a spear. Fellix does-or did, anyway."

"Fellix? The High Commander?"

"That's the one. He appeared in my latest dream," Emesos said. "I found out he was a Battalion Master for Stryne sometime just before the Fourth War started. He got fired and then was hired by Anazan."

"Wasn't Anazan the man you were in your other dream?" Hane inquired.

"He was," Emesos confirmed. They waited for another hour before they managed to write their names in the census book. The Kingdom of Stryne took a census every decade. Emesos let Hane write down the family and they started on their way home. Both of them had finished work that day. Emesos spent the rest of the day reflecting on how holding the spear had changed him even further.

The next two weeks were fairly normal for Emesos. No new dreams had come to him, no magical pulses out of his hands. The only thing that remained was the constant glowing he saw around people. It was something he was becoming used to ignoring. One afternoon he was coming home when he saw a pair of soldiers standing at his front door. His heart skipped a beat. *Are those the soldiers from the market?* Emesos walked closer and was relieved to find they weren't. He tried to enter, but one of the men blocked his way.

"Excuse me," Emesos said. "I live here."

"Are you Emesos?" the soldier questioned with a sense of urgency.

"Yes," Emesos said slowly. The guard turned his head and shouted over his shoulder to someone in the house.

"Lord Erk! We've found him!" Emesos fought the urge to break free and run. His family could be in danger for all he knew.

They could all be thrown in the dungeon for what I did to those guards! he thought.

"Good," said a voice that Emesos figured belonged to the man named Erk. He appeared in the doorway. His hair was a light blond and his eyes an icy shade of grey. His face was sharp and angular, all excess fat stripped from it, leaving him with a taut look. He fixed Emesos with a piercing gaze. "You are to come with us. There's a very important person who'd like to meet you." Emesos swallowed nervously. He was marched between the two guards, with Lord Erk leading the way.

He was taken through the city and, to his horror, the castle came quickly into view. *Oh no, I'm going to the dungeons! Maybe for life! I wish I hadn't beaten those guards!*

They were let through the gates quickly, Erk flashing some kind of document to the guards. In the same manner, they entered the castle's front doors. Erk lead them briskly down a confusing set of hallways. Emesos' dread grew with every twist and turn. Finally, they came to a set of massive doors. Erk showed the guards his document and was quickly let in. Everyone else waited outside with Emesos while the door shut behind Erk.

Who would be so powerful that it would gain us entrance like this? Emesos wondered. *They'd have to be a major political force. Perhaps it's a relative of King Gonra.* He heard Erk yell through the doors.

"Enter!" The doors opened and Emesos was guided to a large room. It was elaborately decorated with wood carvings and statues. Seated upon a large, blocky throne was an old man with a stern expression. Emesos' legs practically gave out from under him.

The two Heavens! It's Gonra himself! He looked around the throne room and saw the king's guard all around the room. Emesos and Erk stopped before the king and bowed. "Your Majesty," Erk said, pointing at Emesos, "We have found him."

Gonra nodded. "Thank you, Erk. You've done well." He turned his attention to Emesos. "I received a report that two weeks ago...you took on a group of the city guard, fighting them in combat with a spear until they were injured, is this correct?"

Emesos nodded.

You didn't speak with a king until he allowed you to. It was an unspoken rule for all of the citizens of Stryne. The king nodded in return.

"I see. My reports also indicate that witnesses say you took on multiple guards at once. Is this also correct?" Emesos felt like he was going to be sick, but he nodded again anyway.

The king paused for a moment and then spoke again. "Where did you learn to fight with a spear?" he asked. Emesos had to cough and clear his throat several times before answering.

"Well, Your Majesty...I didn't exactly...learn from anywhere..." He had to force the sentence out of himself. King Gonra leaned forward slightly in his chair, his eyes boring into Emesos'. Emesos noticed how brightly the king glowed compared to other people he had seen.

"You didn't learn to fight with a spear from anywhere? I find that hard to believe, Emesos Benithis." Emesos' stomach heaved around again, threatening to dislodge his breakfast, but he managed to keep himself under control.

"I know it's hard to believe, but it's the truth." Emesos said with a conviction that stemmed from his honesty.

"*Who* did you learn from?"

The young man braced himself before answering.

"I learned from a man named Fellix, Your Majesty." He watched the king's face carefully. The king did something unexpected. He laughed.

"Fellix? You're a clever one. Why didn't you say you were self-taught?" Emesos breathed a sigh of relief.

If the king wants to think I was self-taught, I certainly won't stop him, Emesos thought.

Gonra stared at Emesos, a twinkle of playfulness in his eye. Despite being old enough to be Emesos' grandfather, he still seemed to have quite a bit of energy.

"Well, Erk, what do you think?"

Erk circled Emesos and nodded to the king. "I think he'd do just fine, Your Majesty." Emesos looked back and forth between the two men. Erk now turned his attention to Emesos. "Emesos, His Majesty and I have given it some serious consideration, and we would like to invite you to become the Elite of the Spear." Emesos was blown away by the news. Part of him was relieved he wasn't going to be punished for attacking those guards. But he was very confused. He knew he was decent with the spear in that line... but not good enough to join the Elite of Kings.

The Elite of the Spear... What a waste! I've only fought once! Why would he offer it to someone like me? he thought.

The Elite of Kings were the best weapons masters in all of the Kingdoms. Stryne had its Elite of the Sword, but the Elite of the Spear had recently retired. Many knights trained for years, hoping to become one of the Elite. And here the king was...offering it to Emesos.

"Majesty," Emesos started. "I'm honored you think that I could be one of your Elite, but aren't there more qualified people for the job?" Gonra merely smiled at Emesos. He snapped his fingers and a spear flew in Emesos' general direction. Emesos failed to catch it and had to pick the spear up off the floor.

"Show me that you're qualified."

Emesos held the spear, but it felt awkward and heavy in his grip. He gave it a few swings, but Fellix's instinct didn't come.

"I'm sorry, Your Majesty, but I can't." Emesos said apologetically. *Why do they think I'm special? Why am I even here?!* Emesos thought to himself.

"Perhaps he would do better with an opponent or two?" Erk asked simply.

The king was nodding, and Emesos' stomach sank.

"That's a good idea. Erk, spar with him."

" I beg your pardon, Your Majesty?" Erk said with surprise. Emesos noticed that Erk clearly wasn't expecting to participate. Emesos' mind was in a state of panic.

Oh no! I'll be crushed! What is the king thinking!? Emesos wondered.

"Face him, Erk," the king commanded. "What better way to match a potential Elite than to put him against another Elite?" Erk gave a quick nod.

"Very well." Erk drew the blade at his waist and Emesos held the spear he had been given. His hands were trembling. He tried to find the instinct that guided him earlier.

It wasn't there.

Erk jumped forward and Emesos barely managed to get the spear up in time. Suddenly, the instinct was there.

He wasn't on a battlefield, he was in a castle. Before him was a large man in black and orange armor that was made of strange, interlocking plates like scales, charging at him with a sword.

Emesos didn't think. He didn't need to.

He dropped the spear and threw up a fist to block the downward slash. The sword didn't slice into his hand. Instead, it stopped with a resounding clank. Emesos charged forward with wicked speed. His opponent in orange and black armor jumped backward. They exchanged a series of blows at wicked speeds. Emesos wasn't deflecting the attacks with a spear, but a black and white sword. He deflected a thrust by him and, in a quick motion, slammed his fist into the knight in black orange armor. The scale-like plates crumpled and bent on the once serpentine helmet. The man shouted as he hit the ground, clutching his face in pain...

Just as fast as the vision had come, it went. Emesos was back in the throne room, a spear in his right hand and a strange, opaque gauntlet around his left. His eyes went wide as the gauntlet faded into his arm. *What was that?* He thought with panic. *Who was I? Was I Fellix or Anazan? What kind of power was that?*

He looked on the ground before him. Erk was on one knee, clutching his nose. Gonra immediately took action.

"Someone get a healer, quick!" A guard gave a slight bow and ran off. Emesos stood there, staring on in shock, his brain still trying to process the transition. Gonra looked at Emesos. The king's face was unreadable to him. "My offer still stands. You think yourself unworthy, and yet I have witnessed a sparring match between yourself and my remaining Elite that has left him in need of medical attention. But you are certain you are not worthy. Why?"

"He wasn't actually fighting. He was toying with me."

"Nonsense."

"I'm not prepared for a large decision like this. May I have a day to think about it? It is a big decision, Majesty." King Gonra nodded.

I have to escape somehow! Emesos thought. *There has to be a way out of this situation! I'm not ready to be a cook, let alone an Elite!* He started to open his mouth to explain to the king when Gonra cut him off and dashed his hopes.

"Yes it is. You will stay at the castle until you decide." He declared. Emesos' eyes widened.

"My parents would worry themselves sick, Your Majesty."

Gonra smiled. "Yes. They'll be informed today. I'll send a runner. Until tomorrow, enjoy the castle and think about the opportunity you've been offered. I'll have somebody show you to your chambers." Emesos bowed, beginning to have an inner meltdown.

I'm going insane! I've got to be. It's the only thing that explains everything that's been happening to me! What am I going to say to Gonra when I reject his offer? What is he going to say when I reject his offer? What would happen if I say no? What would my family think?! How am I going to get myself out of this mess?!

Emesos hoped he would find the answers before his mind gave out.

Four

The king's library was the biggest in the Kingdom of Stryne. It contained more documents on history and nature than any other library in the entire continent of Daclynand. Emesos decided to go there almost immediately. If there was any information on what was happening to him or the people he was seeing and being, he would find it there.

A servant guided him there quickly and left him to his own devices. Emesos stared at the immense library, seeing rows upon rows and shelves upon shelves of books and scrolls. He felt very small next to the enormity of the walls filled with knowledge. Having no idea where to begin, he decided to start with the nearest shelf. He reached for a book and started to pull it down.

"Would you like some help?"

The voice startled him and he lost his grip on the book. It tumbled down and landed on the floor with a *bang* that echoed through the massive library. Emesos blushed with embarrassment he turned around and saw that a young woman was staring at him with steel gray eyes. Her brown hair was done up neatly in a kind of bun.

"Oh," Emesos said, "Um…please…" he tired to keep the plea out of his voice. "I'm a little lost. This is my first time here." He bent down and picked up the book, setting it on the shelf where it belonged. "I'm Emesos." He gave a small bow.

The young woman smiled. "Ah, so you're the one the king kept talking about. I'm Velenry, king's historian." She bowed back. She was wearing pants and a plain shirt. Her hair was thrown back into a simple knot, so that it just touched her shoulders. Emesos figured that she was more practical than stylish. She looked at him with a curious eye. "What are you here to study? I can find you the right book."

Emesos looked around to make sure no one was watching the exchange. "I need information about a man named Anazan. Do you have any books that mention him?" he asked quietly. He figured he'd start on the historical figures before he tried to tackle what was happening to him.

"Anazan? King Orin's advisor? I'm afraid there's not much on him that's in Strynic. We have writings that we think are his, but they're all in Ancient so we don't really know for certain."

"May I see them?"

Velenry gave him a confused look. "Why would you want to see something you can't read? Seems pretty counterintuitive to me."

Emesos adopted a tone that left no room for questions. "It's very important. Please." Velenry flashed him a skeptical look, but answered him anyway.

"Follow me then." He followed quickly behind, her pace was quick. Silence pressed down on the pair. Emesos wasn't sure what to say to her. After almost fifteen minutes of walking, they reached a section where Velenry came to a halt.

"This is the section that contains the Ancient writings." Emesos looked among the books, eager and afraid of what he might find.

Are the answers here? Am I finally going to figure out what's been happening to me? Something inside told him he would at least be one step closer.

"Are you sure these are writings?" he asked.

"No, they're in Ancient. Why is Anazan so important to you?"

Emesos didn't take his eyes off the books. He was looking. Most of them were on King Orin, by authors he didn't know. He finally found an extremely small, plain looking book that didn't have its title printed on the spine. He pulled it out and found it had no title period. "I'm curious about who he was is all."

"Good luck trying to find anything on him." Velenry said teasingly. "There's nothing on Anazan personally in this library other than that he was King Orin's advisor and good friend."

Emesos opened the book. The page of writing on it that was in clear, crisp strokes:

To the one who is reading this:

You have been chosen, my legacy is now yours.

May you bring what was lost back.

I know that you will succeed.

After all, swords don't lie.

May the Divine guide you, my heir,

Anazan

"What is that supposed to mean?" Emesos asked the book, scandalized.

Velenry laughed. "That's what I've been trying to answer. It's Ancient, what did you expect?" she asked.

Emesos gave her an unhappy look. "More information than this gave me. I come looking for historical information or a memoir, and all I get is a bad poem that makes no sense." The statement came out of his mouth before he even thought about it. He kicked himself inwardly.

Velenry's eyes narrowed. "A poem? How do you know it's a poem?" she inquired causally.

"I guessed," he tried to say smoothly. "How am I supposed to know what it says? It's in Ancient." Velenry nodded, a look of disbelief on her face.

"Good point. Well, enjoy the library." She strolled away, leaving him alone. Emesos took a deep breath and let it out slowly.

That was close, he thought, *but what did the poem mean? It said something about an heir… This is so frustrating! Every time I go looking for answers, all I find are more damned questions! I must be the worst scholar in Daclynand!*

To add to his mounting frustration, it took him a full thirty minutes to get out of the library without a guide. It took him another ten minutes to get back to his room. He laid down on his bed and stared at the ceiling.

It took him a few minutes to regain control of his temper. He tried to work out everything in his head and failed spectacularly.

After Emesos passed a few hours by trying to avoid sleep, a servant knocked on Emesos' door. Emesos opened it. The servant had a pile of clothes in his arms and his face was almost hidden. "His Majesty requests that you dress appropriately and join him for dinner. "

Emesos audibly groaned. He took the clothes from the servant and set them on his bed. When he turned around, he gave a jolt of surprise. The man had a familiar face. In fact, Emesos had seen him not so long ago.

"You're the servant I gave the apples to at the parade!" Emesos said. The realization threw off his foul mood. "I never thought I'd see you again."

A look of shocked recognition came over the servant as he remembered Emesos.

"You're the Emesos everyone's been talking about? I never expected it to be you!"

"People have been talking about me?" Emesos asked.

"Of course! You got carted in here by Lord Erk. All the servants were wondering what you'd done. Then we found out that you're a candidate for being the Elite of the Spear! The youngest one in almost seventy years!"

Now, more than ever, Emesos felt completely inadequate.

"Thank you for the clothes." Emesos said.

The servant smiled. "Thank you for the apples." The man turned around to leave when Emesos noticed the man's clubbed foot. Not only that, the man had terrible shoes. They were nearly rags.

"Wait." Emesos said. He slipped off his boots. The servant turned around. Emesos handed the boots to him. "Take these."

"Take them where, sir? The laundry?"

"No, take them for you. They're yours now." The servant's eyes widened.

"Really? Honestly?" Emesos nodded. The servant seemed to take the moment in. He slipped off his rags and slid on Emesos' boots. He flexed his feet a little. It seemed like a good fit.

The servant looked at Emesos with eyes of complete gratitude. "I owe you again...thank you so much!" The servant hobbled off and Emesos smiled as he shut his door. The young man then turned around to stare at the clothes on his bed.

He realized that he would have to grab some other footwear to wear in front of the king. The dress clothes the king had sent him were a fairly simple set. It had brown trousers and a light blue shirt. Along with it was a strange cape that Emesos finally figured out was supposed to clip under one shoulder and be draped over the other. The cape was a much darker blue. He tried in vain to find another pair of shoes, but had no success.

He walked in his stockings down the hallways, asking servants the directions to the dining hall where the king was. He knew his feet were attracting stares, but he didn't care. Emesos only had one thought that ran through his mind like a mantra:

This floor is like ice! I can't even feel my toes!

He finally managed to locate the dining hall and found Erk was there, along with Velenry. The king was nowhere to be seen. An empty ornate chair of leather and bronze was at the head of the table. He bowed to Erk and Velenry and sat at the only open seat at the table that was left. There was a fire that kept the room comfortably warm, crackling away. Stained glass windows allowed the moonlight to reflect off of the torches that kept the room alight.

"Where are your shoes?" Erk hissed at him. "You don't show up to dinner with the *king* of Stryne in stockings!"

"They went to someone who needed them more than I did."

Erk's eyes bulged, but he sat back in his seat and said nothing more. Velenry looked at him like he was insane. Emesos ignored them.

The trio waited for a few more minutes before the king entered the doors. The three of them stood and bowed. The king smiled and gave them permission to sit.

Emesos tried to feel comfortable in the chair. It was well made, but the current situation made him feel restless like something was constantly jabbing him in the back. He shifted around as much as he could without drawing attention. Eventually, he gave up, channeling his nerves instead by gently tapping a senseless rhythm on the table, not daring to take his eyes off the king.

"So…Emesos," he started, "what do your parents do for a living?" Gonra asked.

"They're calligraphers. My brother's a carpenter as well."

The king nodded and clapped his hands to call for food. They sat in an awkward silence until servants appeared with the variety of fruits, bread, and meats. The servants set down a plate in front of Emesos.

"Thank you," he said. The servant girl bowed, blushing. She was joining her fellow servants as they exited to the kitchens when Emesos heard a whisper.

"That must be him." That was all he heard, but he didn't know what to make of it. He ate his food quietly. The king tried to draw him into conversation without success. Finally, when Emesos had finished, he looked at the king and spoke words that had been swirling about his head amidst all of his confusion and anxiety.

"Sire…I still don't think I can do the job." Gonra stared at Emesos, a little confused.

"Why do you think you'll not be a good Elite?"

"I've been in *one* fight. That's not enough for you to judge my skills properly."

"You question my judgment?" The question made the room fall completely silent. Emesos looked straight at the king and got a feeling of familiarity. He was staring at the king, just as Fellix had done in his vision.

"Yes…I am."

Gonra coughed once. Twice. Emesos was practically sweating with anxiety. The smoke of the fire now had an oppressive feeling.

"Well, if that's how you feel, then why not at least *try* being an Elite for a few days and see how you fare?" Gonra suggested reasonably.

Everyone in the room was completely caught off guard. Velenry looked dumbstruck. Erk looked scared. Emesos' heart soared with the suggestion.

Well…it can't hurt to try, can it? Emesos thought. *I just have to be terrible at it for a day or two and be sent off. How hard could that be?*

And he spoke the words that changed his fate forever.

"Your Majesty… I'll do it."

Five

The room was quiet as he spoke the sentence. The king broke into a wide smile.

"What changed your mind?" He asked. "What convinced you?"

Emesos smiled slightly as he looked at his empty dinner plate.

"I just thought it couldn't hurt to try at least." he said. The king raised an eyebrow but said nothing more.

"We'll inform your parents tomorrow of your decision. I'm glad you've chosen to accept this offer, Emesos. Report tomorrow to the throne room to begin your new career." Gonra stood and left. Almost as soon as the doors closed, Erk turned to Emesos.

"I guess we're equals now," Erk said with a slight edge to his voice. Emesos gave a hesitant smile. Erk's next words were just as sharp.

"So, make sure to conduct yourself properly from now on. You're in a different world now. Words can mean everything. Don't foul up your induction tomorrow, lest you make the rest of us look like fools." Erk stood and left, his boots clicking smartly against the stone floor. The door shut behind him.

Emesos suddenly noticed that he was in the room alone with Velenry. She made him feel on edge. She looked at him for a long while. Finally, he couldn't stand it any longer.

"What? Do I have something on my face?"

"Only a set of eyes, a mouth and a nose," she responded.

"You're a very strange woman."

"You're a very strange man." Emesos shifted uncomfortably in his seat.

"How did you learn to read Ancient?" she asked. The question caught Emesos completely off guard. He made up an answer quickly.

"I don't know how to read Ancient. The best scholars in Daclynand can't understand that language. What makes you think I can figure it out?" Velenry gave him a look with one raised eyebrow that let him know she wasn't fooled.

Velenry produced a quill and a piece of parchment from a bag she had on the floor. She walked over and handed them to Emesos along with a bottle of ink. Emesos looked at it, curious.

"What's this for?" he asked, wary.

"I want you to write a speech for tomorrow," she said.

"Speech?" Emesos asked, dreading the word. Public speaking was *not* a strong suit for him. Velenry nodded enthusiastically.

"Yes. It doesn't have to be long, but you should have one at least somewhat planned out."

"Why?"

"It started when Fellix became the first Elite of the Spear for King Orin after the Fourth War. To show respect to Fellix, we keep the tradition."

Emesos paused and gathered his thoughts. He bent over the paper and wrote for a good hour or so, often pausing for long periods between writing phrases. He nodded to Velenry. She nodded back.

"Would you like to speak it for me?"

Emesos cleared his throat. He didn't look at Velenry as he spoke, fearing he would lose his confidence. "I am blessed to receive the privilege to become one of Stryne's Elite. I am aware that it is a rare distinction, and I will do my best to uphold the loyalty and dedication established by my predecessors or die trying." He looked up at Velenry and she raised her eyebrows.

"That's it?"

"You never said it had to be creative or eloquent."

Velenry sighed, massaging her temples with her fingertips. "It's not bad, but you need to speak about something that matters to you, something that shows people how you think. Can you try again?" Emesos nodded.

He set to work one more time. It took him an thirty minutes to write his new speech. When he turned to Velenry, his eyes were alight with a fire that hadn't been there before.

"The speech is ready, if you want to listen." he said. Velenry signaled him to continue. Emesos cleared his throat.

"What have I done to deserve this position? As far as I know, nothing short of being good at waving a weapon around. I am aware that others have worked much harder than I to obtain the position of Elite. It is for this reason I accept the position reluctantly. I have no notion to believe that this will endear me to anyone at this ceremony. I can only promise you a few simple things: First, I accept the position of Elite with absolute humility and regret for the sorrow I have caused from this action. Second, I will work, no, strive, to serve the Kingdom of Stryne in the best way possible. And finally, I swear to respect each and every one of you, whether you be against me or with me-whether you are noble or a representative. These things I promise you, and nothing more. May the Divine watch over you, and thank you for listening."

He looked at Velenry to see her face of slight surprise. "That's a rather daring speech," she commented. "But it's very powerful. Now, I need you to hand it to me, so I can have my apprentices record it." Emesos handed her the speech and rubbed his neck.

"If you don't mind, Velenry, I'm going to my room to get some rest." He stood and bowed, quickly leaving the room. Velenry now looked at Emesos' speech proper. She gasped as she saw it. Her suspicions had been confirmed.

It was unreadable. All of it was a mash of glyphs. Some of them looked familiar to what she had seen near the borders of Rhyth and the werewolf lands. The entire speech was written in Ancient.

She quickly pulled out another piece of parchment and started copying down Emesos' speech the best she could remember. The young man had just given her a direct translation of Ancient. It wasn't much, as she had no idea how the syntax or language structure worked, it was a definite start. Velenry smiled.

He is a very odd man indeed. She put up her quill and all of her other supplies. *I wonder what else he's hiding...*

******

Emesos was standing before a man in a throne room that was covered in black and gold. There was a man standing before him. The being had black hair and golden eyes.

"It is good to see you have fully recovered, my friend." The noble's accent was undefined, but his speech was perfect. Emesos was once again forced to think on his feet.

"I am well, Sire."

The man nodded. "As it should. You are far too valuable to lose, my friend. You are the last heir to Altherai after all." Emesos looked up. For some reason, the statement didn't ring true in his mind.

"I am not." he said.

"Pardon?" The noble said with surprise.

"Altherai has chosen another." Emesos said quickly. The noble seemed slightly frustrated by the news, but he didn't say it outright. "I have dreamed of him." He prayed that the noble didn't detect the lie.

51

"Well, it doesn't matter. Soon, we shall have Rhyth at its knees. The invasion will take place in only a month. And so the Fifth War will begin. And at last, you'll claim what's yours, Sene. And I shall claim what is mine."

Emesos almost froze with terror. He managed to compose himself long enough to respond. "I am forever grateful, Lord Vrasta."

******

Emesos shot up in his bed, his body drenched in cold sweat. *The Fifth War will begin...* he thought. Vrasta was planning on invading Rhyth within a month. War was about to strike the Kingdoms once again. *I have to warn the king...* he thought. *Gonra would want to know about this. But who...would believe me? The last War was over a thousand years ago! And who is Altherai?* He thought and thought, desperately thinking of a person he could tell. The only person he could think of was Hane, and he couldn't be reached. Velenry came up as an idea, but Emesos quickly set that aside, he hardly knew her.

What would I tell them anyway? They'd think I was insane. Emsos sighed in frustration as he laid back in his bed and looked up at the ceiling. He didn't sleep the rest of the night.

It was early in the morning, around dawn, when someone knocked on his door. Emesos opened the door to see the same man he had given the boots standing before him. "Hello, sir. Rough night?" The man seemed much friendlier this time. Emesos nodded, rubbing his eyes with the heels of his hands. The servant held up what looked like a flask. "Here's something to wake you up."

Emesos took the flask and took a swig. He coughed and spluttered as the liquid was icy cold in temperature and spicy tasting at the same time. It flowed through his body, giving him a brief tingling sensation. "What is that?" he gasped as he handed back the flask. The servant smiled.

"We servants call it the Wake Brew." Emesos felt much more alert and energized.

"Well, it certainly did its job. Thank you." He paused for a moment.

"I don't know your name. What's your name?" he asked the servant.

"Mintell, sire." The servant seemed slightly uncomfortable. "But most people call me Min."

"Can you just call me Emesos when no one's around?" Min looked very surprised. "I need someone to treat me normally in this mess. Do you think you can do that?" Min nodded, smiling.

"You're a right strange noble, Sire Emesos."

"So I've been told." The man handed Emesos the clothes of an Elite. It was a smart military-like uniform; dark blue with bronze buttons on the cuffs of the sleeves and a small bronze brooch to secure yet another cape to his back. Emesos noted that the cape was much heavier, and the texture was a little coarse as he ran his fingers down the material, he thought of home, and the similar texture of the paper he used to give to his father.

I wonder what my parents would make of this, Emesos thought. *They're probably worrying out of their minds.* He shook his head to clear it and focused again on the uniform.

There was a bronze helm that had the emblem of Stryne on it: a sun rising behind a flag. He slid the helmet on and fastened it to his head. It was then he noticed a pair of boots were there, a light brown color, polished and ready. He slid them on and Min helped him secure the cape.

Emesos felt like he was in an unfamiliar body, like he didn't belong there. He tried walking around in his room and kept tripping over the cape. He looked at Min sheepishly. The servant could barely contain his laughter.

"Admit it; I look like a moron."

Min now laughed freely. "You're fine. Just make sure to not walk anywhere and you'll look like the perfect statesman."

"You fill me with so much confidence." Still, he felt more relaxed than he had in a while; just talking with Min made him feel more ready to take on his new role. Min guided him to the throne room, still wearing Emesos' boots, limping, but somehow looking more dignified than most people when he walked. Emesos had to hold the cape upward with one of his hands so it didn't trip him up. It was long enough that it just barely caught under his heels when he walked.

He and Min arrived at the throne room. Emesos turned to the man. "Thank you, Min."

Min smiled. "Of course, Sire Emesos."

"It's just 'Emesos', Min."

"Right, sorry…well…goodbye, then." The guards at the throne room door looked at Min oddly as he walked off. Emesos ignored them.

"Do I go in?" he asked one of the guards. The guard shook his head.

"Wait for the horns to sound. Then, you'll go straight up to the throne, and drop to one knee before the king." Emesos nodded. After a few more minutes, he was sweating in his suit, nerves and heat making his temperature rise. The horns blared. The doors swung open, and Emesos began walking at a reasonable pace. He managed to get halfway to the king before the cape tripped him up. He stumbled forward. He heard quiet laughter from the back of the room. His face flushed red in humiliation.

He got up to the king. The king rose and mouthed a single word.

"Kneel."

Emesos dropped to one knee. Emesos heard a faint *whoosh* as the king summoned his Blade. Emesos felt the pain in his arm again. It was searing, burning. His hand was crackling with the same faint light that appeared during the parade that seemed so long ago. He grasped his wrist as it flared in pain. He suppressed a moan.

The Blade touched each of his shoulders. Emesos felt like his arm was going to explode. The king asked him a question he didn't hear. All he could hear was the throbbing of his pulse in his ears. The king asked another question he didn't hear. Emesos managed to faintly hear one statement.

"As my Blade proclaims my right to rule from the Divine, may the wielding of the Blade be seen before all in this room." The pain in Emesos' arm intensified. This time, he let out an audible scream. He tasted blood and blacked out.

Six

When Emesos regained consciousness, he woke up, staring at a swirl of a strange mist above him. *Mist? I'm indoors...mist doesn't make any sense.* The mist then did the unexpected. It slammed into him. It felt like a cold wind. He gasped. In an instant, Erk's face was over his.

"He's awake!" Erk called over his shoulder, staring back at Emesos. "You have some explaining to do," he muttered to Emesos. "The king is livid you ruined the ceremony."

"Not my fault," Emesos protested. His tongue felt awkward in his mouth, heavy and resistant. "I have no control over it. It's his Blade..."

"What?" Erk seemed surprised by that statement. He didn't get to ask any more questions. Emesos heard a door fly open. Erk snapped to attention. As an Elite, Erk only had to do that to one person: the king.

"Is he awake?" the king asked. The tone was rapid, curt. He expected an answer, and quickly. Fortunately, Erk was ready.

"He is Sire. Would you have him sit up?"

"Please."

Emesos was helped upright with Erk's firm hands. He was glad he had Erk's assistance. He wasn't sure if he would have been able to sit up otherwise. Emesos looked at the king and saw his outraged expression. "I'm sorry, Sire."

The king now unleashed what Emesos figured had been building up in his chest for at least a few minutes.

"Do you realize you've made me the laughingstock of the nobility of Stryne?" he shouted. "Almost all of my enemies are practically cackling with glee at this! They say I've now lost my wits, that I picked a handicapped person to be an Elite! Not only that, but your image is-"

Words burst out of Emesos' mouth, without his bidding. He cut the king off. "I said there were people more qualified than me." Emesos said quietly. "You were the one that refused to listen. This blunder is of your own making."

The king turned red faced. "You dare talk back to-"

"Yes I dare!" Emesos now thundered back at the king. He got out of his bed and stood level with the king. His weakness from earlier was gone.

A fiery anger seared through his body. "I dare speak against someone who refuses to acknowledge his mistakes!" The king had adopted a strange look of shock, but Emesos plowed on, not caring. "You insisted on making me an Elite despite my objections!"

"You refused to acknowledge your potential! You could be one of the greatest servants of the king of Stryne!" Gonra bellowed.

Emesos now snapped completely. He slapped the king across the face. Erk let out a cry of shock.

"My *potential*? Am I just a servant to you? Some...*plaything*? I'm a person! Yet all you care about is what your new *toy* can do for you! You didn't bother to listen! You shame Orin's legacy by acting in such a fashion!" The king stumbled backward, his eyes still filled with surprise. He fell back into a chair.

"Divine save me…" The king whispered. "What are you?" He seemed to have a moment of panic and then started shouting.

"Guards!" A set of well armored men came crashing into the room, grabbing Emesos' arms. Emesos didn't resist. He just stared at the king and made one final statement as he was guided away.

"Don't make the mistake Orin's predecessor did."

Emesos was hauled off to the dark, cold dungeons and tossed in a cell with a few other people in it. The door was slammed shut and locked behind them. He looked at his cell companions using the dim glow the single candle in the cell gave him. One of them had a beard, one of them did not. That was about all he could see.

"What are you in for?" asked the man with the beard, "Haven't seen guards that scared before."

"I yelled at the king. I also collapsed in the middle of a ceremony."

The man with the beard stepped into the light. His face was covered in dirt, he was missing a couple of teeth, and he looked like he could use a good meal or two. He smiled.

"Name's Kast," he said with an easy air. He nodded over to his companion. "This here is Zafen. He doesn't talk much. So…you yelled at a king and got away with it? How?" Emesos told them his entire story. He left out nothing. Not even the lights and moments of feeling others' emotions.

The two prisoners gave him looks of disbelief. Emesos didn't expect them to believe him. He just needed to tell somebody. How they took the story was their own problem. It was then that Emesos received his second surprise of the day. Zafen stepped forward.

"Can you feel my emotions?" he asked in a quiet monotone. Emesos nodded slowly.

"Give me your hand." Emesos instructed. Zafen extended his hand and Emesos took it.

****

Emesos was in the middle of a battle. A much younger Zafen was there, wielding a bow with deadly precision. "Aim!" Zafen called. More archers raised their bows in unison. "Fire!" The arrows released in a wave that plowed into the opposing army...

He saw Zafen clamped in shackles before king Gonra. "This is the peasant who led the revolt, sire," a guard stated. "He is the one who is responsible for the death of your nephew." Gonra stood and slapped Zafen hard across the face. Zafen's lip split and started to bleed.

"Life in prison. No hope for release." Gonra declared. "Make sure he isn't in a comfortable cell." Zafen shouted one final statement as he was being dragged away.

"It's your fault! If you had ruled better, he wouldn't have died!" The king grasped his throne for support as he leaned back into it. Tears ran down his face.

******

Emesos let go of Zafen's hand and opened his eyes. He wasn't even aware he had closed them. Zafen looked at Emesos, his eyes almost pleading. Emesos looked back at him and spoke briefly.

"It's unfortunate that the king's nephew had to die. I don't think he's forgiven himself for letting that revolt happen."

Zafen was shaking slightly. He covered his face and slumped to the floor. A sob erupted from him. Kast looked at Emesos and spoke.

"I don't think he's forgiven himself either." Emesos looked at the man on the floor and pitied him.

Emesos didn't know how long he had been locked in the cell. Time had no definition, stretching on for what felt like an eternity. At one point, he was sitting up against a wall, staring into the darkness. Kast came over and sat next to him.

"Are you alright?" he asked. Emesos turned to him and changed the subject.

"You know what I hate most about being in the cell? All it does is give you time to think. Time to brood and sleep."

"There are worse things to suffer than boredom," Kast pointed out. Emesos shook his head.

"Not for me. All I can do is think about those...dreams? No, 'dreams' isn't the right word for them... neither is 'nightmare;' but they aren't 'visions' either. More like flashbacks, but they're not mine. What do I call them? What's happening to me?" He let out a grunt of frustration, slamming a fist on the ground. "I'm so tired of being confused!"

He turned to Kast. Kast had seen many weary men before, but never had he seen one more stretched than Emesos. The boy's skin was rapidly becoming pale in the darkness of the prison. His hair was a tangled mess. His lips were drawn tight against him. But his eyes were the worst. They were bloodshot from lack of sleep and anxiety. *He looks like he's hanging on by a thread,* Kast thought.

"I would call them 'experiences,'" Kast suggested. "After that, try mentally organizing your thoughts and feelings. Sort things using the straw we have for beds if you have to. You need to get control over your own thoughts before anything else." Emesos looked as if a massive burden had been lifted off him.

"Thank you."

Kast watched him for a long while after that as Emesos took small pieces of straw and twisted them into various shapes, laying them in a small section of the floor. He was muttering to himself as he did the task. *Perhaps the thread has already snapped,* Kast thought. He drifted off into an uncomfortable sleep against the wall, the only sound in the cell the rustling of straw as Emesos worked.

He was wakened by the clang of the cell door. Kast opened his eyes and saw that a guard was standing there. "Emesos?" the guard said. Emesos looked up from his straw work. "Come with me," the soldier commanded.

Emesos got up and silently followed the soldier, waiting for him to shut the door before they walked off. Kast looked over at what Emesos was working on. Zafen did the same. They were both very confused. On the ground was a mass of straw, twisted and laid out in shapes they didn't understand.

Maybe there's more to that boy than meets the eye...

Seven

Velenry stared at the speech Emesos had written, then back at the translation she had written. The glyphs Emesos had written were inconsistent in many cases. Certain repeating words had different glyphs. She assumed the symbols were different to show things like accusative or narrative case, but she wasn't sure.

She needed Emesos to write other things. Simple sentences, so she could at least get the core of the language. Velenry knew that Ancient would be very complex, but she hadn't expected to count over forty different symbols in just a few lines.

No wonder Ancient was supposedly 'untranslatable.' There were no obvious consistencies. She looked up from her work when she heard the door to her study open. In between two soldiers was a being so beaten down and ghostly, she wondered if it was even human.

She was horrified. *Emesos has only been down in that prison for a week! What happened to him?*

"Emesos?" she asked hesitantly. *Surely this isn't the same person I met in the library.* The figure lifted his head. Her heart sank.

"Hello, Velenry," he said quietly. "It's good to see you." She inspected his face and saw no falsehood, only pain. There were very large dark circles under his brown eyes. The eyes themselves were bloodshot.

He hasn't been sleeping, she thought. *Why?* The soldiers went to move Emesos roughly into a chair, but a sharp look from Velenry softened the movement. Emesos sat in the chair, staring off into space, his eyes distant.

"I need to ask you a few questions," she said to him, firmly but gently. Her voice seemed to snap him back into reality.

"What do you need to ask?" he returned back. "I'm afraid I'm very short on answers right now."

Velenry grabbed Emesos' speech and put it in front of him so he could see it. "What's this?" he asked. Velenry rolled her eyes.

"It's your speech. The one you wrote. You were lying to me. You *do* know Ancient." She got a peculiar reaction from Emesos. His eyes dilated, his face an expression of horror.

"I did that?" he whispered. "How did I do that? It doesn't make any... where did this...Anazan? No...I never..." Emesos looked at Velenry. The shadows of his eyes were much deeper than before.

"I *don't* know Ancient, Velenry. The truth is...I have no control over...anything." He seemed to say this to himself with such misery it made the soldiers uncomfortable. Emesos looked at Velenry.

"I haven't told you everything." He spoke slowly, as if forcing words to emerge that didn't want to surface. "I randomly write Ancient. I see lights..."

"Lights?" Velenry said with worry. *Has being in prison made him lose his mind?* she wondered.

Emesos nodded. "Yes, lights. A kind of glow surrounds everyone I see, like a faint candle. Did you know I haven't slept properly in over three weeks? If I do...*they* come."

"Who are 'they?'"

He groaned. "The experiences. It's like every time I've tried to sleep, I get thrown into a dream. Only it's not a dream. It's like

I'm living as somebody else; and they're so *real*. Last time, I was a man in a throne room...a man named Sene. And I was talking with Vrasta, something about an Altherai and a Fifth War. Vrasta said he was going to invade Rhyth in a month. But a week has already gone by."

"It was just a nightmare, Emesos."

"Was it?" he snapped at her. "That still doesn't explain the time I was Fellix, or the time I was Anazan; and I was in actual historical events. They weren't just dreams. Dreams don't make chronological sense like that." Velenry's eyebrows came together in confusion. Emesos continued his explanation

"I'd never heard of Anazan before my first incident three weeks ago. I certainly didn't know Anazan wasn't from Stryne. I'd heard of Fellix, but I didn't know he was ordered to leave his post by the king of Stryne." The soldiers seemed shifty now, on edge. Velenry wondered if Emesos was sane. But Emesos went on.

"I can't touch people either. Otherwise, I learn things I really didn't want to know."

"What do you mean by that?" Velenry asked. *This is all going so wrong! I just wanted him to write a few sentences, not have a debate!*

Emesos turned around rapidly in his chair and gripped one of the soldier's arms. The other soldier went to beat Emesos over the head, but stopped short when Emesos let go. Emesos looked at the soldier and nodded. The soldier's eyes widened. Something seemed to have joined between them in that single touch.

"I wish it could be different." Emesos said to the soldier he had grabbed. "You're a good person. It's not your fault she wound up the way she did. It was her choice." The soldier broke down, losing his iron discipline and started crying and shaking. The other soldier went forward to hit Emesos, but the crying soldier caught his companion's spear.

"Don't hit him." the soldier said to his friend. "I'm fine." The other soldier slowly took his weapon back, looking at his friend with unsure eyes.

The soldier turned to Velenry. "Ma'am," the soldier said. "what he says is true." Velenry raised an eyebrow.

"You could have easily been bribed by him to act this way," she stated. Emesos flew forward into sudden movement. He grabbed Velenry's arm.

A violent swirl of images flew through her mind. She didn't know what they were; they went by too fast to see. A sudden upwelling of emotions...

Emesos let go of her arm. He was smiling. "You really don't hate him." She was confused.

"What?"

"You don't hate him. You like him. Quite a bit, I might add. Of course, I should probably learn about him before I say this, but you two need to stop dancing around each other. It's driving Erk mad, the game of hide and seek you play."

Velenry's heart jumped into her throat. Her head was pounding. *How did he...there were no rumors... what just happened? How?* She shook her head. "I don't know what you're talking about."

Emesos gave her a knowing smile. "Come on, Velenry! Now which one of us is lying?" She ordered the guards to take him away after that and she was left with her own thoughts.

What Emesos had said was completely true. She was attracted to Erk, she always had been. But Erk was so stiff and formal with her that she had reacted in kind. *Could what Emesos have said been true?* She wondered.

"Velenry?" She jumped when she heard the voice. It was Erk, standing at the door in her private study. Fear gripped her.

"How long have you been standing there?" she asked quickly.

"Long enough to hear Emesos," Erk said. Velenry thought she was going to be ill. A slight blush crept up her neck.

"What about him?" Velenry asked. Erk came in and sat down across the desk from Velenry. He looked more serious than ever. But something else had been added to his sharp face. It was a brooding look, and it made him that much more magnetic.

"I believe him," Erk declared.

"What?" Velenry was shocked. Erk, Stryne's greatest cynic, was believing a prisoner?

"You didn't have to duel with him, Vel." Velenry felt a strange tingle run up her spine. Did he just call her 'Vel'?

"He was like a monster with a spear. But he acted like he wasn't there. His eyes were *closed* the entire time. And when he was yelling at the king before he was locked up...he was shouting in Strynic and first, but then it changed into some language I've never heard before. But the way he was speaking... it rang in your ears." Erk traced the outline of the wooden grain of Velenry's desk as he continued.

"You didn't have to know what he was saying to get the point. He doesn't have control over what's happening to him. And from what I can tell, it only comes up when he's under pressure. If those symptoms are true, then the other ones could be true as well, right?" Velenry nodded.

Erk grabbed her hand. She jumped a little, but did not pull away. He stared at her in a different way. "Velenry. He was right...about the other part too...I...I'm tired of..." He was fumbling for words, so unusual for him. He shook his head, trying to get a grip on his mind. "The point is...I need you."

She raised her eyebrows. "What about the court? You're very important, and people will talk."

"I don't care!" The words were forceful enough to make her lean backward. "I don't care what they say!"

"But the king's reputation-"

"Is in shambles already, so what's one more brick removed from the ruins?" he sighed and squeezed her hand. She squeezed back.

"I suppose I have to go and thank Emesos," Erk said. Silence filled the room between the two of them until he cut the silence unexpectedly.

"Damn, why is it always the troubled people that fix the world?"

Velenry smiled at him before replying. "Because... They stay troubled so they can fix other people's troubles."

"I guess that makes sense. Still, I hope he manages to hold on in that cell. The king won't budge, no matter what I say. But a Teacher of the Divine is coming tomorrow to talk to Emesos."

"That should be interesting."

Erk nodded. "Indeed. I get the feeling that Emesos is just the beginning of something much bigger though."

"Let's hope his mind lasts long enough to witness it."

✳✳✳✳✳✳

Emesos was in a dressing room. A figure was standing before him, a crown on his head and utter panic on his face. "Fellix!" he cried. "Help me, please! I don't think I can go through with this!"

So I'm Fellix this time, *Emesos thought. He looked at the young man before him.* This must be Orin again.

"Don't worry." he said encouragingly. "You'll be a great king. And if you feel overwhelmed, take a few deep breaths and think of something that grounds you."

"Like what?" Orin seemed desperate for something to hang onto. Emesos rapidly thought back to what his dad had once told him. Then he answered.

"A simple moment. Nothing extravagant or worth noting. Something like skipping stones in a pond on a spring day; or eating the first apples of fall." Orin closed his eyes for a moment, whispering the advice under his breath. Then, he took a few deep breaths and opened his eyes, smiling at Emesos.

"Thanks, Fellix. It's just like you told me that one time right? 'Try to think about too much at one time; and you'll just ruin your ability to get anything done.' Emesos nodded.

"Yeah... sometimes I should learn to follow my own advice." he said. They both laughed. Suddenly, a soldier came in.

"Your Majesty, it's time." The excitement in the soldier's voice was obvious. Orin looked at Emesos and gave him a huge smile.

"Well, I guess it's time for us to get to where we're supposed to be." Emesos nodded. Orin went to walk away, but then he paused.

"What's wrong?" Emesos asked. Orin turned around. He stepped up to Emesos and gave him a hug. Emesos returned it after a moment of surprise. Orin whispered a final statement in his ear.

"Thank you so much...father."

Eight

Kast jumped backward rapidly as Emesos shot upward from his sleeping position on the floor, his straw symbols next to him. Emesos took in another gasp of air and blinked a few times to bat away the remains of his experience. Kast noticed that his friend's eyes had turned completely white. He blinked a few more times and they returned to normal. *So he was telling the truth...he does have those strange dreams when he sleeps.*

"What did you see?" Kast asked Emesos. Emesos gave him a smile that seemed to lift the burden off his shoulders. Something in that smile made Kast want to smile back.

"I saw Orin...I was Fellix."

"As in the legendary High Commander?"

Emesos nodded. "We were standing in a room talking. I gave him some advice before some important ceremony and he gave me some back. But then, he hugged me. He...called me 'father.'"

Kast recoiled. "But none of the stories say Orin is related to Fellix...They clearly note that Fellix had one child named Ross. Orin's parentage is clearly mentioned too. He was from Stryne and his mother was Bellan, his father was Wesk."

Emesos paused for a moment and thought. "I don't know what he meant by calling me 'father.' Maybe he and Fellix were close enough to have that relationship." Kast gave him another look.

"What?" Emesos asked defensively. "It was just a theory."

"You're really different, you know that? What I would give to watch how your life plays out."

"You are going to see it play out. I'm stuck here in this cell with you, remember?"

Zafen spoke up in his quiet voice. "No you're not. Not once the Teacher of the Divine meets you. Half the Congregation will be clamoring for your release."

Emesos crinkled his eyebrows. He hadn't thought of that. "You mean a Teacher of the Divine is coming here?"

Zafen nodded. "Of course. He appears for all the new prisoners. Doesn't like me much though; never have been one for religion."

Kast nodded in agreement. "The Teacher will be very interested in you. He'll think you're a person who's been blessed by the Divine; or maybe a Prophet; they like having those."

Emesos shook his head. "But I'm not a Prophet. I don't see the future, just the past."

Kast now made his point. "But doesn't every experience you have somehow reflect the present?" Emesos paused.

He's right! Emesos realized. It all fell into place: Fellix leaving, and then he left for the castle himself. The advice he had gotten from Orin, when he needed it most. The vision of the celebration came the day of the festival. Dread gripped his stomach when he thought about his conversation with Vrasta.

"Vrasta's going to invade within a month." Emesos whispered. "If my experiences reflect the present...that means Vrasta's going to invade within a month. Oh, Divine help us..." Kast's eyes widened and Zafen's head shot up when they both came to that realization.

"You have to tell King Gonra, Emesos." Kast said

"They all think I'm insane, remember? This would just be the final proof. Besides, I don't think Gonra's in the mood to listen to me." Emesos and his companions fell into a long silence.

That silence was broken as they heard footsteps coming toward them. They were slow, uneven sounding. And before their cell was someone Emesos never expected to see again.

"Min? Min, is that you?" Min nodded.

"Sure is. I figured you were a little lonely, so I came to visit." Emesos got up and walked to the bars that separated him and Min. Min's tanned face looked more alive than when Emesos had met him. His brown eyes had a different shine in them.

"Thank you, Min," Emesos whispered. He tried to silently show Min how much he appreciated his visit. Min seemed to get the message. Emesos spoke more loudly now. "So, how are you? Anything strange happened recently?"

Min smiled and scratched his head. "Well, there's been rumors around that Historian Velenry and Lord Erk are courting. And there's been plenty of talk about you too. Most of them think you have a strange illness and are hammering away at Gonra for picking someone so 'unstable' as they put it."

Emesos winced. Gonra would definitely not want to hear him out now more than ever.

"Hey, Min? Mind if I ask you something?"

"Of course."

"What did you need those apples for?" Min smiled.

"Oh, the apples? I used them to feed the king's horses! The king even gave me extra wages for it!" The two were quiet for a while. As Min turned to leave, Emesos asked him for one favor.

"Hey, Min... If anything strange or worth noting occurs, would you please tell Lord Erk?"

"Sure, it's the least I can do!" Min bade him farewell, quickly walking away. Kast spoke as Emesos watched the man go.

"See, I told you you're different."

"Oh, shut it."

They spent the rest of the day doing nothing; just staring at walls. The next day, Emesos met the Teacher.

The man was very thin and pale; his robes looked to be far too big for him. He wasn't just a Teacher, but a Listener as well, a person who was supposed to find signs of the Divine's will. He stood at the bars and spoke with authority.

"I come seeking the one they call Emesos," he said. Emesos stepped forward.

"That would be me." The Teacher looked over Emesos with a keen eye.

"And would you care to explain why you shouted at His Majesty so unjustly?"

Emesos grew angry just thinking about it. "It wasn't unjust! It was the same situation Fellix was in with Orin's predecessor! He wouldn't listen and others paid the price for it! Once again, a King of Stryne rejects a person who tries to make them see reason. But right now, we have a bigger problem to worry about."

"And what problem would that be?" the Teacher challenged.

Emesos looked directly into the man's eyes and spoke with no hesitation. "Vrasta is coming again. He's going to invade Rhyth in just under a month. But Gonra won't listen to me now, so what's the purpose of warning him?!"

"Vrasta is long dead, boy," the Teacher said scornfully. "It has been over a thousand years since he's invaded the Kingdoms."

"He's alive!" Emesos shouted. "He's still alive, damn it! I saw him with my own eyes! He's coming again and all you care about is me? Did it *ever* occur to you that Vrasta also led the Third War as well as the Fourth?" He stopped in the middle of his rant in surprise. *How do I know that?* He thought. *I didn't know that before...*

The Teacher tilted his head. "The leader of the Third War was never known. Why do you claim Vrasta was the leader?"

Emesos answered quickly. "No one else has control over that many werewolf tribes. No one else would have been able to orchestrate such a large assault with such a conflicted force." The Teacher's eyebrows rose.

Once again I'm getting knowledge or power that isn't mine. Emesos thought. *Where am I getting them from?*

"Those are interesting theories, but I'm here to talk about you. I was told you were making strange symbols and speaking in a different language. Would you care to demonstrate for me?"

Emesos gripped his hair in frustration. "I don't have control over it! It just happens; like the experiences!"

"Experiences?"

"Yes, experiences. When I sleep, I get strange dreams. It's like I go back into the past and *become* a person in the dream. It's so realistic... There not really dreams, or visions, so I just call them experiences."

He could see the Teacher didn't believe him, and it bothered him. He grabbed the Teacher's hand. The man tried to jerk away, but Emesos held him fast. "Maybe you'll understand better if I show you."

It felt like memories were pouring out of him and flooding in. The priest's emotions and memories were coming, and his were going. He let go as a soldier struck him backward with the butt of his spear.

Emesos hit the ground hard and looked at the Teacher. The man's eyes were wide with shock. He was staring at Emesos.

"Well?" Emesos asked.

"You...you..." The Teacher couldn't seem to find words to say. "How?" He managed to ask.

Emesos shrugged. "I told you, *I don't know*. I don't know what's happening to me. I just know I have to take it as it comes and not to reflect on it. Orin was kind enough to mention that. Otherwise, I would have lost my mind." This statement seemed to shock the Teacher even more.

"It was...interesting to talk to you, Emesos." The Teacher left, his robes making a flapping sound as he walked away. Kast broke into laughter behind him.

"Oh, his *face!* If we ever get out of here, remind me to buy you a drink! That was priceless!" Emesos couldn't help smiling. Zafen was grinning widely as well. The three of them broke into laughter that lasted a long time.

It would be the last time Emesos would laugh in quite a while.

Nine

It had been two weeks since Emesos had been put in prison. Erk was walking down a hallway when he saw a servant hobbling toward him, a look of anxiety on his face. Erk grabbed his shoulder. "What's wrong?" The young man nodded toward the window.

"There's a gathering happening down in the market square. The Teachers are talking."

"About what?"

"They say Emesos is a herald from the Divine! They're telling people that Emesos is Stryne's great Prophet. They're displaying the soldier Emesos grabbed and the Teacher he talked to as proof!" Erk cursed. He was afraid something like this might happen.

"Does the king know yet?" he asked. The servant shook his head.

"No, I was finding you so you could tell him." Erk exhaled.

"Alright." The servant bowed and walked down the corridor. Erk headed in the direction of the king's study. When he arrived, Gonra was reading a tome. He looked up and shut the book when he saw Erk's expression.

"What's the matter?"

"The Teachers are talking about Emesos in the market square. They're claiming he's a Prophet of some kind." The king looked down for a moment and then looked back up at Erk.

"The more I think about that, the more it would actually make sense." Gonra said.

Erk's mind was sent reeling. He had expected the king to be angry, or displeased at best. Instead, he was *agreeing*.

"Why would you say that, Your Majesty?" Gonra tapped the book in front of him with his index finger.

"Because everything he's talked about has happened before. The dreams he was telling Velenry about actually *did* happen. I looked through the Historian Archives myself." Erk was slightly taken aback. The king continued his explanation.

"In addition to that, I witnessed firsthand some of the things that he had described. He was yelling at me in another language, unaware of the change. His eyes turned completely white when he was yelling. And the speech Velenry showed me actually was written in Ancient. She managed to find a somewhat consistent pattern. The only thing that's not explained is the incident at the ceremony." Gonra let out a deep sigh.

"He's so strange, but damn it, Erk-" The king slammed a fist on his desk. "That boy's changed so much in such a short time. That soldier he touched now is getting married soon with the girl he's always loved! And you and Velenry..." He smiled at Erk. Erk grinned back. The king's face became serious and he stood.

"So I'm going to publicly pardon him," he finished.

Erk was once again surprised. This would be the first public pardoning of Gonra's reign. "But I have to apologize privately first. Care to come with me as I humiliate myself?"

"Certainly, Sire."

Gonra glared at Erk. "You agreed far too quickly to that."

Erk followed Gonra to the dungeons, where they arrived at Emesos' cell. Emesos looked up and Erk visibly flinched at what he saw.

Emesos' ankles were raw from the shackles around them. He was pale and his cheekbones prominent. But it was his eyes that were the most disturbing. They were bloodshot from exhaustion. Emesos blinked a few times. He stood, the chains clinking on the stone floor.

"Your Majesty," Emesos bowed. "I'm honored to see you. I would like to apologize for what I said to you...I spoke out of turn." Gonra shook his head.

"Save your apology. I was in the wrong. I would like to apologize for putting you in here. You will be officially pardoned and released in a few days." Emesos was very surprised by this.

"What made you change your mind?" Emesos asked.

"Well, the Teachers of the Divine have been declaring you as a Prophet, so it would stand to reason that I should release you before they demand your release themselves. I wouldn't want to appear easily influenced by the Congregation by releasing you after they demand it."

Emesos laughed softly. "You have to save what little reputation you have that I didn't destroy, right?" Gonra held up a finger.

"Actually, I'll be credited with discovering the next great Prophet."

"I'm not a Prophet," Emesos protested.

"Like it or not, you are Emesos. The Teachers have declared it. Now, what are you supposed to predict? I have to have some basis of a Prophecy, or some other excuse, to release you."

"It's interesting you should mention that..." And so Emesos told Gonra and Erk what he had learned from the past, and of the conflict that was to come.

Darkest Siege

Ryan Wilshusen

Part Two:
The Outcast

Ryan Wilshusen

Ten

"Let yourselves be open to the Divine, and He shall enter your hearts and come to call them home." Ishik was transfixed by the Teacher's lesson. The other acolytes were packing up their things to leave. Ishik remained, lost in his thoughts.

He didn't leave until the rest of the acolytes had gone. He didn't belong in their circle of friendship. He didn't belong to anybody's circle of friendship. It didn't bother him, though; he was used to it. Even before joining the Congregation, he had always been alone. It was something he had grown accustomed to.

It was time to go to the lesson on the Forces. It was his first time going there. He hoped it was as interesting as the Theory of Morals lesson he had just attended.

He arrived at the lesson and sat up front, where he could get a good view of the board. The rest of the acolytes were there, talking to each other. Ishik stayed silent and waited expectantly. The teacher soon walked in, a thin man with little hair left. "Hello. Today, we shall learn how the Divine views the Forces." The other acolytes fell silent.

"Now, let's review what the four Forces are that govern our lives. They are as follows: gravity, friction, heat and substance. Each one is essential to our daily life. Now, the Divine chooses to bless each of the Kings with limited control over these Forces through their Blades."

"What about other people who control Forces?" a boy asked. "You know, those who don't have Blades?" The teacher's face grew serious.

"They are not chosen by the Divine. Many say they can Manipulate the Forces, but almost all of them lie, hiding behind tricks and slight of hand. But those that can truly Manipulate the Forces are desecrators of the sacredness of the Blades and therefore desecrators of the Divine's will."

"If they can Manipulate the Forces, could they not also be blessed by the Divine?" Ishik asked. The teacher shook his head. His eyes bored into Ishik.

"No, for it is written by the Prophet Teacher Parapas 'He who controls the Forces without a Blade in hand brings shame to the Divine's great plan. That is all for this lesson. I hope to see you all tomorrow." The acolytes got up and left, Ishik pondering the Teacher's words as he went.

After lessons, the rest of the day passed quickly. It was just service, then reflection, then bed. Ishik was about to go to bed and was praying his evening prayer to the Divine, his eyes closed.

Divine; please, accept my humble prayers of thanks. I am but a mere mortal placed here by your hand. All I ask is that you give me another day and a sign that you are with me.

He opened his eyes and found that he was no longer at the foot of his bed. He was above it.

But I'm still on my knees, Ishik thought. *That doesn't make any sense.* He looked down, and discovered that he was floating above the ground.

He let out a gasp and dropped to the ground, his knees hitting the floor hard. He was in denial. Surely what he had seen was merely a trick of the eyes. He crawled into bed and slept peacefully.

When he woke up, he said a quick prayer, got dressed, and went to morning Service. It was a good lesson on how the Divine favored those with discipline, like Fellix, the great High Commander of Stryne. Nothing strange had happened to him then.

It was during farming hours that the issues began. It was fall, and apples were ready for picking. Ishik went with his basket and tool to remove the apple from the tree. He went to cut down an apple. He sawed it free and let it drop in the basket, it landed with a slight *thunk*, one of Ishik's favorite sounds. He quickly acquired an entire basket's worth.

He was carrying his load of apples back to the storage rooms, where they would be preserved for the coming winter months, when he saw an acolyte struggling to keep a grip on his basket. The acolyte tripped over a rock and the basket went flying from his arms. Ishik dropped his own basket, lunging forward to catch the other man's load. Only, he didn't catch it. It floated above his hands, as if repelled by an invisible force.

The other acolyte was staring at him, eyes wide, and his mouth open. Ishik felt a surge of panic. He quickly grabbed the load of apples and placed it in the man's hands. Ishik went over to his basket and finished hauling his own load, avoiding eye contact.

While he was walking from the orchard, Ishik saw the area where he had stopped the other acolyte's apples from falling. It set him on edge.

Divine, what's happening to me? He asked. *I am lost and in need of guidance. Please, help me find my way.* Ishik kept on working, pretending nothing had changed.

That night, the evening service was on honesty. Afterward, he knew that they would be expected to profess their mistakes and mishaps out loud in front of others, as it was the third day of the week. They admitted them out loud together; that way, there was nothing hidden among them, so they were truly unified under the Divine.

It had never bothered Ishik to admit his mistakes, but this was the first time he had something to hide.

People were standing as their turns arrived, going down the chapel's rows, confessing. Mostly it was unholy thoughts. It came to Ishik quickly. He stood and spoke. "I confess that I have tried to control things that are in the Divine's hands alone." The others nodded in understanding.

"You are forgiven, please be seated." The teacher leading the service declared. Ishik sat down, relieved. It wasn't a lie, but it wasn't specific either. That night, he was at the foot of his bed again, praying with as much force as he could.

"Divine! I beg you; please send me a sign of what I'm to do? Is this my penance for not worshiping you like I should? I need your guidance, a simple sign... *please?*" He whispered under his breath. He opened his eyes and found himself floating yet again.

No! he thought. *This can't be happening. What's making me do this? It might be a sin! Surely the Divine wouldn't make me sin!* He dropped to the ground after a few seconds, managing to catch himself this time. Ishik went to bed, pondering his predicament.

The next day was worse. He woke to find himself floating above his bed. Then, at morning service before breakfast, Ishik had to hold himself down to keep from floating in his seat. At breakfast, he had to keep a tight grip on his bowl and spoon to keep *them* from floating.

He was walking down the hall trying to get to one of his lessons, his mind still in a panic.

There has to be an explanation for this? Divine, what am I supposed to do?

A young acolyte was walking by and dropped a quill. The acolyte didn't seem to notice, so Ishik grabbed it and went to pat the young man on the shoulder. "Excuse me." He patted the acolyte's shoulder twice.

The young man was suddenly airborne. He slammed into the ceiling hard enough to leave cracks, then fell back to the ground with a *thud*. People were staring. One ran forward and put his fingers to the acolyte's neck to check for a pulse. "He's dead!" the man cried.

No! Ishik thought. *No...this isn't happening...* People were staring at him with fear in their eyes. Ishik knew then, that it was the end of his time in the Congregation.

******

A week had passed since the incident. He had been turned out of the Congregation and left to fend for himself. Ishik couldn't help but think about it at night.

He was starving, slowly but surely. Food was hard to find in Rhyth's rocky, pine-forested terrain. Even if he could find some wild animals, he knew next to nothing about hunting.

I've been rejected by the Congregation, he thought as he was walking down a slope near a river, trying to keep his balance. *But, rejected or no, I still need to eat something! Anything! Divine...please...I know I made a mistake, but I really need your help now more than ever.*

He jumped and landed on a nearby rock, losing his balance.

He was about to fall in the stream, but he stopped just above it, floating, being held upward by that invisible force. *Force!* he thought. The realization hit him. *I'm affecting the Force of gravity!*

A dead fish floated to the surface of the river. Ishik silently thanked the Divine and set about cleaning and cooking the fish.

There was plenty of wood for a fire and he managed to find some flint. He ate the fish with relish, enjoying the taste of food for the first time in nearly a week.

I could live like this, he thought to himself. *Out in the wild...* The more he thought about it, the more attractive it sounded. *I won't have to be around anybody. I could have my problems...and nobody would know...*

He decided that was what he was going to do, until he managed to find a town. Ishik looked around for a stick that was large enough to use as a support. He managed to find one after searching around the river for fallen branches. It was slightly curved, but it would do.

Ishik looked around for a sharp stone and managed to sharpen a point on the end of his stick. After that, he heated it over the fire, like they did for the sticks used for pilgrimages. Then, he found another stone to use to carve a rough grip into the sturdy branch.

Ishik stood, flexing his neck. He inspected his work and was pleased. He had to pick a direction to travel, but he wasn't sure which one to pick. He knew a small village called Biere was southwest of the monastery, but he had traveled in a random direction when he was put out of the Congregation. Using what he had learned from his Stars lessons, he oriented himself southwest and started his walk to Biere.

It was isolated in the wilderness, but Ishik felt a sort of ease that he hadn't found in the Congregation. He had joined upon his mother's death, much to his father's joy. Ishik thought back to how excited his father was. *"This could be the next great step in your life, Ishik. Maybe you'll finally have some friends to talk to."*

Ishik shook his head. *He really didn't care. He just wanted me away from his merchant friends so I couldn't embarrass him on accident.* He sang the Five Prayers to the Divine as he walked. The rest of the day passed quickly and Ishik managed to find some berries to eat before he fell asleep.

He continued traveling this way for another week, slowly becoming more like the land itself: rugged and wild. The cold sun had tanned his skin and less food with more exercise had made him much stronger.

All the while, he had been searching himself and the Divine for answers. Ishik prayed to Him still, even though the Congregation had rejected him. It was written by the Prophet Qien: *"For the Divine never turns away from a mortal soul."*

At the same time, his control over the Force of gravity was getting stronger and stronger. He was now crossing streams by walking over the water. He caused fish to fly out of rivers and become his dinner. He could make things float briefly, but he hadn't figured out how to control directions yet. Ishik had come to accept his ability.

Maybe the Teachers are wrong. If the Divine didn't want me to have this ability, He wouldn't have let me exist. I have these abilities for a purpose; I just have to find out what that purpose is. For now, it's a blessing of the highest honor, a blessing bestowed to kings. Yet I have it. Why?

He was walking through a forest he didn't know the name of when he saw a log in his way. Ishik didn't feel like lifting the log. A wild idea struck him. He backed up from the log and got a running start.

He made his feet to reject the Force of gravity as he came close to the log. It worked too well, sending him soaring twelve feet in the air.

Ishik saw the ground getting closer. He rapidly tried to make himself reject gravity again, before he hit the ground and broke something. It bent to his will and Ishik managed to land hard, but safely on the other side of the log. He was red in the face, adrenaline searing through him. But looking ahead, he saw something that made his blood run cold.

A hairy creature with large fangs stood on two feet before him, its arms having large hands with five fingers and sharp nails. Its face had a large snout and red eyes, with ears were surprisingly human looking, but they were pointed. Its hair was pure white, completely covering its body.

Before him was a creature of nightmares and myth.

Werewolf!

Eleven

The werewolf didn't react for a moment. Neither did Ishik. Then the beast shot forward, lunging for Ishik's throat. The young man's reaction was instinctive. He rejected gravity from under his feet and was hurtled upward, over the werewolf's lunge.

As the beast looked around for his prey, Ishik landed behind him with a loud thud. He scrambled off the ground and managed to turn in time to see the werewolf lunging again. It grabbed him by both shoulders and slammed him into the ground. Ishik could smell the blood on its breath.

He managed to get a boot into contact with the werewolf's foot. He rejected the gravity that held the werewolf to the ground.

It was sent flying backward, its howl of surprise filling the forest. It landed on the ground hard just a few feet away. Ishik rushed forward and slammed his walking staff onto the werewolf's chest. He now made the werewolf's body accept the Force of gravity more than normally possible. Its arms and legs were pinned to the ground. The werewolf tried desperately to move about, but it was unable to; gravity was keeping it firmly in place. After a few minutes of struggle, it gave up.

Ishik was smart enough not to take his eyes off the creature. There was a disturbing quiet in the forest. Even the birds had fallen silent. Finally, the werewolf looked at Ishik and spoke in passible Rhythian.

"You are very strong." Ishik said nothing in return.

The werewolf kept talking, having to force out the words because of the pressure on its chest. "Never has a human bested a son of the great Nanali tribe. Kill me, human. The shame is too great."

"No!" Ishik said emphatically. "What makes you think your life is worth sacrificing for someone else's reputation?"

There was genuine fear in the werewolf's eyes now. "You must kill me," it said. "Otherwise...I will be banished from my tribe!" Ishik thought for a moment and then replied.

"I was banished from my home for killing. You really think I'd do it again?"

The werewolf shook its head. "I will be banished, human. I shall never be mentioned again, my memory and life forgotten! Surely you would not subject me to that!"

Ishik looked at the werewolf with cold eyes. "I can't kill you. I'd never forgive myself."

"But humans have had no problems killing my kind in the past. What stays your hand?"

Was it mercy? Was it hate? Or maybe curiosity? He wasn't sure what emotion stayed his hand. But words came out of his mouth, fueled by honesty and something else he couldn't identify.

"The need for a friend." The werewolf seemed surprised. He was clearly not expecting that answer.

"You wish to be friends with me, human? It will never happen."

"Why not? Give me a reason," Ishik challenged

"I'm a werewolf," the creature said. "You're a human."

"Look at my face and see if I care." The werewolf looked at him under close scrutiny. The answer was plain on the human's face.

"Human...you and I cannot be friends...we'd be rejected from both our homes..."

"You're rejected already, remember? I won't kill you. I'm already rejected anyway, so what's stopping us?" The werewolf actually paused. It finally answered.

"What's stopping us is the fact you have me pinned to the ground." Ishik smiled and finally stopped manipulating the Force of gravity. He extended a hand to help the werewolf up. The werewolf took it. The werewolf's hand was surprisingly soft, covered by little hairs. Ishik hauled the werewolf upright.

"I'm Ishik," he said with an easy air.

"My name is Kiraj." He pronounced it with extra emphasis on the end. The werewolf's mind was full of questions.

Why did this human let me up? Why didn't he kill me? I could attack him right now...but why did he do this to me? Why did he let me live? I will stay with him for now...until I fully understand how strong he is.

Ishik smiled and they began walking. He would have to revise his plans, but at the moment, he didn't care. He had a friend, and that was enough for now.

Twelve

riendship, Ishik discovered, was a wonderful thing. Having someone to talk to while he was walking made loneliness go away and traveling lighter. It also made him quite a bit faster. Keeping pace with a werewolf was no easy task. While running, Ishik learned that werewolf culture was just as complex as human culture. No human had actually ever gotten the chance to learn about it. The two groups were too interested in killing each other.

Ishik and Kiraj had sat down for a breather. The pine needles were prickly and dry against their backs as they sat next to an ancient evergreen. The noon sun provided little heat, and Rhyth's infamous winter was approaching. *I have to find a pelt or a coat of some kind.* Ishik thought. *The snow will be starting soon.*

"So, werewolves have a tribal culture?" Ishik asked.

Kiraj nodded. "Yes, we do." he said. "There are twenty-three different tribes, each with its own guardian ancestor."

"Guardian ancestor?"

"A great hero of ancient times. There were twenty-four of them that fought in the First War, against Vrasta's masters. Twenty-three freed our ancestors from slavery. It is to them we owe our lives."

"What about the last tribe?"

Kiraj nodded with a sense of reverence. "That is the greatest of the tribes. It is the only tribe to be named after a hero that's not a werewolf. The mighty Anazan, the greatest Manipulator of Forces."

Ishik paused for a moment. The name sounded very familiar. Then he recalled that Anazan's name had appeared when they learned about the Kingdom Stryne's history. Anazan was said to be the famous King Orin's advisor after the Fourth War. *How could Anazan be in both the Fourth and First War?* Ishik wondered.

"Anazan is also famous in the human land called Stryne." Ishik told Kiraj. "He's said to be a great hero of the Fourth War." Kiraj quickly noticed the same issue Ishik had thought of just moments earlier.

"Humans do not live that long, though. How could Anazan...? He was extremely powerful...but such a long life...it's impossible. Maybe there was another person named Anazan in the Fourth War? I know humans often name themselves after each other."

Ishik merely nodded, opting not to argue the point. He decided to move on with the conversation. "I bet you have quite a few children named after your heroes then?"

Kiraj shook his head. "It is forbidden to name a cub of a tribe after the twenty-four heroes. They shall remain the only of their kind. None may take the name of a Great One unless they have done something of such great value that it surpasses the original owner of the name."

"So, werewolves are able to change their names multiple times?"

"Of course. Why would you ask?"

"Humans are only allowed to have the name they're given."

The werewolf looked shocked. "How can that be? How do humans measure accomplishments? The more names you take, the greater you are in the tribe."

"We use stories, and things called books to record our accomplishments," Ishik explained.

"What is a book?"

Ishik, being raised in a family of merchants, and then living in a monastery of the Congregation, couldn't fathom not knowing what a book was.

As they moved on, Ishik described in great detail how a book was made. Kiraj seemed slightly confused by the process. "This *book* sounds very difficult to make. Do you all make a book for yourselves each time you have an accomplishment?"

Ishik shook his head. "No. In those books, after we make them, we scratch down symbols that mean words. We say who accomplished what with those words. It's like having a silent storyteller for a very long time. With books, you can learn so many things! It's like having thousands of years of storytellers at your fingertips. My name actually comes from the word *Ishikai* which means *Living Story* in Gyllithian; that's another Kingdom south of Rhyth."

Kiraj looked at Ishik and seemed to be reforming his opinion of the man. Finally, he spoke. "So your first name is Ishik...It is a rare honor to find out a tribesman's first name. Kiraj is my third name."

"I'll find out the other two later, I hope." Ishik said.

"You'll have to earn the right."

"I like challenges."

As the sun set, they set up camp in the shade of a large oak tree. They ate silently and Ishik fell asleep. He was sleeping easily, his staff next to him.

After a few hours, a strange howl filled the air. Ishik snapped awake and shot up, staff in hand. Kiraj was just as alert.

"Was that you?" Ishik asked. Kiraj shook his head and bared his fangs.

"That is a tribal howl. It's the howl for assembly."

"Friendly?"

"No."

Ishik made sure the fire was lit. He wanted to be able to see if any enemies showed up. Sure enough, he and Kiraj soon found themselves surrounded by a pack of other werewolves. One of them stepped forward in the fire light. It was covered in grey hair and considerably larger than Kiraj. It made a face Ishik thought was similar to sneering.

"Well, well, what have we here? Kiraj, have you stooped so low as to accompany a human?" There was a round of short growls that must have been laughter. Kiraj snarled at the other werewolf.

"Have you stooped so low as to take orders from Vrasta?" he challenged. The other laughter stopped, replaced by a lower, more threatening growls.

"Vrasta is six times more powerful than these humans!"

"Then how do you explain us humans beating Vrasta two times?" Ishik said, coming to the support of his friend. The werewolf finally paid attention to the man.

"He was merely testing them. Humans only won because they were unified. But now, they are divided, and so Vrasta shall claim them and put them in their rightful place!" The werewolves howled. Ishik was growing irritated. He had heard enough.

He slammed his staff on the ground. Gravity was rejected all around him. Kiraj was prepared this time and manipulated his fall to land on his feet. The rest of the werewolves weren't so lucky. All of them went flying backward and up into the trees, slamming into them with an impact that could have broken bones.

"I'm only going to say this once, so listen!" he shouted. "Stay away from my friend! Now, go!" He heard the sounds of howls growing fainter and fainter. He turned to Kiraj. The werewolf was staring at him.

"What?" Ishik asked. "What's the matter?"

Kiraj pointed at him and spoke with a respectful tone. "You sent an entire pack flying with one strike of your staff. Surely you must be a great warrior among your people."

Ishik shook his head. "I'm considered evil, a heretic to the extreme among my people."

Kiraj shook his head. "That is an awful mistake." Outrage filled the werewolf's eyes. "One like you should never be cast away!"

"Why were you talking about Vrasta with the other werewolves?" Ishik was extremely curious, and nervous.

Kiraj now looked Ishik directly in the eyes. "Vrasta is on the move once more."

Ishik's eyes widened. "Wouldn't he would be dead by now? It's been over a thousand years!"

Kiraj shook his head. "No. Vrasta is not human. And with his power he has managed to ally himself with twenty of the tribes of my people." Ishik's eyes widened even more. Kiraj nodded.

"You understand his motives then: Invasion. What better soldiers than us, we who love to kill?"

Kiraj sat down on the ground and Ishik did the same. The werewolf continued his explanation. "Vrasta is going to invade Rhyth within the month. What we encountered here was just a scouting party."

Ishik responded immediately. "What do we do about it?"

Kiraj lowered his head, then raised it. "The tribes will follow the strongest leader. To them, Vrasta is the strongest, so they follow. But...if we were to find someone stronger, we could free the tribes from future enslavement."

"Vrasta's not someone who likes to throw away perfectly good servants, is he?" Ishik asked. Kiraj shook his head. Ishik thought for a moment. Frustration coursed through him. He could come up with usable solution. Kiraj's head shot up.

"You!" he said. Ishik threw him a confused look.

"What about me?"

"The opposing werewolf tribes haven't had a champion to rally around. They need someone strong enough to take on the challenge."

"Me? Sorry, I'm not a good candidate."

"Why not? Look what you did to that entire pack! Let me tell you something, Ishik. I've been around many a Force Manipulator. None of them come close to your power. Every Manipulator I've met had to have some kind of life force to drain out of something to use their powers, be it grass or animal. But the energy to manipulate the Force of gravity seems to come only from you. No other Manipulator has done that. Not even Anazan."

Ishik was extremely confused. "I thought you just did it; you focus a little and the Force does what you want? And I'm definitely not as strong as Anazan. Anazan controlled all four Forces. I can only control one."

Kiraj was impatient. "You misunderstand. Anazan had years of training and practice. He drew his power from grasses. Even with all of his practice, he was still limited. Look at what you just achieved, by instinct. And when you used your power...I felt...more alive than I ever have. You are definitely strong enough for the tribes to at least listen to you."

Ishik was stunned by Kiraj's earnestness. "But I'm an outcast. What would I do if I were to rally those other tribes, anyway?"

"We fight." Kiraj said with a firmness that left no room for doubt. "We fight against Vrasta and the other tribes."

"Kiraj...I'm not sure I could do it."

"You would save countless of your race's lives!"

Ishik had never had so much faith put in him before. He threw up a prayer in desperation. *Divine! Please give me an answer!*

Do it. Something whispered in his head. *Do it for the sake of all the people...*

Another part of him whispered as well. *Don't do it! You took a vow of nonviolence.*

Should I kill one to save a thousand? Ishik thought to himself. *Should I kill again, this time to save?* A kind of fire rose up within him. His heart felt more ready than ever before. Combat was to be his. He would crush the enemy. He would unite the tribes, and he would win. His sudden inner eagerness both surprised and disturbed him.

"What direction is it to the four tribes we need to rally?" He asked Kiraj. Kiraj looked up, and recoiled.

"What happened to your eyes? They're pure white." Ishik blinked a couple times.

"Any better?" he asked.

"Yes. They're brown again." Ishik was disturbed. Something had changed in him, or something had changed for him. He shook his mind. *Now is not the time.* the voice in his head whispered. *You must go to the tribes at once!*

"I'll do it, Kiraj. Let's set out tomorrow. We need to hurry if we're going to fight Vrasta." Ishik doused the fire.

Kiraj's red eyes peered at him in the darkness. "Why the sudden change of heart?" Ishik thought for a moment and then answered.

"It feels like the right thing to do." He went to bed, and for the first time in a long while, he dreamed of home.

✴✴✴✴✴✴

"Dad," he asked. "Can I be a scholar?"

His father laughed. "Why would you ever want to be one of those useless little paper scribblers? No son of mine is ever going to be one of those. You'll learn to be a merchant, like your father and your grandfather."

The scene changed again. He was standing as a teen in his father's tent. His mother was before him, looking stern. "Mother, why can't I learn to be an archer? I want to serve Rhyth!"

"You'll do no such thing!" she said sternly. "There's no good in becoming a simpleton who can shoot sticks!" She shook her head in disappointment. "I don't know what's wrong with you."

✴✴✴✴✴✴

You never gave me a choice. Ishik thought silently. *You never let me be what I wanted to be. But you can't stop me this time. This journey is my choice to take on. And when I succeed, you will be the ones who will be stunned. You will be the ones who won't have a say. I'll make my own path. I've had enough of other people telling me what to do. It's my turn to give directions.*

Kiraj woke to find Ishik had already made breakfast. Kiraj was actually happy at the change of pace. His friend was moving with a

101

sense of purpose and single minded determination. They now took watches, in case any more packs were hunting after them.

Whenever they had a break, Ishik practiced his new found powers. Soon, he could guide a stone through branches with amazing speed. But his powers weren't the only thing that got stronger as they traveled northwest to werewolf territory. Ishik was now more muscled than Kiraj thought a human could ever be.

He really is a living story, Kiraj thought as he observed Ishik floating a large, lichen-covered stone around in a gradual oval. *I wonder how the story will change as time goes on...*

Another week passed this way and they soon found themselves at the walls that guarded Rhyth from werewolf attacks. Soldiers were standing guard, on edge, and there was such a large number that Ishik came to a conclusion.

They might have found out about Vrasta's plan. Now, how do we get over that wall? He looked for a lightly guarded spot, but he couldn't find one. He had to figure out how to get Kiraj through without sounding an alarm. Getting over the wall would be easy. He just had to reject gravity to fly over it. But how would he avoid being seen?

That's when he heard a cry: An almost otherworldly scream; like metal edges grinding against one another. It was followed by a methodical *thump* that repeated at a steady rhythm. Then, he saw it in the horizon. It was a black beast with two giant claws, wings and a long neck that connected a massive, sinewy body to a hideous head full of teeth. He heard the soldiers on the wall cry out.

"Drake! Ballistae! Drake! Sound the alarm!"

All of the soldiers crowded to the right of the wall. Ishik saw his opening. "Let's go, Kiraj! Don't stop running!"

They took off across the open land between the forest and the wall. The soldiers didn't see them. As they came close to the wall, Ishik held out his arm. "Grab on and don't let go!" Kiraj latched onto his arm and Ishik rejected gravity under his feet. They were sent flying over the wall. Ishik saw how close the drake had gotten to the wall.

Help them, pleaded the voice in his head. *If that drake gets through, disaster will sweep through Rhyth!* Ishik looked at Kiraj. His friend knew what he was going to do, by the look on his face. Kiraj nodded and took off for the refuge of the nearby forest.

Ishik took off at a run. He was almost under the drake, and then he rejected gravity in a way he never had done before. He rejected all the gravity he could that was holding his body to the ground.

He was sent soaring, high above the wall, all the way up to the drake. No one was on top of it. He held out his staff and braced himself. He landed on the drake, winding himself and nearly having one of the monster's back spikes skewer his head. He then stood upon the drake and slammed his staff into its back.

He could tell the drake was getting ready to throw him off. Ishik reached out and made the drake's body accept as much gravity as it could. It was as if an invisible hand reached out and pulled the drake straight to the ground. It slammed into the ground with a crunching, massive, earthshaking boom. Death was instant.

Ishik managed to keep himself from breaking anything by rejecting gravity off his body at the last moment. The soldiers were looking around for the cause of the drake's sudden demise. Ishik took off, bolting for the forest. He didn't look back to his homeland; rather, he looked ahead into the wilderness that was the start of Werewolf Lands. He couldn't worry himself with the past. Right now, he had more important things to do.

Thirteen

He is the one, Kiraj thought as he saw the drake slam into the ground. *He is the one who can do it. Once the tribes see the strength he has, there is no doubt they will work together.*

Kiraj saw Ishik bolting toward the forest. He ran over to the edge, so Ishik could see him. Ishik slowed down as he approached him.

"Thanks for waiting," he said, breathing heavily. "That drake had to be stopped." Kiraj nodded in understanding.

"Come, we shall go to my tribe first. It is about nine days of running to reach it from here."

The two of them began running through the forest, not halting until darkness forced them. It continued on that way for eight days. Snow was falling on the ground. The pine trees were much older and more menacing. Fire went from being a luxury to a necessity. Kiraj managed to kill a few creatures and skin them to give his more vulnerable companion some protection against the merciless cold. Ishik felt like he had taken a step back in time, to when the world was primitive and young.

On the ninth day, they were running when a pack of werewolves surrounded them. Ishik held his staff ready, but Kiraj held up a hand. "Peace, they are from my tribe." Ishik lowered his staff.

A white werewolf with red eyes stepped forward. It looked similar to Kiraj, but had more scars and was much bigger.

"Kiraj," It said, "Why do you dare guide a *human* into our tribeland?" Its voice was deep, and almost unmistakably male.

Kiraj stepped forward. The other werewolf lunged, closing a claw over Kiraj's throat, lifting him off the ground. The werewolf snarled. He yelped in surprise as it found itself flying backward, slamming into a tree. Kiraj fell to the ground, wheezing for air.

Kiraj looked behind him and saw Ishik, staff raised, a look of rage and death on his face. His eyes were pure white.

It confused Kiraj how someone who was so opposed to killing now looked so ready to commit violence.

"Touch my friend," Ishik said, his voice low, "and I *will* kill you, got it?" His white eyes were glowing and there seemed to be a hum of icy energy about him. The werewolf managed to get back onto his feet. He was staring at Ishik through narrowed eyes.

"Who are you?"

"I'm Ishik, a fighter against Vrasta. I've come to unify the four tribes not under his control. I'm trying to help save your race while we have the chance." Ishik heard growls and rumbles come from the pack that surrounded them.

The werewolf who had grabbed Kiraj now tilted his head. He then threw back his head and let out a blood-chilling howl of five descending notes. He looked at Kiraj, then at Ishik.

"You will follow the pack, human. We will take you to the elders. They shall decide your fate."

Ishik nodded. *It's a start,* he thought.

With another howl, the pack gathered together and moved out. Ishik ran at the rear. Somehow, he managed to find the strength to keep pace. When they took a break for the night, he was covered in sweat and scratches.

The large werewolf directed Ishik to sit with them. Ishik sat down, tense and waiting to be attacked. There was silence among the group as the fire crackled. An awkward air surrounded the group. Finally, the large werewolf spoke up. "So, how long have you been Manipulating?"

"A month," Ishik said. "Maybe a little longer if you include my time in the Congregation of the Divine." The pack broke into short growls and grunts. Ishik wondered if it was laughter. The lead werewolf leaned forward.

"Packs from the Jurnsik Tribe reported that a single figure near the border took down a fully grown drake. Do you know anything about another Manipulator that may be following you? Possibly one of Vrasta's servants?"

Ishik shook his head. "No one's following us. I was the one who took down the drake." He described the brief fight he had with the monster. The pack seemed engrossed in his recount.

"But where did you draw all of that life force from?" the large werewolf challenged. Ishik wrinkled his brow in confusion.

"I just did it. I didn't draw from any life force." The pack seemed uneasy with this answer. Kiraj looked at Ishik in surprise.

"What I meant," said the lead werewolf, "is where did you find all of the life force to reject that much gravity? There's hardly any life in that area between the wall and the forest."

Ishik shook his head. "I never used any life force. I just did it." The pack now broke into heated discussion in their language. Ishik looked at Kiraj questioningly. Kiraj shrugged. The pack leader silenced his followers. It was then he spoke to Kiraj.

"Kiraj, forgive me for my aggression toward you earlier. I did not know you found him."

Ishik was confused. "Found who, exactly?"

The werewolf nodded at him. "You, Anazan's heir."

Ishik recoiled in surprise. He wasn't expecting that answer. "What? Anazan's heir? I'm from Rhyth, not Stryne. I didn't even know I could Manipulate until a month ago! I can only control one Force. I'm nowhere near as powerful as Anazan; but I'm here and willing to help."

The werewolf held up his hand. "It is said among the legends of the tribes that Anazan would be reborn, freeing the tribes from oppression once and for all. Anazan was a master of all the Forces; but even he had to draw from some kind of life force to Manipulate." Ishik recalled the explanation Kiraj had given him before he had set out on this journey to unite the tribes. The pack leader continued talking.

"If you killed a drake with control of just one Force, you are definitely strong enough to be his heir. Most of the tribes said that Anazan's heir was Vrasta; but some of us did not believe. So, Kiraj was selected by the Great Moon to find the true heir... And here you are before us."

Ishik blinked a few times, soaking in the explanation. Somehow, it felt right.

Here is your chance, the voice whispered in his head. *Take this and make it something to rally around.* "So, what do we do now?" Ishik asked the lead werewolf.

"We tell the other tribes that the true heir has come, and then, we go to war against our last oppressor."

"Vrasta?"

"Yes."

Ishik nodded. *This is so much...I didn't realize I'd be this important,* he thought. A heavy feeling came down on his shoulders. He looked at the lead werewolf. "What's your name?" Ishik asked.

"My name is Nan. I am leader of Nanali's Tribe. Kiraj is my brother." Ishik extended a hand. The werewolf looked at it, confused.

"You're supposed to shake it." Ishik explained. "It's a human greeting. It means you're friendly." Nan took Ishik's hand and shook it once after some brief hesitation. The werewolf's grip was gentle, as if he were afraid of breaking Ishik's hand.

"How do werewolves show they're friendly?" Ishik asked.

"We put our heads on each other's shoulders." Ishik got up and put his head on Nan's shoulder.

Nan paused for a moment, and then returned the gesture. The pack howled in approval.

And now, my journey really begins, Ishik thought. The voice inside him only said a single word.

Good.

Ryan Wilshusen

Part Three:

In Foreign Lands

Ryan Wilshusen

Fourteen

Cold was a prominent feature of Rhyth, much to Emesos' displeasure. He pulled his cloak closer to himself, trying to keep out the chilling wind. He was riding beside Gonra and Velenry. They had been traveling for nearly two weeks, and finally, they had arrived near the capital.

The air was biting into him and it was hard for Emesos to breath. The trees were very strange to him. They were covered in little things Gonra called "needles." So far, the only thing Emesos liked was the sky. It seemed to always be a bright blue until the sun set, and then it just turned a deep violet, a breathtaking sight.

Emesos' discovery of the Fifth War was kept secret until it was declared officially to avoid frightening the public. But to his dismay, word of Emesos being declared the next great Prophet by the Congregation had spread ahead of them. Emesos had to keep his face hidden at all times. Even that didn't work too well. Everybody was asking him questions he didn't know the answer to. Worse was when they asked for him to touch their hands. During those times, he learned so much about people he wanted to scream and curl up on the ground in a ball until his mind settled down.

After about an hour, they finally reached Rhyth's capital, Wrin. A herald had been sent to the King of Rhyth, Hasin, to announce their coming. They rode through the city. Many people paid no attention to the visiting king or his honor guard.

Instead, their attention was fixed on the normal figure in plain blue cloak and hood. Emesos kept his head down the best he could as people were lining the streets. They were all silent and staring. The only sound on the street was the sound of horse hooves clacking on the stone walkway. One voice rang out of the crowd from a location Emesos couldn't identify.

"Hail the Prophet!" The crowd broke into wild cheering. Emesos raised a hand in recognition. Their cheering intensified. They shouted his name, his title and compliments.

If only they knew, Emesos thought. *If they only knew what I was predicting...Divine help them...* He shuddered when he recalled his vision of Vrasta. The time was close now; the invasion was just around the corner. It weighed on him like a heavy mantle.

They reached the castle gate and showed the royal seal of Stryne. The guards let them in and took their horses. They were guided down hallways to what looked like a throne room. The man on the throne was pale, as if he didn't spend any of his time in the sun. He had a pale silver beard, cropped close to his face. His green eyes glistened.

This must be Hasin, Emesos thought.

Hasin nodded to Gonra. "It is good to see you, my friend. And I hear you decided to have the new Prophet accompany you." He nodded at Emesos. Emesos bowed respectfully. The king's Strynic was spot on, with just a slight clipped, accent.

"I have met many who claim to be a Prophet," Hasin said. "Is he truly one of them?" Gonra looked at Emesos, the command in his eyes as he spoke.

"Maybe the Prophet could show you." Emesos stepped toward the king and cast off his hood. The king seemed very surprised.

"Hold out your hand, please." Emesos said quietly. The king held out his hand and Emesos took it.

The explosion of images and sound happened again. Too many to keep track of. Emesos felt a blend of emotions that wasn't his. He felt

*himself stretching out and touching the king's mind. The king did the
same.*

Emesos let go of the king's hand and groaned softly, grasping
his head. He started to fall, but Hasin supported him with a firm
grip. "It is unfortunate the Divine chose one as young as you to
bear such an ability," he said softly. Emesos bowed and returned
to his place beside Gonra.

"So, do you believe his message now?" Gonra asked. Hasin
nodded.

"Of course, I'd be a fool not to. But you realize what this
means, Gonra? We must hold a Council." Velenry gasped. Emesos
was confused. Gonra nodded.

"We must. And Emesos, I'm afraid you'll have to come with."
Emesos nodded. "Might we stay here until the Council occurs?"
Gonra asked the King of Rhyth.

"Of course, Gonra," said Hasin. "You are always welcome
within these halls." Gonra nodded and everyone was shown to his
quarters. Gonra quickly visited Emesos after everyone else was
settled.

"Your Majesty," Emesos said with a bow. Gonra sat down and
spoke with a weary tone.

"Emesos, what Hasin and I were talking about in the throne
room was called the Council of Kings. It's when all of the kings of
the Kingdoms gather together to discuss major events, such as the
coming of another War. I'm afraid you'll have to go along and
speak to us of your dreams. I know you've been through a great
deal already, but I'm afraid I must ask for your assistance once
more."

Emesos nodded, "I understand."

"You must also be aware that all of the kings will summon their Blades before the council begins." Emesos felt another kind of chill seep through him; fear.

"Your Majesty, the summoning of *one* Blade made me pass out. I don't know if I could survive *four*." Gonra nodded.

"That's what I fear as well. You seem to have a reaction to Blades that is very strange. That is why I want you to practice with Hasin and I to practice resisting that problem." Emesos nodded. It made sense, but it didn't make him any less afraid.

"I'll do it. When do we start practicing?"

"Right now, if you're willing." Emesos nodded once again.

"Brace yourself." The king warned. He then summoned his Blade. Emesos screamed, clutching his left hand as it crackled with energy. Blackness came at him. He fought it off with a grim determination. He blinked back tears.

When his vision cleared, he wasn't in his room with Gonra. He was in a large grand hall, a symbol of an eye on a banner. On his left arm was the strangest sword he had ever seen. It looked like two long swords, one black and one white, had been fused to each other. It had a single black and white handle, long enough for two hands. It had four bars, two black and two white, as a cross guard. The blade of the sword had four edges. The blade itself was a clash of swirling black and white patterns.

Emesos blinked again and the vision was gone. Gonra looked at him with a serious face. "You remained conscious this time, but your eyes turned white. Did you have a vision?" Emesos nodded and described it the best he could for the king. Gonra's eyes narrowed. "That is strange...I've never heard of a sword like that before. I wonder where and when that vision's from."

"I don't know," Emesos said. "I didn't get any information from it, except a weird banner that looked like this." Emesos grabbed a piece of parchment and gave the king a rough charcoal sketch of what he had seen. The king stared at the symbol and his eyes widened.

"I know this symbol," he said. "This is a symbol Velenry saw in ruins found on the border of Stryne and Rhyth. I wonder what that sword you saw had to do with those ruins."

Emesos shrugged. "Well, if I see anything else, I'll let you know. I think I'm done for today." Gonra stood and gave him a pat on the shoulder.

"We'll continue this tomorrow." The king left, leaving Emesos to reflect on his experience. *I have a few theories,* he thought. *I just hope they're wrong.*

Fortunately, he practiced for a week without another vision, although the other results were the same. Gonra would summon his Blade, and Emesos would nearly pass out, but hold onto consciousness. Sometimes, Hasin would join Gonra and they would summon their Blades at the same time. Emesos barely managed to get through the pain during those sessions.

The day for the Council of Kings finally arrived. Emesos didn't feel ready, but he didn't have a choice. He had to convince the other kings of Vrasta's invasion. At the same time he was preparing, Rhyth and Stryne were mobilizing everything they had. Erk was back in Emesos' homeland, rapidly preparing the Kingdom for all-out War.

Emesos was at the council, dressed in plain white clothing that had been donated by the Congregation of the Divine. He accompanied Gonra, continually preparing himself, going over what to say in his head to the four most important men in the Kingdoms. When he arrived, he made note of everyone there. Each king had his historian with them.

Gonra was there, so was Hasin, but he saw the other two kings as well. Lokus, King of Ollou, and Yanata, king of Gyllithia.

Lokus was a very tan man who was large. His beard was longer than the other kings, its brown tangles going to his collarbone. Yanata was clean shaven, his pale green eyes sharp. His skin was also dark, though not as dark as Gonra's or Lokus'.

Gonra took his seat. Emesos stood behind his throne alongside Velenry, who was rapidly writing. All of the kings had sheaths next to their thrones to hold their Blades, but first they had to summon them. The coming moments filled Emesos with enough nerves to make him nauseous.

Hasin spoke the words to begin the Council, as he was the oldest king. "Let us show our right to be here at the Ninth Council of Kings, by showing our right to rule." Hasin raised his hand. His Blade flashed into existence. "Rhyth," he said calmly, looking at Emesos. Emesos was clutching his left arm, gritting his teeth, trying not to make a sound.

Gonra raised his hand. His Blade appeared. "Stryne," he said. Emesos fought the urge to be sick as his fist now crackled with more light and energy. He wanted to beg them to stop, but he could not speak without fear of crying out in agony.

Lokus raised his hand. His Blade appeared in his hand. "Ollou." His voice was now filled with concern as he saw Emesos' pain.

Yanata raised his hand. *No!* Emesos pleaded inwardly. *Please no! Don't-*

His thought was lost in a new level of agony as Yanata's Blade flashed to life in his hand. "Gyllithia," he said, his voice worried, his attention turned to Emesos' crackling hand of energy.

Emesos felt his arm shoot up, out of his control. He spoke a word in a voice that wasn't his.

"Anazan!" he cried. A sword flashed into view. It was black and white, the blade four-edged. It was the sword from his vision. He grabbed onto its handle as it plunged into the stone floor of the

Council room. He sank to his knees. *Not a sword*, he thought, *this isn't a sword.*

As he toppled into unconsciousness, the realization hit him. The weapon before him, the weapon in his grasp, wasn't a sword.

It was a Blade.

Fifteen

The landscape was wild and dangerous in the werewolf lands. Ishik had nearly been strangled by at least three vines of a plant the werewolves called Miklin. More strange and terrible creatures existed here besides werewolves, as Ishik learned from the random growls and shrieks that pierced the night. All in all, he had learned more about survival in his past few days of travel than he had in his entire life. Not to mention that he had gotten a cold and had to suffer through it the best he could.

All the while, the pack was watching him, like they were waiting for something. It made Ishik uncomfortable. Kiraj seemed more relaxed than ever now that he was back among his people.

It gave Ishik that same feeling of isolation he had gotten his entire life. *Maybe I'm meant to be alone*, he thought. *Maybe it's the Divine's plan for me to be by myself.* He was walking as he was thinking, when suddenly he heard rumbling. All of the werewolves paused, sniffing the air. After they had finished, they looked afraid. The rumbling sound now came with vibrations under foot.

Ishik swallowed and looked at Kiraj for an answer. The werewolf's eyes were wide he barked out orders. "A wurm! We need to-"

The ground exploded before them. A massive thing, covered in a mix of brown scales and slime, in one long, continuous body. The head consisted of a gaping maw with no teeth, only tentacles that writhed about as it roared. The tentacles lashed out among the werewolves. They scattered into the trees. Nan was caught by the foot by a tentacle that rapidly dragged its victim into a gaping mouth.

"No!" Ishik screamed. He charged toward the wurm, staff raised. Rage filled him. This creature was eating his friend. *You're dead!*

An intense pressure seemed to build up in his hand and he let it go. A blast of light hit the wurm. Ishik heard multiple cracking sounds and snaps. The wurm collapsed, dead.

Ishik heard more cracking and then saw Nan had managed to extract himself from the dead beast. The werewolf was slightly blackened, but he managed to move around fine.

Nan spoke, his tone carefully neutral. "So, you not only have control of the Force of gravity, but the Force of heat as well." Ishik shrugged, flexing the hand that the light had burst out of.

"I guess. I've never done that before."

Nan shook his head. "And yet you don't draw any life to use your powers. The elders will find you very interesting, I think." He then gave the howl for the pack to form up and start moving again. Kiraj and Ishik brought up the rear.

"Nan has a very strange way of thanking people for saving his life," Ishik noted. Kiraj nodded.

"Nan never has been one to thank others verbally, but he is grateful." They continued their journey without incident for the rest of the day.

When they stopped for the night, Ishik was sitting in the circle with the werewolves when Nan spoke to Ishik. "Ishik, tell us a story that you enjoy."

Ishik was taken by surprise. He had never been one for storytelling, but he collected himself and started to speak words that came into his head.

"Once, there was a young man. He wanted to contribute to his..." Ishik paused to find the right word. "Tribe. However, people wouldn't let him. Anything he tried to do to help his tribe, they wouldn't allow. The man didn't understand, so he kept trying, but he was stopped... *every single time*. But, when the man was old enough to journey, he went to another land so he could return and share its secrets with his tribe." The werewolves nodded to each other in approval of this hero. Ishik continued his story.

"In this far off land, he learned ancient secrets and powers that he never dreamed he could wield. But when that man returned to his tribe, he was banished." The pack growled in surprise and unhappiness for the man of the story. Ishik continued, the firelight they had lit growing dimmer.

"Angered, the man set out on a journey to find a new tribe. He was determined to belong to a place that wanted him. But as time passed, he was rejected again and again, left alone. In one last desperate act, the man set out on one last journey, to do what others considered evil: he fought in battle in disguise. Everyone praised his efforts, even those who had rejected him; even though they didn't know him. The man was still alone, but at the very least; he wasn't truly forgotten. And with his task of helping others complete, he died." There was silence for a long while. Nan broke it.

"That is a sad story. Are all your legends this somber?" Ishik shook his head and laughed slightly.

"No, but those kinds of stories are the ones that can mean the most." And with that Ishik went to bed, having no dreams. The rest of the pack slowly did the same except for Kiraj and Nan.

Kiraj looked at his brother and spoke in a soft voice. "I don't think that story was entirely a legend." The fire was flared as Nan prodded it gently with a stick.

Nan shook his head. "I don't think so either. This human has been through so much." He stared at Ishik, who was fast asleep, his staff by his side.

"To be rejected not from just one tribe, but more... he must suffer great shame. But to fight for them still... his loyalty is greater than I would have thought possible from a human. Perhaps he truly is Anazan's heir."

"That is for the elders to decide. But for his sake, I hope you're right." The two brothers went to sleep next to the dying fire, its last fluttering sparks and crackles piercing the black silence of the night.

The pack rose in the morning and continued their journey. Ishik noticed that the pace was gradually increasing. He was barely managing to keep up. In this wild land, being behind meant a smaller chance of survival. Ishik was slowly learning to control the heat he had used on the wurm. He could only control small amounts of it, but he knew he was making progress. The voice in his head was now in constant communication with him. He was worried about it, but he had learned to deal with it for now.

I hope we reach the first tribe soon, Ishik thought. *Time is short.*

You will conquer this challenge, the voice whispered. *Have faith, and the Divine will keep you.*

Faith hasn't gotten me very far, has it? The voice had no answer for that statement. Ishik kept running, having to reject gravity in small amounts to keep up.

Finally, as the sun started to set, the pack came upon a clearing in the middle of the forest. A large number of huts and dwellings in trees were scattered in a haphazard fashion.

"This is the tribe," Kiraj announced. "The tribe of Nanali. We have arrived, Ishik." Ishik nodded. The pack walked into the village. Ishik drew multiple stares, along with growls and barks.

He held his head high, staff in hand. His clothes were in an even worse state from days upon days of harsh travel through wilderness. The cold wind bit into his skin, but he didn't show that he was cold. He didn't show he was afraid.

He couldn't let it show.

The pack stopped before a large hut and Nan walked into it. He heard an exchange of growls and grunts and Nan emerged out of the hut. A giant werewolf followed. Its white fur was glossy, and its stature was large, even by werewolf standards. It gave a low growl in friendly greeting to the pack. Then, it saw Ishik and froze. There was silence in the village. The werewolf bared its fangs at Nan. It leaped forward.

Ishik's reaction was immediate. He tried to reject gravity under the werewolf. It continued its leap unabashed. Fear ran through Ishik. *It's immune to Force Manipulation?* he thought. He saw claws come up and descend toward Nan.

"No!" Ishik screamed. He rejected gravity under his feet and flew forward. He slammed into the werewolf in a vicious tackle from the side, barely managing to avoid the claws seeking to tear out his throat. The claws raked across his chest. He cried out in pain, and that pain was transformed into rage. He and the werewolf were circling each other, each waiting for the other to make the next move.

The werewolf charged forward. Ishik brought his staff upward and rejected gravity under his arms. His staff collided with the werewolf's chest, sending it flying backward. It slammed onto the ground with a thunderous *boom*. It scrambled back onto its feet.

Ishik looked the werewolf straight in the face. "If you have an issue with me being here, take it up with me personally. But don't go attacking others for something that's not their fault!" The werewolf howled and charged again. Ishik screamed, running forward. The werewolf jumped. Ishik stopped abruptly and let his staff be grabbed by the werewolf. He grabbed the werewolf's hands and using the attacker's momentum to turn it over, putting himself on top of it. He then made his own body accept gravity. The duo crashed into the ground.

Ishik's body had effectively pinned the werewolf to the hard earth. "Now, would you mind listening to your pack's explanation instead of blindly trying to tear out throats?" he demanded. The werewolf snarled. Ishik heard someone approaching behind him.

"Great elder," Nan said, "you were right to attack me under normal times. But this human is not normal. Kiraj has succeeded in his quest. This human is Anazan's heir." The werewolf looked at Ishik with a piercing gaze. Ishik wondered what he saw. Finally, the werewolf spoke.

"Surely the Moon would never leave a burden like this on one as young as you," the elder said. Ishik let out a laugh.

"The Moon might not, but the Divine sure did, cruel bastard he was..." The werewolves around Ishik yelped in surprise. Even the Elder looked shocked at that statement.

"But humans always have held their precious Divine in such high regard!" The elder said. "Have humans changed so drastically?"

Ishik couldn't shake his head because he was still making his body accept gravity. "I'm a little different. My abilities are *hated* among humans; utterly evil. I am hated religiously for what I can do. I was cast out of more than one tribe."

The pack gave another growl of surprise. "But this is my last chance to redeem myself. This is my last hope." Tears were now spilling down his face, flying down onto the werewolf's neck from increased gravity. "I can't have this taken away from me! Not this time! Not this chance!"

Ishik released gravity and got off the werewolf, holding his head in his hands, his knees drawn to his chest. The pain of so many years of defeat and ordering now crashed into him like a wave. He cried for a long time, in undignified, hiccupping sobs.

I've never been in control of my own life, he thought. *Always told what to do, always defeated. Isolated from others because of my attitude and now my abilities. Every gift I've gotten has either been ripped from me or despised. Is even this journey my own?* The question bothered him. The werewolves were staring at him as if he were a wild animal that could attack them at any moment.

There isn't time to mope, you must unite the tribes! The voice whispered in his head. Ishik's rage grew. He smashed into the voice's source with a strength driven by rage and regret.

Shut up, he thought. *I don't need you to tell me! I know! Get out of my head!*

The tribes-

Out!

The tribes-

I said 'Out!' He pressed on the voice's source more than he thought was possible. Suddenly, a weight seemed to lift off his chest. His strength seemed to soar. He tried rejecting gravity and found himself still able. Inside, he felt freer than he had in his entire life.

He got up and stood tall. The werewolves were looking at him like he was insane. *Maybe I am, but it won't stop me.* Ishik smiled. *Vrasta's going to wish he had never bothered the tribes when I'm through.*

Ishik walked to the nearest tree and started to tend his wounds the best he could. Kiraj stared at his friend. Nan did the same. The elder soon joined them, speaking in his gruff tone.

"His mind is nearly shattered, just like Anazan's was. He very well could be Anazan's heir. But... is his mind strong enough to bear this burden?"

Kiraj sighed. "He's the only hope for our race at this point. It has to be..." Nan nodded in agreement.

"War is coming soon. We're going to find our answer quickly. I just hope it's the right one."

Sixteen

The halls were black and familiar. *I'm in Vrasta's place.* Emesos thought. *I'm probably one of his servants.*

He saw a figure in orange and black armor kneeling before Vrasta. Vrasta was surprisingly human looking. The only thing that unsettled Emesos was the man's long, razor-sharp finger nails. "Sene, the boy forced me out. I could not control him. His mind is too fractured, too random." Vrasta shook his head. "He's borderline insane! Never have I seen a human so powerful. Never have I seen one so close to losing their mind. This boy is fascinating. Not since your brother has there been a Manipulator so powerful."

Sene raised his head. "My lord," he said, his voice controlled and heavy. "Surely he could not match him. He's had no training, nor lived as long."

Vrasta looked at Sene with his golden eyes. "You have not felt this boy's strength. No training, yet he managed to take down a drake. No training at all, but he crushes me out of his mind. No training at all, but he controls gravity as if he's done it for years. He's quickly teaching himself how to control heat as well."

Sene looked at Vrasta and stood. "Are you saying that he is stronger than my brother? Such a thing is not possible for someone who is not Altherai's heir. You've never been one for exaggeration. There must be something more to this boy that you're not telling me." Sene took two steps forward and looked at Vrasta.

Who is Altherai? *Emesos wondered. He recalled himself crying it out when he summoned a Blade.* And why is he so important to Sene?

Vrasta answered without flinching or blinking, something Emesos grudgingly admired. "The boy uses some kind of energy that's near infinite to Manipulate."

Sene's face was covered by a helmet, so Emesos couldn't see his expression. The armored man turned and spoke without looking back at Vrasta.

"I must find him."

"You will not—"

A Blade flashed to life in Sene's hand and he held the massive black and orange blade in his hand, ready to swing. "You will never command me, Vrasta. My loyalty lies only to Altherai. And it seems that the heir apparent has been chosen."

✳✳✳✳✳✳

Emesos shot upward, in a cold sweat. He was always cold after an experience. A girl he didn't recognize was staring at him and he didn't have a shirt on. Emesos immediately felt self-conscious. "Um, excuse me...where am I?"

"You are in a medical wing," she said in clipped Solic. It wasn't her first language, but she spoke it quite well. "You have quite a few questions to answer, dear Prophet."

"Emesos."

"Pardon?"

"My name is Emesos. And I'm not a Prophet."

"Velenry said you were strange, but she didn't tell me you were so straight forward... Or in such harsh physical condition. You look like you've missed a week's worth of meals."

"I've missed about a month and a half's worth, but that's beside the point. Who are you?"

The woman smiled, her teeth flashing. "My names is Lanita, but most just call me Lani. I'm Rhyth's current historian. I was told to question you when you were ready."

"Can I get food first?"

"Not until you answer the questions and talk to me."

"I'm ready." Emesos said. He talked about what he had seen and heard, word for word. Lanita was copying with rapid speed that was born from practice. When he had finished, she set down her quill and flexed her hand slightly. She then picked up the quill again and started asking questions.

"So, what's your interpretation of this vision?"

"I call them experiences," Emesos said. Lanita nodded and made a note of the statement.

"So, what do you think is important about the experience you just had?" She asked. Emesos thought for a little bit and then answered.

"The biggest thing about that experience is that I have to figure out if it's from the present, or past."

Lanita's head shot up in surprise. "You have 'experiences' of the present?" Emesos nodded. "That's never happened before with Prophets... sorry, continue please."

"Well, the reason I say I need to find out is that both Vrasta and Sene were in an experience I've had in the present. But Vrasta and this man could also be in the past, because of a long life or something similar. If it's in the past, then there was an unsung hero in one of the previous Wars. Vrasta said something about a Manipulator that drew on his own energy that was nearly infinite." He paused to let Lanita to catch up before continuing. When she looked up he started speaking again.

"Supposedly, the Manipulator was on par with Anazan, or even better, but was also borderline insane. If he's in the present, then we could possibly have a huge ally. But what bothers me more is that Sene has a Blade. It's large, and is black and dark orange, like a massive broadsword."

Lanita continued to write without looking up. "Anything else?" She asked.

Emesos nodded. "Yes, Sene was determined to find the Manipulator, and he said to Vrasta his loyalty belonged only to Altherai. I've never heard of this Altherai before, so I don't know if it's a person or a thing; or anything else about it really. Whatever or whoever this Altherai is, I have the feeling that Altherai is at the heart of this entire War. And what's happening to me." Lanita merely nodded as she finished her writing.

"Now...let's get you some food."

"And a shirt too, please." They walked down a hall where a shirt was found for Emesos and then Lanita guided Emesos to the kitchens, where Emesos encountered Rhythian cuisine. He was served a strange kind of fish that was bitter, a salty bread, a strange shelled food called oysters, and some kind of sauce that burned the inside of his mouth and caused him to sweat.

After he had eaten, Emesos realized that he had consumed four plates of food. It surprised him that he was that hungry. Finally, Lanita broke the silence. "You can wield a Blade," she said quietly. Emesos nodded slowly.

"Well, not really wield," he said, "I just learned I could summon one. No one recognizes what Blade it is anyway."

"May I see it?" she asked.

Emesos held out his hand a safe distance from anyone. He concentrated, envisioning it in his hand. In a flash of light, the

Blade appeared. Only it wasn't the same as it had been when it was first summoned.

It was a black and white clash of colors, but it was now backwards in his hand. The sword was pointed downward. The actual edge of the sword was slightly misaligned with the handle and guard. The edge itself was just a single blade now. The handle was white, the guard was black and there was a mash of colors on the cutting part of the Blade.

Emesos' eyebrows narrowed. "That's not what it looked like before...what happened?"

Lanita stared at it with interest, making yet more notes. "Blades adapt themselves to their owners to a shape and style that best assists the owner's fighting. This Blade, it's adapted to you. But I've never seen a sword so strange..."

"That makes two of us." Emesos said. He willed the Blade to vanish and it did. He realized everyone in the kitchen was staring at him. *I shouldn't have summoned it here!* he thought in a slight panic. *I hope this doesn't cause a problem!*

Lanita quickly guided him away. "I was told to guide you to a private area for your training in Blade fighting."

"Training? I don't like the sound of that..."

"King Gonra's going to train you, so it won't be that bad."

"I don't think that statement's entirely true," Emesos said. Lanita smiled.

"Well, we're here," she said. Emesos looked at the room; it was square and had a fence that looked like a kind of arena. There were no other things in the room other than a set of armor made of leather and chainmail.

Lanita smiled. "Well, this is goodbye for now, Emesos. I hope it goes well for you."

Emesos nodded. "Thanks. I hope I get to see you again." The words came out of his mouth before he could stop them.

Lanita's smile widened. "I hope so, too." She walked off. Emesos turned around to see Gonra standing in the arena, Blade in hand, in a similar suit of armor to that which was in the room.

"Welcome to your first lesson." Gonra said. "First things first, you have to get your armor on." He gestured to the armor that Emesos had seen when he entered the room. Emesos put on the armor and the first thing he noticed was the amount of weight it added. He entered the arena and stood waiting for instruction.

Gonra nodded. "Good, now summon your Blade." Emesos did so. The Blade did not change like it did when he showed it to Lanita. It was in the same, strange shape it was in before, in his hand backward. Gonra paused and stared at his Blade. He then summoned his own, that Blade made famous by Orin striking down the Darkest Knight in the Fourth War.

"Let's fight a little, just so I can see your style." Emesos nodded and flipped his Blade around in his hand. It was awkward to hold normally. Gonra came forward and started to do basic strikes that Emesos kept blocking or barely dodging. His sword was heavy and strange in his grip. He jumped away from Gonra and put his Blade backhand in his grip once more. It immediately became more comfortable. Gonra raised an eyebrow.

"You do realize there has never been a somewhat decent backhand fighting style?" Emesos shrugged. He charged forward, his Blade flashing behind him. Gonra adopted a defensive stance. Emesos swung his Blade in diagonal patterns and strange angles that caught the king off guard. The king was back peddling around the arena, trying to get a hold on the situation. Emesos waited for an opening to appear. The king executed a broad, horizontal sweep. Emesos saw his chance and dropped to one knee, letting the Blade fly over him. He brought his Blade up to the king's leg, stopping it before it hit.

Both men were sweating profusely. Gonra willed his Blade to vanish and Emesos did the same. Gonra smiled at Emesos. "That was fantastic! Whose memory did you use to fight like that?" Emesos thought on it and was surprised. No memories had entered his mind.

"It was just me..." Emesos said, surprised. "I did that. But...how? I've never had a sword in my life, let alone fought with one! I expected my Blade to look like a spear, so Fellix's memories would fight for me...but... I don't understand."

Gonra smiled. "Well, a Blade has been known to help a wielder before, but actual skill comes from the person. I think you'll do just fine with a Blade. But there's something very important I have to tell you: No one knows you have a Blade besides the kings and their historians. It's being kept a complete secret, to avoid political upheaval."

"Political upheaval?" Emesos asked. "Why would my Blade cause upheaval? It's just an ability." His mind flew back to the kitchens. The panic started to rise again.

Gonra shook his head. "You don't understand. A Blade is the distinguishing mark of a ruler of a Kingdom. It's the symbol of our right to rule. Your Blade shows that you are to be a ruler of a Kingdom, at least to common folk. They would, in fact, expect you to claim a Kingdom. However, we kings know that you aren't very keen on the idea of ruling much of anything."

Oh no, Emesos thought, *I hope I haven't done anything. It was so stupid for me to summon it in the kitchens! What was I thinking?*

Emesos laughed half-heartedly. "Being a supposed Prophet is hard enough. No, I think keeping it secret is the best idea for now, too." The two of them smiled and nodded in understanding.

Finally, Emesos thought, *things are starting to give me more answers than questions. But I still wonder, when is Vrasta coming? And did I just create a massive problem for the kings on top of this*

War? He shook off his thoughts for now and tried to enjoy making causal conversation with the king, joking and laughing as they walked down the hall toward their chambers.

Seventeen

The tribe of Nanali accepted Ishik into the village slowly. With Kiraj at his side, Ishik managed to get by. Many of the werewolves just asked him to perform building tasks, like lifting large stones or logs by rejecting gravity. He soon learned how much his powers were respected among the tribe, which surprised him. The elder, whose name he learned was Ruk, told him how the tribe viewed his powers.

"You are simply the strongest human the tribe has ever met. You also are the strangest. You actually care about the pack. You show no attachment to other humans. Yet at the same time, you seem afraid of yourself and have a desperate need to be with others." Ruk then asked a question Ishik knew he was building up to. "Why are you so attached to Kiraj?"

"He was there. He was willing. He listened."

"I do not understand," Ruk said, his eyebrows narrowed in concentration.

"Can I tell you a secret?" Ishik asked as he sat down next to the Elder. Ruk nodded. "I don't know who my real parents are. The people who raised me were some merchants that took me in." Ruk thought for a moment, considering this fact before responding.

"How could parents ever abandon a cub? That is the highest evil among the tribes."

Ishik shrugged. "Well, I was. I don't know why. But I was always different from everyone else around me. I looked different from them, but that wasn't a large concern for me. I managed to see things that others didn't. I also asked too many questions. I always wanted to know how things worked and why."

He flashed a smile as he recalled all those times he was little, asking questions nonstop.

"The first time I spoke, I was six years old. I spoke in complete sentences. Anyway, you get the point. I didn't have any of the qualities of a good merchant, so I was always assigned to putting things in and out of the cargo wagons."

Ruk gave a disapproving growl. "That is wrong. One as strong as you should never be a beast of burden."

Ishik shrugged. "Well, I tried to convince them to let me be a scholar, archer, anything else, but they wouldn't let me. But I finally found a way to escape. I joined the Congregation of the Divine. But even there, I was the odd one out. I guess when I saw Kiraj, he was so different...I thought he was different enough to understand me. Turns out I was right."

Ishik grabbed a rock and made it slightly reject gravity. It was floating in the air above his palm. "And now that I have these abilities, I'm more of an outcast. But these tribes...I've felt more at home here than I ever have anywhere else." He let the floating stone drop into his palm and he squeezed it with conviction. "And I'll be damned if Vrasta's going to take that away."

Ruk gave a light growl Ishik interpreted as laughter. He stopped after a while. "I know why you are here, Ishik. You seek to unite the tribes against Vrasta so we may avoid enslavement and suffering for both humans and pack. The sons and daughters of Nanali will join you in this journey. But first, you must go through the Naming." Ishik nodded.

"Whatever it takes, I'll do it."

Ruk held out a hand. "Give me your arm. This is going to hurt." Ishik took his arm and the Chief used his claw to gently cut a symbol on his skin. Ishik hissed in pain. When he had finished, blood was running down his arm and dripping from his hand.

"This is the symbol for getting your Second Name. This is the name you'll use in public. Your first name is reserved for your greatest friends and family alone." Other werewolves had gathered around them in a rough semicircle. They were watching carefully. "From this day forward, your second name shall be Urbak." The pack howled in approval.

"Thank you." Ishik said. They spent the night celebrating around a large fire, where some kind of large wild animal was cooked over a spit. Ishik and the others jumped around the fire, howling, growling and yipping. Ishik also tried to teach the werewolves a dance called the Country High Step that resulted in hilarity and much laughter.

Ishik woke up the next morning and walked out of the hut he was sharing with Kiraj to see Ruk standing there with some sort of large, porcelain-colored walking stick that was covered in scratches and had a rough leather handle.

"Urbak," Ruk said, "You must hurry if we are to reach the other tribes in time. But before we depart, we would like you to have this." He handed Ishik the giant stick. Ishik took it and held it with a sense of awe. It was lighter than he expected it to be. "This is the staff used by your namesake, Urbak, our tribe's last known Manipulator."

Ishik looked at the staff carefully and gave it a few swings. It was fairly balanced. Ruk continued his explaining. "The staff is made out of a piece of drake spine. He slew the drake with heat, but at the cost of his own life. You slew a drake, but lived. It is for this reason you have surpassed him and proven yourself worthy of his name."

"Thank you." Ishik said. "Where is the nearest tribe that we're traveling to?" Ruk pointed over to the west.

"The nearest tribe is the tribe of Lok. They have agreed to join Vrasta later this month, so you have to reach and convince them quickly." Ishik nodded. Ruk now gave a howl that no longer sent a chill down Ishik's spine. He recognized it as an assembly howl. Soon, the entire tribe was before Ruk. Their numbers surprised Ishik. They were all silent and waiting for their elder to speak.

Ruk spoke as loudly as he could. "Sons and daughters of Nanali! I have called assembly for a single purpose: Anazan's heir, Urbak, is departing. He cannot journey alone, for our land is full of dangers, even for a Manipulator. Therefore, I wish to ask you for volunteers to accompany one of the few humans who dare look out for our kind. I ask you to go with this man who seeks to free the tribes from their oppressor! Now, who will join him?" Kiraj stood and came forward immediately. Ishik couldn't help but smile.

"Back again, I see," Ishik commented. Kiraj gave a light growl of laughter. Several others stepped forward, including some he had met while traveling in Nan's pack. Ruk nodded to Ishik.

"Well, Urbak, we have your pack that shall accompany you. They will lead you to the sons and daughters of Lok. Farewell, Urbak. We wish you and your Pack good hunting."

As Ishik and his new companions bounded off in the wilderness, there was a loud, unified howl of farewell.

Eighteen

A horseman was crashing through the capital of Rhyth. He charged up to the capital gate. The soldiers on duty saw he was covered in blood. "The king!" the man gasped. "I need to see him!" He flashed his seal. The guards on duty recoiled in shock. It was Wiln, Hasin's son.

The gates opened as quickly as they could. Wiln took off on his horse, pounding through the castle courtyard. He dismounted near the stables and took off in an undignified run. He reached the throne room in a short time. The guards recognized his seal and let him in, looks of concern about their faces.

Hasin was there, with Gonra and someone else Wiln didn't recognize. It was someone that was very young, maybe four years or so younger than himself, with dark hair and a brooding look. Hasin was immediately on edge, his face full of concern.

"Wiln, what's happened to you?" he asked, urgency in his voice. Wiln took a few moments to catch his breath before responding.

"Father, there's been an attack on the northern border defenses of the wall. The attackers were not human. They were werewolves, in numbers I've never seen before. They tried to cleave into us, but we managed to hold firm, just barely outlasting them."

The young man with brown hair looked at Hasin with a knowing expression. "So I was right..." he said. "What I would have given to be wrong..."

Hasin nodded. "It seems that you were right, Emesos," he said to the young man. He now turned to his son. "Wiln, this is Emesos, the newest Prophet."

Emesos bowed respectfully. "It is an honor to meet you, Young Sire."

Wiln nodded to him. "The same, Prophet." Wiln turned back to his father. "Father, what do you make of this attack? It was very organized and well planned."

Hasin sighed, making him look older than ever before. "Son, you have been rather isolated these past few months. The Kingdoms of Stryne and Rhyth have created a wartime alliance. Messengers were sent out to Gyllithia and Ollou asking for the same pact. Maybe our Prophet would care to explain to you the situation."

Emesos looked uncomfortable but did as he was told anyway. "We are on the cusp of entering the Fifth War. Vrasta has mobilized for invasion, and that attack on the border was just the start."

"What?" Wiln whispered. His mind was sent reeling. A War... in his lifetime? It was like the worst possible nightmare had become reality. He had had a deep suspicion in his mind as he had ridden to the capital, but he had tried to convince himself that he was just over-exaggerating. Now his father had stripped him of that wishful thinking to make him face cold reality. It sent chills up his spine. The young man named Emesos continued speaking.

"I am a supposed Prophet, given the cursed task of telling you that Vrasta is coming and leaving nothing back. He's attacking again and the invasion will happen within the next few weeks, most likely. What's worse is he has a Blade wielder on his side, with a monstrous black and orange blade. That is what's happened and is going to happen."

"You saw this in a vision?" Wiln asked.

Emesos shook his head. "No. I don't see the future, only the present and the past. And if I've learned anything in these past few months, it's that history has a nasty tendency to repeat itself."

Wiln turned to Hasin. "Is this true, father? Is Vrasta invading again?"

Hasin nodded to his son. "It is true. Vrasta is just beginning his assault. The Fifth War shall begin." Wiln sagged, as if the air had been knocked out of him. Emesos nodded in understanding.

"If Vrasta has already started, we have no choice. The civilians must be evacuated," Hasin said with weariness. "And I'm afraid, my son, you must rally the troops and pull all the resources you can. For the first time in ages, Rhyth shall march to War."

"With Stryne alongside it," King Gonra added with conviction. Emesos shook his head and sighed.

"The past may have been bleak, but the future looks worse. For once, I'm glad I don't see into the future. I'd just depress myself."

"It'll be better this time, Prophet," Hasin said. Wiln looked at Emesos and waited for his answer. After a long wait, Emesos looked at the king and spoke a simple phrase.

"I guess we'll have to wait and see." Emesos stood and continued talking. "But I've never really been one for waiting around. So... what are we going to do first?"

Wiln couldn't help but smile. This Emesos had a strange personality. He was burdened and downbeat, but he put on an optimistic face. Hasin smiled as well.

"You will go with my son Wiln and start preparing everything for evacuation. He'll know what to do." Emesos nodded and walked toward Wiln and bowed.

"A pleasure to walk with you." Wiln bowed back.

"Thank you, Prophet." Wiln noticed that when he spoke those words, Emesos' face tightened and his brown eyes sparked.

"With all respect, Young Sire, I'd prefer to just be called Emesos." Wiln nodded and proceeded briskly down the hallway with Emesos.

"So why don't you like being called a Prophet?" Wiln asked quietly. "It's a prestigious position."

Emesos shook his head. "There's nothing prestigious about seeing the destruction of entire Kingdoms, or knowing that you're going to survive, but others you care about won't."

Wiln's eyebrows crinkled. "I thought you could only see the past and present." Emesos gave a hollow laugh.

"It's nice to get someone who pays attention for once. I do only see the past and present. But the past chose me. Memories of from other people in the past can take over my mind, and I'm never sure when it will happen. It terrifies me." Wiln nodded.

"That makes sense." A somber silence fell over the two. The only sound that was heard was the two pair of boots hitting the granite floor. Emesos finally spoke up.

"Shouldn't you change clothes?" Wiln shook his head.

"There's no time. We have to start preparing right away. I'll worry about my clothes once we make some progress."

They stopped at the castle scribe room. Wiln jerked his head toward the door. "Come on, we have a War to prepare for."

Ryan Wilshusen

Part Four:

Invasion

Ryan Wilshusen

Nineteen

Ishik and the chosen pack that accompanied Ishik made fantastic time. He quickly learned how to keep up and they took turns standing watch at night. All the while, Ishik was slowly mastering heat. He could now control a limited amount at will, but it wasn't as good as his control over gravity. It would have to do for now.

They were to reach the next tribe in just a few days. With help from the werewolves, some shorter but more dangerous routes were chosen to take the shortest amount of time. Ishik had nearly fallen into the trap of a giant spider, fallen down a ravine, and almost drowned in a river.

It was hard for him to adjust being called Urbak. He kept looking at his new scar on his hand and thought of what he had done.

He had taken a second name. *And I guess,* he thought, *I've taken a second life.* He went to sleep that night, dreaming he was flying among the stars, changing their gravity and making them collide in beautiful and shocking explosions.

When he woke up, he continued with his journey and managed to use gravity to escape a rather large bear and lift a werewolf out of a pit of some deadly looking snake. They stopped next to a waterfall to get some water and rest for a while.

Snow was falling and it was fortunate that the water moved fast enough it didn't freeze. Ishik filled his canteen and washed his hair, shuddering as icy water ran down his back. He looked around for Kiraj and saw the werewolf fashioning an object out of some kind of skin. Ishik walked over and Kiraj greeted him with a growl.

"Urbak, this is for you." He held out the material and Ishik noticed it was a kind of mantle or cloak, bound with some kind of bone. He put it on and immediately felt warmer

"Thanks Kiraj. What's it made out of?"

"It's made out of the skin from an animal called a-"
The werewolf paused suddenly. Ishik tensed. He knew from their stance that the werewolves listening and smelling for a potential danger.

Suddenly, a massive figure jumped from the top of the waterfall and crashed into the pool. Waves erupted skyward. The pack quickly formed a half circle around the pool, growling.

Ishik stood just behind Kiraj, waiting for the mysterious being to emerge from the pool. The water crashed again as a massive figure in black and orange armor stood. Water poured from every gap and opening. Ishik tried to reject the gravity under the figure, but it didn't work.

"I'm immune to your Manipulation," the figure said in Rhythian. It wasn't his native language, Ishik could tell by the accent he couldn't identify.

The armored figure held out an arm and a massive orange and black Blade flared to life in his hand. Ishik shouted immediately.

"Get back!" he shouted at the pack. "Nothing you've got can beat a Blade!" The pack slowly backed away. Ishik stepped forward. "What do you want?" he demanded from the figure.

The armored man pointed his Blade at Ishik. "I want to test you." he said, his voice rumbling monotone. Despite having no emotion inflected into the words, Ishik sensed a strange anticipation.

"It's a test you want?" he said, secretly summoning the Force of heat. "Then it's a test you'll get!" He released the heat and projected it at the water around the knight. It exploded into steam, obscuring the man's vision. He now shouted orders to the Pack. "Get back and stay back! He's mine!" The pack bolted away into the nearby forest. They were keeping their eye on Ishik, watching him eagerly.

The knight quickly recovered and moved forward, Blade in hand. Ishik tensed, ready for the knight to strike. The knight lunged and Ishik rejected gravity underneath himself.

He flew out of the way. The knight followed him with a speed that betrayed his massive size. His blows were equally fast and there was no way to match the knight's sheer power; so Ishik didn't try to block, he just evaded. He was looking for an opening and multiple times he had to reject gravity to distance himself from the knight.

The knight stepped on a large stone and Ishik saw his chance. He rejected gravity under the rock with as much force as he could. The knight flew backward and slammed to the ground. Ishik grabbed a stone and tossed it onto the knight. He made it accept as much gravity as he could, pinning the knight down.

"Impressive." the knight commented.

The knight moved his body through the rock, passing through it like he was air. He jumped up and brought his sword forward in a vicious stab. Just before the Blade touched Ishik's skin, it vanished in a flash.

The knight seemed surprised. "So, you are a son of Altherai." The knight backed away, staring at Ishik. "We will meet again, Manipulator."

"My name's Urbak. And if you get in my way, I *will* destroy you."

The knight turned around. "I will find you again, Ishik. Following you this time was actually rather easy." And with a few quick steps, he vanished into the forest.

The pack came forward out of the forest. Kiraj looked at Ishik and spoke with seriousness.

"Urbak," he said, "That was one of Vrasta's fighters. The tribes have known him for years. Never has anyone beat him in a fight. When the other tribes hear of this, you will surely win their loyalty."

Ishik took a shuddering breath. "He knew my name," he said. "How did he know my name?" The question bothered Ishik. As far as he knew, he had not mentioned his actual name for quite some time.

"I wonder how long he has been following me... and what the hell is 'Altherai'? He said I was a son... but I don't know anyone named Altherai."

Kiraj shook his head. "Do not ponder on his words. He has lied in the past. We should get moving." Ishik nodded and after gathering water, the pack was on its way. Ishik and the others made it to Brin's tribal lands later that day.

There were no obvious marks that Ishik could see, but Kiraj assured him that they were in new territory. When they stopped for the night, Kiraj seemed unsettled.

"We should have been greeted by now," he said to Ishik. "Something is wrong." Ishik nodded. Everyone went to sleep uneasily and woke up uneasy. Ishik could see the other werewolves in the pack had the same feeling Kiraj had. They traveled on regardless and eventually came to a clearing not unlike the one Kiraj's home was in.

There was one problem.

"Divine help us..." Ishik whispered. "They're all dead." Werewolf bodies were everywhere. But they looked cut, not clawed. Something had sliced cleanly through them. Kiraj and the rest of the pack howled in sorrow. Ishik looked at the bodies, confused and horrified.

"I don't know anything that can make a clean cut like this. Not even the sharpest sword can go through werewolf bone in one swing; at least that's what Rhyth's stories say."

Kiraj nodded. "That is true. But there is a sword that can cut like this: a Blade." Kiraj lowered his head. "This must be the work of The Darkest Knight in service to Vrasta. The neutral status of the tribe of Brin cost an entire tribe their lives."

Ishik turned to Kiraj. "What about your tribe? Maybe the knight will do the same to them." Kiraj shook his head.

"Our elder, in his infinite wisdom, had us hide our tribe deep in the wild. None but a select few know where our tribe is now." Ishik nodded. He then stared at all the bodies.

"What do we do with the bodies? Do we burn them? Do we bury them?" Kiraj looked around and shook his head.

Ishik spoke, his tone somber. "We depart immediately for the next tribe. The sons and daughters of Anazan could be in danger," He saw the pack form up and stare at him. Ishik swallowed and spoke loud enough for everybody to hear. He tried to find the right words to say, words honoring the dead, but he couldn't do it. Instead, he put all his emotions of grief and fear into two words. They rang out across the group like a bell calling warriors to arms. "Let's move!"

The pack roared in unison. Kiraj took the lead and Ishik followed closely behind. Together, they left the terrible carnage behind, determined to prevent it from occurring again.

The sense of urgency was greater than ever before over the next two days of travel. Now, it was more than need that drove them forward. It was a matter of survival. On the second night, after Ishik had practiced his control of heat, he noticed that he had much more control than he had before he had arrived at the Brin tribe.

It's like desperation or panic is the key, he thought. *Maybe my emotions are an opening. The more I panic, the stronger I become. If that's true, how far do I have to be pushed before I gain complete control of heat?* It was a question he wasn't sure he wanted answered.

He noticed a figure stopping before him. Ishik looked up and saw that it was the werewolf known as Gren. Gren was a very quiet werewolf, and mostly kept to himself. Ishik had never actually heard him speak. "What can I do for you, Gren?" he asked.

The werewolf shuffled about shyly for a little bit, looking strangely small despite his massive size. Gren wasn't the usual brown or white; he was had a pure black coat that glistened in the firelight. "Urbak..." he said, hesitant. "I...I was wondering...So were the others...would you mind doing a ceremony for the tribe of Brin? Or at least speak for them?"

Ishik was surprised by Gren's request. "I don't know any werewolf customs for dealing with their dead. Are you sure you want me to do it?"

Gren nodded and bared his fangs. Ishik was taken aback for a moment and then realized the werewolf was trying to smile. He smiled back. "Alright; get everyone around the fire and I'll do my best. Just warning you, it won't be perfect."

Gren padded back over to the rest of the pack. Ishik heard a few words. "He said yes." The pack gathered around the fire and Ishik stepped into the loose circle, the blaze warming his back in the frigid winter air. He started speaking, not bothering at going on and on. He didn't like being fancy with his words anyway.

"I don't know how it stands among werewolves, but where I come from there's nothing sadder than the murders of the perfectly innocent. But we can't let the death of the tribe slow us down. We have to show others, no, *prove* to others that the tribe of Brin made the right choice, not the easy one."

Ishik took a deep breath and waited for their reactions. There was silence in the pack. A rustling sound came from beyond the view given by the fire. Everyone immediately went into a defensive stance. A werewolf came into view. Its eyes settled on Kiraj.

"Kiraj, it's been a long time since you've visited." Kiraj swallowed, but said nothing. Ishik turned to Kiraj with questioning eyes and then back to their unexpected guest. The werewolf had a brown coat and a leaner build, along with a softer, more eloquent voice. Ishik realized this very well might be the first werewolf female he had ever encountered. She now turned a green eye on Ishik.

"And what is this...*thing* doing in our territory?"

Gren poised to jump forward, but Kiraj held up a hand to make him pause. "He is not a thing... he is a human. His name is Urbak." The brown werewolf raised her eyebrows in recognition.

"You've seen fit to give this human a second name? And what prompted you to do that?" she challenged.

Kiraj gave an answer almost immediately. "He fought off Vrasta's knight without a Blade and won. He spared my life when he could have taken it and decided that he would save us from enslavement to Vrasta. He also took down a drake and saved Nan's life."

The female gave Kiraj a skeptical look. Kiraj continued his explanation. "He isn't just a normal human! He's a Manipulator. He's mastered two Forces on his own and he takes no life from others to use his abilities. He's Anazan's heir."

Ishik felt like Kiraj was being a little too generous with his praises. Their definitions of the word *mastered* must be completely different.

The female's expression grew serious. "That is a very bold and reckless statement." Her eyes narrowed on Ishik. "And I doubt Anazan's heir would be so...inexperienced."

Ishik resisted the temptation to reject gravity under her feet. The she-wolf continued. "And what about a Blade? Anazan had a Blade he could summon at will. If this boy cannot produce a Blade?"

Oh no, Ishik thought. He started to panic slightly. *What am I going to do to get out of this mess?!* His arm shot up on its own accord and exploded with pain. Suddenly the pain was gone and something flashed into his hands. It was a large Blade. It looked like a long sword, meant for two hands. It was made of different shades of grey except for the hilt which had a rough leather grip wrapped around it that was brown and tattered. The grip was haphazardly on the sword, with a knot tied into the back, the ends of the pieces of leather slightly longer than the length of his hand. It was boring to look at, but it filled Ishik with a sense of wonder.

I just summoned a Blade! How did I summon a Blade? He looked at the weapon again.

I've never even heard of this one. He now thought about his state of mind before the Blade appeared. *Once again, I panic and something comes to my rescue. I'm sensing a common pattern.* Ishik lowered his hand and Kiraj shot him a look of utter surprise.

Ishik shrugged. He had no idea he could do that; it just happened. He looked to the female werewolf and waited for a reaction. Her face was a mask he couldn't read. Finally, she spoke.

"That Blade is very old. It's the oldest one in fact... The last time it was seen was at a large battle. Its wielder walked off the battlefield and was never see again. The Blade in your hand was the first one, before the large conflict you humans had."

Ishik's eyes widened in surprise. "Are you talking about the First War?" he asked. The female werewolf nodded and made a motion with her head.

" I am the legend keeper of my tribe. Come, I shall guide you to the tribe of Anazan. We'll talk there." Ishik looked at the Blade and started running, amazed by how light it was. They ran through the night, which was much more frightening than running in the day. There were so many roars and growls in the night, Ishik wondered how the werewolves got any sleep.

After what seemed an eternity of running, they arrived at another clearing that marked the beginning of the werewolf living area. It was dark and they slept outside for the rest of the night, too exhausted to even bother finding a place to sleep with a roof.

The next morning, Ishik woke up and realized that the Blade had not disappeared. He wasn't exactly sure how Blades worked but he was pretty sure that they would vanish when willed to go away. He tried to will the Blade away, but it didn't move. He tried concentrating harder, but it still didn't disappear

Ishik took a look at his surroundings now that it wasn't nighttime. It looked almost identical to the rest of the werewolf settlements he had seen. The brown werewolf he had talked to earlier was staring at him. Ishik looked down and noted that almost all his clothes were rags. It occurred to him that he hadn't changed clothes since he had been kicked out of the Congregation of the Divine almost a month and a half ago.

"Hello," he said tentatively. The she-wolf said nothing. She just stared at him. "Is there something I can do for you?" he asked. She gestured to a large log.

"I need this lifted and put on the other side of the village." Ishik nodded.

"Sure," he said. Ishik gripped the new Blade tightly and forced the log to reject gravity. It came off the ground easily and he quickly walked with the log floating behind him to the other side of the village and set it down. "Is here good?" he asked her. She merely nodded. Ishik had an inward feeling that this was just the start of a series of tests.

"Good, now, I have something else that I need you to do." The female said. Ishik nodded and followed her. She pointed to some vines that were wrapping around a hut. "I need you to clear these away." Ishik nodded and summoned the Force of heat.

Ishik was glad that he practiced controlling it, because this was a precision job. He spent the next fifteen minutes carefully burning away the foliage. When he finished, the she-wolf inspected his work and seemed satisfied. She looked at him and spoke again, in a commanding tone.

"Now you will kill a criminal." Ishik's insides went cold. He didn't have to think about a response. His answer was automatic.

"No."

"Pardon?" the werewolf asked. Ishik knew she had heard him perfectly fine.

"I said no."

"I am head of the tribe of Anazan, and as his heir I command you-" Ishik acted rapidly. He made her body reject and then accept gravity so she was pinned with her back to the ground. He then pointed his Blade at her throat.

"I don't take orders from you," he said, his voice low. "I don't take orders from anyone, got it? I won't kill someone who's done nothing to me." For a moment, Ishik saw something in the werewolf's eyes. It was a glint of outrage.

"You dare disobey—" she started to growl.

"Yes, I do." Ishik cut her off ruthlessly. "And when are people going to learn that *I don't care what their position is?*" he asked rhetorically.

"I don't care if you're the ruler of all four Kingdoms. I don't take commands from anyone without a reason, understand?"

She nodded and Ishik released the control he had on gravity. He turned around and walked back to where Kiraj and the others.

"You are very similar to Anazan, human." The statement made Ishik pause. The pack leader walked up beside him, a fierce light in her eye. "But you are like the other man more."

Ishik was confused. "What 'other man' are you talking about?"

"Only two other humans besides you have dared enter our tribe lands and lived: Anazan, and the one before him."

Ishik's eyebrows narrowed. "What do you mean... there was someone before Anazan?"

The female werewolf nodded. "Yes. His name is one that werewolves from the tribe of Anazan fear above all others. Before the Great Collapse, humans tried to kill our kind. Before the Collapse, humans were massive in number and extremely strong. When almost all were dead, a single human rose to fight. In his hand, he had the very Blade you hold now."

Ishik flexed his fingers over the worn leather. "And what did he do?" he asked.

The werewolf leader's eyes glimmered with the excitement of the tale. "He killed almost every human on the battlefield that day. He spared only two people: A messenger, and Anazan himself. Then he walked off the battlefield, never to be seen again."

"He must have been an amazing warrior. What was his name?"

"His name was Ishik. None in the history of the tribes have even considered taking that name. He saved our race from extinction, an achievement no one else has accomplished."

Ishik's mind was sent reeling. *Is that where my name comes from?* He wondered. "My first name..." He whispered to himself.

"What is wrong?" the leader asked. "You seem ill."

"What's your first name?"

The pack leader was taken aback. "You haven't earned the right to know my first name. You may refer to me as Yeznia."

"Want to know my first name, my *actual* name? I think you've earned the right."

"What is your first name then?" Yeznia said in an exasperated tone.

"My first name is Ishik."

Yeznia gave him a look of disbelief. "Humans don't remember that legend. It's impossible for you to be named Ishik."

Ishik slammed his sword into the damp, cold earth. The Blade sank deep into the ground. "My name is Ishik. I want to help your people survive. If you don't believe me, ask Kiraj. Fight for your freedom or not, it's your choice."

Yeznia went over to Kiraj and spoke to him in native werewolf tongue. The conversation slowly grew faster and louder as time went on. Yeznia walked back to Ishik, her face one of shock.

"You...you were telling the truth. Your first name is Ishik... And so the promise has come true...just as Anazan said: *'One day, another man named Ishik will come to save the tribes. Fight with him.'*"

Yeznia looked Ishik straight in the eye. "We will join your fight, Urbak. It is time for the sons and daughters of Anazan to take action." Yeznia walked off from Ishik to go tell her tribe the information she had just acquired.

Something inside Ishik told him that the real test was just beginning.

Twenty

Rumors were flying around the Kingdom of Rhyth about the crown prince and only son of King Hasin quickly befriending the Prophet Emesos.

Unlike most rumors however, this one was completely true. Wiln and Emesos had found something neither were expecting: a close friendship. Around Wiln, Emesos could drop all formalities. He was just Emesos, a normal person with an interest in cooking.

And around Emesos, Wiln was a normal man who liked to run in the rain. Even though both of them were practically run ragged doing errands and messages to work on mobilizing and evacuating to prepare for the Fifth War, they somehow managed to have dinner together and make each other laugh.

Just now, they were walking down the hall to the Grand Council Gathering that all the kings and their children would attend so an overall plan could be agreed on. Emesos looked down on his plain white robes in disappointment. "They really need to use a color or two," Emesos said to Wiln as they walked down the hallway. Wiln looked at his own, heavy dress clothes that were bright red and green.

"And make them easier to wear," Wiln added. Then they were stopped at the door by an announcer.

"Hold, please," the announcer said. "Surely you weren't expecting to enter without female companions? That just won't do for people as important as you." Emesos groaned inwardly. He could see Wiln was in a similar state.

"Who are to be our companions?" Wiln asked. The announcer clapped twice and two women came out of the shadows. One of them was a rather attractive girl in a green dress that Emesos didn't recognize. Judging by the color that left Wiln's face, Emesos guessed that the prince recognized her.

"Zelda..." he said. "I-It's good to see you. You-you look great." Zelda tilted her head and her blue eyes sparkled with pleasure.

"It is good to see you to, Majesty." She spoke in Rhythian, but Emesos understood what she was saying. *How do I understand Rhythian?* Emesos asked himself. The answer hit him like a brick. *Anazan... just how many languages did he know?* Zelda then turned and curtseyed at Emesos. "And it is an honor, Prophet."

Emesos bowed and smiled. "Likewise. Please, just call me Emesos." Zelda's eyes widened in surprise.

"I see you've learned Rhythian," she commented. "I'm impressed." Wiln gave Emesos a confused look that said *when did you have time to learn?!*

Emesos shot him a look back that said *I'll explain later.* The other woman, the one meant to accompany Emesos, stepped forward.

Emesos' heart skipped a beat. Her brown hair and green eyes shined. Her violet colored dress was simple, but it worked. Her smile revealed white teeth. "Wow, Lanita...wow..." he said. "You look stunning." She raised an eyebrow.

"Since when did you learn Rhythian?" Lanita asked. Emesos gave her the same look he gave Wiln. She seemed to understand. He stopped himself from grabbing her hand and felt his neck grow warm. The announcer brought them in and announced their presence. Emesos took her hand and guided her in.

He saw a small girl, sitting at a desk with parchment and a quill before her. She was writing miniscule runes onto a sheet of paper, humming tunelessly to herself as she worked...

He quickly dropped her hand as Lanita gasped. She shot him an extremely confused look. After Emesos and Lanita finished greeting people who tried to swarm them, Emesos guided Lanita to a place where they could talk in relative privacy.

"Look," he said, his voice quiet and earnest. "You felt that strange feeling when I grabbed your hand." Lanita nodded. "The Congregation calls me a Prophet because I have visions. But I don't call myself a Prophet because they're not visions. They're *memories*; other people's memories that somehow wind up in my head. My skill with a spear doesn't come from training or talent. It comes from the memories of Fellix. I don't know a single bit of Rhythian. *Anazan* knew how to speak Rhythian." Her eyes widened. Emesos continued his explanation.

"I can't touch people for too long; otherwise, I gain some of their memories and feel their emotions. I seem to gain skills from memories as well."

"Like spear fighting and languages?" Emesos nodded. Lanita stared at him in amazement. "This is so strange," she said. "It's like the Divine has combined the talents of all the heroes of the last War into one person." Emesos rubbed the sides of his head.

"I'm glad someone's thought the same thing. But, I feel like I'm missing pieces." Her eyebrows narrowed. Emesos elaborated. "More and more, I'm finding things are tying into Anazan."

"Anazan? The old advisor from Stryne?" Lanita asked.

Emesos nodded. "That's the one," he said. "Only, he wasn't from Stryne. He could speak fluent Stryne, Rhythian, and Ancient. Not to mention he was the one who hired Fellix after he was rejected by the ancient king of Stryne."

Lanita did not seem surprised by this. "Velenry told me that you knew more than you were letting on. So, what does this have to do with the Fifth War?"

Emesos sighed. "I'm trying to figure that out. But nothing's coming together!" He noticed that the music had picked up and people were dancing. People were staring at them. Emesos held out a hand. "Shall we dance?" Lanita curtsied with a mischievous smile and Emesos guided her out to the dance floor.

Suddenly, his mind was elsewhere. He was standing before a beautiful woman with brown hair and gold eyes. She was smiling. He smiled back. Then, behind them, he saw a large stained glass window shatter. A massive figure in black and orange armor leapt through it and landed on the marble floors with a crash. He summoned a massive Blade that matched his armor and surged forward...

Emesos shook his head and gasped. Lanita was smiling at him. Behind her was a large, stained glass window. He knew what was going to happen. "Get away from the windows!" he screamed. "Get away from the—"

The windows crashed and the large, black and orange knight came charging through. He landed on stone floors with the same crash. He summoned a Blade and dove forward, cutting through a nearby victim. The four kings were immediately there, Blades in hand. The four of them attacked with all the skill they could muster, but the knight held them back with almost contemptuous ease.

"You really are pathetic compared to him." The man's voice was the exact same as the one Emesos had seen in the vision of Vrasta. "A son of Altherai has risen to reclaim what is his. Step aside, or be cut down." The knight slammed his Blade down and three of the kings were sent flying. Hasin managed to stand his ground, his feet oddly bound to the ground. The knight easily disarmed the older man. Emesos saw the man's Blade descending on the king's neck.

"Sene!" he bellowed. Everyone turned to look at him. Emesos let go of Lanita's hand and ran toward the man. But before he could reach the knight, the man's Blade cleaved through Hasin's neck with ease. The king gave no gasp and fell to the ground in a sad, silent death.

Screams and cries rang out. Emesos heard Wiln's cry, and it filled him with rage. Sene now looked up at Emesos and held his Blade in front of him.

"So, you are the Prophet," Sene said. His Strynic was incredibly accurate. "I expected someone a little older." Emesos gave a cry and his black and white Blade flashed to life in his hand. Emesos charged forward and went into immediate combat with the knight. After exchanging a series of blows, the knight jumped back and stared at Emesos' Blade.

The knight's stance changed. The massive orange and black Blade shook in his fist. His entire body seemed to be shaking. "No...Why...How...How dare you wield that cursed sword in front of me! How could it choose another!? How?! You don't deserve such a burden!"

"Enough!" Emesos yelled, resuming his attack. He and the knight exchanged more blows. The kings were getting up and rushing back to the fight. The knight slammed his Blade on the ground and the kings were strangely immobile, as if someone rooted them to the spot.

"No one interferes with this fight," the knight said, his deep voice rumbling through the hall. Emesos was now all over the place, weaving patterns and attacks the best he could. The knight held him off and made him go on the defensive. Emesos was barely holding on. He jumped back away from the knight and they circled slowly.

Emesos was in a combat situation. The knight was staring at him. Emesos looked down and saw he was armored. The knight charged forward and Emesos threw a gauntleted fist in his chest, sending him soaring backward...

Emesos snapped out of his vision in time to see the knight go flying, a huge dent in the chest plate of his armor. Emesos looked down at his arm and saw that an opaque, whitish glove covered his hand. In fact, the white substance covered his entire body, like some kind of armor. It coupled strangely well with his Blade.

The knight landed on the ground with his feet beneath him, skidding back several feet. He looked at Emesos for a long moment before speaking.

"You have no experience, yet you have summoned the armor... the 'integration' has already begun." He looked at the other kings still struggling to move, held down by an unseen force under the knight's control. He then turned back to Emesos and did the unexpected. He bowed.

"We shall meet again, Anazan's heir. Until then, long may you live, and may Altherai live through you."

"Wait!" Emesos yelled. "I need answers!" The knight ignored him and using some strange power, jumped through the window, leaving cracks in the floor. There was silence in the ballroom, then, a dry sob. Emesos looked back to see Wiln kneeling next to his father's body. Emesos went over and knelt down beside him, putting a hand on his shoulder.

"He...he was the only one," Wiln whispered. "He was the only one to stand his ground." He looked at Emesos, his watery eyes blazing. "You have to kill him," he whispered vehemently. "You can stop him. You have to..." His voice lost what little strength it had. Emesos nodded and embraced his friend.

After what felt like hours of shared agony, for Emesos felt the emotions of grief and separation as he embraced his friend; they broke apart and stood. Wiln quickly and quietly ordered soldiers to carry out his father's body. He turned to the crowd that was staring at him. It was a mix of royalty and servants. Emesos was amazed that Wiln managed to actually speak with volume and conviction.

"This party is concluded. I shall speak before this gathering tomorrow at noon." He paused for a moment and then continued.

"There shall be an immediate Council of Kings, now!" Wiln walked off, Emesos followed him. The crowd was buzzing. Eventually, the other three kings and their historians managed to filter out. Emesos followed them and they came to the Council chamber. Emesos halted. Gonra looked at Emesos.

"What are you pausing for?"

"I'm not a king, or a historian, so..."

"You have a Blade." Gonra said sharply. "You fought off that monster of a swordsman. Get in here before I have to drag you." Emesos hurried inside the chamber, Gonra shaking his head behind him. "Honestly, you are sometimes too humble for your own good."

Each of the kings summoned their Blades and plunged them into the slots. They looked at Wiln. Wiln concentrated, and sure enough, Hasin's Blade flared into his hand. Wiln was now officially king of Rhyth.

They now looked to Emesos. He stared at them blankly until Gonra gestured to his own Blade. Emesos understood and summoned his Blade. He merely held it; there was no slot to put it in. Wiln now broke the silence by asking Emesos a question.

"What was said in the conversation between you and that swordsman?" Emesos was surprised. He raised an eyebrow and looked at all the kings.

"I was speaking Strynic," he said. "You heard what I said." Velenry, who was behind Gonra's throne, shook her head and spoke out.

"Emesos, you were speaking Ancient." With that statement, all the kings looked shocked.

"You can speak Ancient?" Yanata, king of Gyllithia asked with interest in his voice.

Emesos shook his head. "I can't speak it, but Anazan can." He then launched into a very detailed description of everything that happened to him and all of the abilities and theories he had acquired only a short time ago. To him, it felt like an eternity. When he had finished explaining, all of the kings looked very concerned.

"So, this knight...you've had...what do you call them... '*experiences*' before?" Gonra asked. Emesos nodded and responded with a sour note in his voice.

"The knight's name is Sene. He used to serve Vrasta, but apparently he has his own agenda now. I'm not entirely sure if he's still allied with Vrasta or not. He said that his loyalties lie only with something or someone called Altherai. Apparently there's someone who's an heir, and he's out to find him. But it appears I'm connected to this Altherai, too. I'm so confused about this whole thing. I've been trying to puzzle it out for ages, but I haven't got any solid answers on what Altherai is or what Sene has to do with it."

The kings looked at each other and seemed to reach a silent but unanimous conclusion. "We must return to our homelands and ready them for War on the Rhythian border. We will stay for Hasin's funeral, though," Yanata stated. "He was a great king and a good man."

Wiln gave Yanata a look of silent thanks and, for a while, all that was heard was the scratch of the historians' quills on parchment. Emesos suddenly felt dizzy. A massive headache gripped him. He gave a small moan and tried to get the pain to go away, but it merely increased. Suddenly, he felt a rush of air, and then saw black.

******

Emesos was in a long, high and very plain corridor. There were no colors, windows, or banners, not even a rug. Instead, just plain, smooth grey stone. Emesos hurried through it, trying to figure out where he was.

"Hello?" he called out softly. "Hello? Is anyone there?" He came to the end of the hallway and suddenly, a tall man was there with a flash of a great smile. His hair was completely white, his eyes blood-red. He was very thin, almost skeletal.

"H-hello, M-majesty. W-what can I do for you?" The man flushed red with humiliation as an uncontrollable stutter came through. He seemed to brace himself for a glare or mockery. Emesos just smiled at him and gave an expression of gratitude. "Can you start with your name?" The man's face lit up.

"M-my name is Rhyth." Emesos' insides flipped.

Rhyth! *he thought.* Who would name their child after a Kingdom? *"I assume you're from the Kingdom of Rhyth," he said. The man shot him a strange look.*

"S-sire, what are you talking about? T-the only land I'm from is the Empire. That's the o-only land anyone's from! Are you feeling alright?" he asked.

Emesos' mind reeled in shock as he processed this bit of information. An Empire that was as big as all four Kingdoms. This must be before the First War! Anything and everything I can gather information-wise could matter.

"I'm fine, Rhyth. Say, do you know where my family is? Is my father around here?"

Rhyth gave him a pained expression. "Lord Qwen is currently not available. And your brother Sene is not in the mood to see you." Emesos' eyes widened.

"Could you take me to him? I need to see him, right now." Rhyth gave Emesos a strange look, but he led Emesos down several twisting corridors. Finally, they stopped at a door. Rhyth knocked on it politely. Emesos heard a very similar voice to the one he encountered at the ballroom.

"What? I'm very busy right now, leave." Rhyth gave Emesos a questioning look, wondering what to do next. Emesos now knocked on the door, heavier than Rhyth had done.

"Sene, it's me," he said. "We need to talk." The door opened and Emesos saw Sene for the first time. He was somewhat tall, very well-muscled. His dark hair was tousled and his strange, orange colored eyes were filled with impatience.

"What? What do you need?" he said. His snappish attitude made Rhyth cringe, but Emesos held his ground.

"Don't snap," Emesos said; his voice firm. "You're royalty after all. I need to ask you a few things."

Sene rolled his eyes and beckoned Emesos in. Rhyth bowed and walked away. Sene shut the door. Emesos looked around Sene's room and saw it was covered in papers, some with sketches of swords, others crammed with miniscule writing. One of the swords looked very familiar. Then, Emesos realized that it was the Blade that Wiln summoned, just a little while ago. "What's this?" he said as he gestured to the paper with Wiln's Blade on it.

Sene now actually looked embarrassed. He blushed and looked around. "It's nothing, just a project I've been working on in my spare time." Emesos then realized something shocking.

Sene is designing the Blades! *He turned to his 'brother' and gestured to the entire room littered with drawings, writings and books.* "This isn't 'nothing', Sene. It's fantastic!" *Sene looked at Emesos like he had sprouted a third arm.*

"You really think so?" he asked. Emesos nodded enthusiastically.

"You can change the course of history with these swords!" And then, everything seemed so far away...

******

Emesos woke up and stared at the ceiling of what looked like a medical wing. Two facts were certain: Things just became more dangerous, and things just became much more confusing. *Sene designed all of the Blades...how old is he? If it's the same person I faced in the ballroom, then he'd be incredibly old...* Emesos thought in silence, thinking and lamenting about how much more complex this experience would make things. On top of fighting a War and warning others of conflicts to come, he had to unravel a few mysteries as well.

Twenty-One

Kiraj saw the marching mob. Hundreds upon hundreds of werewolves were moving out; hundreds upon hundreds of his kind were walking into slavery.

He then looked over to Ishik, who was staring at it too, his face an expressionless mask.

"We've have gathered two non-bound tribes, so what next?" Ishik asked. They had managed to convince the tribe of Anazan of Ishik's superiority just two days ago. Almost all of the fighting werewolves had joined their pack, including Yeznia herself. Ishik's mask broke and disgust was clear on his face.

"This is sickening." Ishik said. "Come on, we have better things to do. We still have one more tribe, right? What are they called, and what are they like?" He grabbed his staff and his Blade that had been driven into the ground.

Kiraj looked at the rags that barely covered Ishik anymore. They were covered in muck and grime, stained by days of hard travel. His brown hair was cut roughly, as if he had done it on his own with a knife or sharp rock. He was covered in minor scratches.

But the minor scratches were nothing compared to the large amount of muscle that Ishik had acquired. Every part of him seemed to have become as hard as iron since Kiraj had first met him. Among humans, he would be a barbarian abomination. Among the werewolves, he was what humans could be at their full potential. The others held him in a special spot in their hearts.

And even though he didn't say it, Kiraj was fairly sure Ishik felt the same.

"The last free tribe could be the hardest. They are the sons and daughters of Ragnok. They are the strongest fighters of all the werewolves. The only reason Vrasta couldn't ally with them by force is that they managed to kill almost all of his soldiers in the brigade he sent. No doubt their elder will want to challenge you."

Ishik nodded and gave a jerk of the head, staring at the marching werewolves with scorn. "Come on, let's get going. I might be ill if I look at this any longer." The two of them came back to where the rest of the Pack was waiting.

"Let's move." They formed up and with a single howl from the werewolf on point, began their trek to visit the last free werewolf tribe. The journey wasn't easy, but it was certainly more manageable since Ishik had his Blade.

Any Bloodvine that tried to strangle or trip up someone was quickly sliced. Predators were nowhere to be seen. They encountered a wurm and the wurm actually ran away once it saw Ishik. This led to a lot of good-natured joking about looks and faces. And soon, Ishik found himself laughing and joking along with them.

I wonder why I can do this with werewolves but not humans, Ishik thought as he maneuvered his way through the wilderness. *Maybe I'm less human? Or are they just more reasonable?* Ishik shrugged. He wasn't going to question too much. What mattered was that he had friends.

Their journey lasted just three days before they arrived at the place the tribe of Ragnok called home. There was a werewolf there, ready to greet them. "We were waiting for you." The werewolf's hair was gray and it was undoubtedly the biggest, most ferocious looking werewolf Ishik had ever seen. It was a little while before Ishik managed to speak.

"It's good to meet you," Ishik said. "It's nice to meet the strongest tribe. At least, that's what I've been told."

The werewolf glared at Ishik, then turned back to Kiraj. "Why did you bring this *thing* here?!" he yelled. Kiraj's eyes hardened. A slight snarl crept on his face.

"He is not a *thing*, he is a human. And he is stronger than Vrasta, and the Dark One. He seeks to fight Vrasta, and thought 'who would be better to fight him than the finest warriors?'"

The werewolf sneered at Ishik. Ishik merely gave the werewolf a small smile. So far, being underestimated had been his biggest advantage, and this was the place he could take the largest advantage of it.

"Are you saying I'm in the wrong place?" Ishik said. "I was sure this was where Ragnok's people are."

"You are pathetic," the werewolf taunted. Ishik said nothing in response. "You think we would help a weakling like you." The werewolf turned to Kiraj and the pack. "Or weaklings like th-"

The werewolf's sentence was cut off as Ishik leaped forward and slammed his fist into the werewolf's throat. He then flicked the Blade up to the werewolf's neck.

"Taunt them again, and I will gut you like the wurm you are. I'll tolerate insults at me, but not them. If you want to insult someone, go insult the twenty tribes that didn't have enough spine to say 'no' to Vrasta."

The werewolf grabbed Ishik's Blade and growled. He yanked it out of Ishik's hands and let out a sound that sounded like a scream. The Blade seemed to burn the werewolf. He dropped it and stared at his scorched hands.

His eyes flashed to Ishik in anger. Then, they widened in shock. "You-you are-" The werewolf turned and ran. Ishik looked to Kiraj, confused. Kiraj shrugged. Suddenly, the werewolf returned with a much larger one that was covered with scars across his torso. The colossal werewolf peered with gray eyes at Osjol.

"So...you are the one who claims to be stronger than Vrasta?" it asked in a soft voice. Ishik nodded in reply. "What makes you think you are stronger than Vrasta?" the werewolf asked.

Ishik replied immediately. "I have a shred of honor, something worth fighting for, determination, a Blade, and some of the best fighters in the entire continent behind me. I also can Manipulate the Forces of gravity and heat."

The werewolf laughed. "And you think that matters?" he challenged. "Humans are so weak. They dare not face us without their tools or armor. They hide behind shields and cower behind Forces, not daring to fight us one against one. Not even Vrasta himself could beat me in an honest fight."

Ishik planted his Blade in the ground. He dropped his staff and stretched. "I'll do it; whatever it takes to convince you." There were many cries from his pack. Many of them just said his name. Kiraj actually grabbed him.

"Urbak, you can't! This is madness! Not even other werewolves can best him," he explained, in a soft, urgent whisper. Ishik took Kiraj's hand off his arm and spoke.

"I have to," he said just as softly. "We need to have them with us; otherwise, we could be crushed. We're desperate enough for help as it is. I'm not going to miss this chance."

Ishik now looked at the werewolf before him. "I challenge you, to a fight. If I win, you have to help us. If you win, you get me." The pack was silent and the locals gathered around in silence, waiting for an answer from the large werewolf.

The large creature was nearly double Ishik's height, and half-again as broad. He gave a roar, then stared at Ishik with amusement. "Fine then, *pup*; let's start." A large circle of werewolves quickly formed around them.

Ishik crouched low, ready to face the werewolf. It lunged forward, claws bared. Ishik jumped out of the way. The werewolf turned to lunge again, and Ishik continued to evade him. This pattern continued until the werewolf made an unexpected turn in midair. The claws raked at Ishik's side and back. Ishik cried out in pain and the werewolves around the circle howled. Ishik managed to get out of the death grip in which the werewolf was trying to ensnare him.

"You humans are so weak," his opponent taunted. "One or two little scratches are enough to immobilize you." Ishik looked at his opponent, his hands slick with his own blood. The werewolf now flew forward and pinned Ishik to the ground by his arms, driving all the air from his chest. "And you are so easily pinned." The claws came down, raking Ishik's chest. Ishik's body now surged with adrenaline as he planted his feet on the werewolf's chest.

"Get off!" he yelled, pushing as hard as he could. The werewolf was thrown off balance. Ishik took the opportunity to get back up off the ground and throw a punch to the werewolf's face. His fist collided, knocking his opponent's head away, allowing Ishik to move out of the range of those devastating claws. The werewolf now looked at Ishik with newfound respect.

"Well human, it seems you have some will." The werewolf lunged again. Ishik wasn't quick enough to evade the tackle completely. The claw scratched his cheek, causing him to bleed. Ishik wheeled around to see that his opponent had flown past him. When the werewolf landed, Ishik was now the one to dive forward. He proceeded to punch every part of the werewolf he could reach. The werewolf threw a single punch to his abdomen, sending Ishik flying backwards.

Ishik was sure that one or two ribs broke when he hit the ground. The pain was enough to make him dizzy. Soon, the werewolf had picked him up and tossed him again. When he landed, he heard ringing in his ears.

"Give up, human!" his opponent said. "You are in no state to fight anymore." Something in those words gave Ishik the strength to stand. He hauled himself off the ground slowly. He heard the sound of growling. He could hardly see out of one eye, and he was fairly sure that his left ear was ringing still. His opponent spoke to him again.

"Stay down, human! You have lost and you know it." Ishik stumbled forward and threw a punch the werewolf easily countered, sending Ishik to his knees. "Stop fighting. You know there is no hope."

Slowly, Ishik got back to his feet, swaying slightly, coughing up a little blood as he did so. "I...can't...give up," he managed to say. "I...have...to save...you all..." The werewolves now exchanged looks of confusion.

I need to help them. Divine...please... he pleaded. His body was begging for him to collapse, but Ishik denied it. He would not fall. He didn't have a choice. He had to succeed. His body stopped swaying at these thoughts. He remembered all the times he had been denied by his family: all of the times he never got a chance, all the opportunities others had taken from him, all of the times people had made him give up and taken in his place. But now...now was—

"My turn!" he yelled. Strength born from years of hatred, regret and sorrow propelled him forward. His opponent was clearly not expecting this. The werewolf went for a simple slash. Ishik grabbed the arm and yanked. The werewolf toppled forward and Ishik threw his other fist upward to collide with the werewolf's face.

His blow landed with enough force to lift the massive creature off his feet. When he landed, Ishik jumped on top of him and landed another blow on the werewolf's throat, making him gasp. With his opponent stunned, Ishik proceeded to rain blows on his opponent's face, his fists beating out a violent, bloody rhythm.

As swiftly as it had arrived, the manic strength left his body, and he felt drained; more exhausted than he ever had felt in his life. Ishik gave a small smile.

"I did it," he said softly.

He toppled over and the world went black.

Twenty-Two

Wiln stared at the battle report, his eyes fixed on the numbers. "So we lost four ballista and one hundred soldiers? How many did they lose?" The soldier who had delivered the message paled and answered.

"Nine drakes and twenty werewolves." The words made Wiln want to cringe. *And all those soldiers were behind a massive wall. I'd hate to see what happens when they face werewolves in open combat.* Wiln looked at the soldier.

"How soon do you think we could get more supplies and troops up there?" The soldier thought for a moment and then answered.

"I'd say about a week, sire." Wiln thought for a moment and then nodded.

"Well, that will have to do. I'll make sure to get you the things you need and get you back there as fast as possible. Dismissed." The soldier snapped to attention and walked off.

Wiln put his head in his hands. They were now a week into fighting and already taking heavy losses. The other nobles seemed awed that Wiln hadn't asked for help from the other kings yet. *They're like sharks,* he thought. *Circling around and waiting for me to give.* The speech and funeral for Hasin were devastating to the people's morale. On top of that, Emesos had fallen into a coma for the past week as well.

Wiln hadn't gotten much sleep. Lanita chose to remain with Wiln at all times, except for when he asked to be alone. At least she was on his side. There were stacks of documents that needed his seal to be executed. Wiln was at his desk, facing that pile of documents with a kind of grim determination to make some progress.

Wiln picked up the first document and began to read. At that moment, Lanita burst through the door to the study. Wiln's head shot up, concern on his face.

"He's awake," Lanita said breathlessly. "Emesos is awake! Oh, and he says he has quite a few things to tell you." Wiln stood, leaving the documents behind and started down to medical wing with Lanita.

"What does he have to say?" He asked.

Lanita shook her head. "I don't know. I think he had an experience during the coma." When they arrived at the medical wing, a very pale Emesos was sitting up in his bed. Wiln went over and knelt next to Emesos' bed.

"Emesos, I'm here. What do you need?" Emesos looked at Wiln and swallowed a few times before he spoke.

"You're not going to like this." Emesos explained in detail everything that occurred in his experience. He paid particular attention to Sene, and the servant named Rhyth. Wiln looked stunned and so did Lanita. After he finished, Emesos looked at the ceiling and sighed. Wiln looked to Lanita for answers.

Lanita finished copying what Emesos had said and then spoke. "We have no information on anything before or during the First War," she said. "To hear that there was an empire and that the Blades came from it is new to me."

Emesos shook his head. "You're missing the important part," he said. "*Sene* made the Blades." Wiln's eyes narrowed.

"Who's Sene?" he asked in confusion. "I've never heard that name before." Emesos looked at the ceiling and took a small breath before speaking.

"You did, Wiln. I shouted it at the knight in the armor. That's his name; Sene." Wiln shook his head, and his face became one of unhappiness mingled with anger from the resurfaced memories.

"I didn't know. You weren't even speaking a language I knew. He spoke a sentence in Strynic and that was all I knew. The rest was in gibberish."

Emesos came to the conclusion he had been speaking Ancient again. He moved on. "What we said wasn't important. What *is* important is that Sene made the Blades."

Wiln's eyes widened. "You think they're the same person?" Emesos nodded. Wiln thought some more.

"Oh, but he could be like Vrasta! That makes sense. If Sene were like Vrasta, they're both probably the same age!" Wiln now turned to Lanita.

"Lanita, is there any mention in the history books of a knight similar to what we saw at the ball?"

Lanita paused for a moment, biting her lower lip. "I guess that I could look, but who would be there for your assistance?" Emesos shook his head.

"No. I think Lanita's best helping you tackle the mountains of papers and preparations you have to do. I, however, don't have nearly as much on my hands. I'll go to the library and look through what I can. But I'm afraid I might not be able to stay too long."

Wiln's face fell. "You're leaving soon? Why?"

Emesos shook his head. "I'm not leaving soon. I was talking about staying in the library. According to Lani, the head librarian is something of a monster." Lanita blushed, but didn't say anything. Wiln laughed, and Emesos smiled.

After a little while longer, Wiln bid his friend goodbye and went to check with the healer to see when Emesos could leave. He was pleased to find that if the healer didn't find any complications, Emesos could leave tomorrow and start delving into the mystery that was Sene.

Wiln went back his study with Lanita to tackle the mountain of papers and notices piled on his desk. They spent the better of the next two hours signing and looking over documents. Wiln went to shift a pile of completed documents off of his desk and noticed a small piece of paper had fallen onto the floor. "What's this?" Lanita asked. She picked it up. Wiln took it from her and opened it. His heart seemed to squeeze under a pressure in his chest as he recognized his father's handwriting. Wiln's eyes were completely focused on the words before him.

Dearest Son,

I write this with a heavy heart. I wish to tell you all of this letter's contents in person, when you take the throne. But given what history has told in the past about these Wars, I know that I will most likely be killed before I get the chance. The historians have been misguided into believing that nothing survives from the First War. That is not true. If you were to seek some evidence for the First War, look no further than the Blades.

Yet, there lies an even greater secret. Their original wielders were the first rulers of the Kingdoms. But I feel that the knowledge we kings have held close to our hearts lacks compared to what the Prophet can reveal. The Divine did not send us his chosen by accident. I get the feeling that this Fifth War is not just a battle for freedom, but a door that ancient secrets have chosen to hide behind.

The Prophet is the key to that door. Trust in his counsel; he listens to the past so that you may create a better future for the Kingdoms and their peoples.

Love always,

Your father Hasin

Wiln read over the letter twice more, hardly believing the words. But somehow, they felt right inside. He smiled as he looked at his father's rough, tight signature and folded it back to the shape in which he had found before tucking it away in his pocket. Lanita looked at him with concern.

"What is it?" she asked.

Wiln was still smiling as he shook his head.

"It's nothing." He stared at the papers on his desk, sat down, and got back to work.

Twenty-Three

A warm breeze was the first thing Ishik was aware of. The rest of the senses came back slowly. Next was the sound of a crackling fire. He felt a soft, fur cover on his body. Then the smell of smoke and herbs. His mouth had an oddly metallic taste to it. He blinked a few times and then a ceiling to what looked like a hut.

He tried to turn his head, but a firm, warm hand held it in place. "Don't move," said a female voice. "You've been through a rough time. Try to move as little as possible." So Ishik followed her instructions and did nothing. He heard some shuffling around and an exchange of friendly growls.

"It is good to see you alive, human," a deep male voice said. Ishik recognized it as the opponent he had faced in combat. "I hoped you would survive."

Ishik opened his mouth and spoke, softly, as though his voice had nearly left him. "I lost..." There was silence between the two of them for a while. Finally, the werewolf spoke again.

"My name is Zysk. What is yours?" The question made Ishik realize that he had never given his name to Zysk.

"My name is Urbak. So...I lost...that means I'm yours to command, right?" Silence filled the room again.

"Well...not entirely." Zysk said with a vague air.

"What's that supposed to mean?"

He heard more shifting around and an uneasy cough. "Well, we in the tribe decided to not make you follow through on the agreement." Ishik could hardly believe what he was hearing. He had lost, but they were letting him go.

"Why not?" he asked hesitantly. Ishik wasn't sure he wanted to hear the answer. But Zysk gave him one anyway.

"You fought me with no assistance, no weapons, and no powers. I thought I was going to have an easy time. And I did at first; I practically ripped you apart. But, every time I threw you to the ground, you got back up. Every time you fell, you rose again. You refused to give up, despite injury and almost no hope for victory. You could barely stand. You refused to lie down. 'Why?' I said to myself. 'Why doesn't he stop? There is no reason for him to fight now; he has already injured his pride.' The answer you gave shook us all. Why would a human ever want to save a werewolf? Then...you flew into an offense, one fiercer than I have even seen from humans. There was nothing to stop you, as you pounded your fists into me."

"The tribe quickly went to try and save you. You were on the gates of death, but you were talking. You said only a few words: 'Save them. Have to." You repeated this over and over."

"I did?" Ishik said, shocked. *Dying...* the realization left him incredibly aware of his own body. The air seemed even more vivid and sharp than before.

"Yes," Zysk stated, "you did. The strongest in the tribe then got together, once you were fairly safe, and began discussing your fate. After much heated talk, and a few well-chosen speeches, we have come to the decision to not make you a servant. Kiraj and the others that followed you here were adamant about you being safe. Therefore, we decided not to kill you either."

Ishik made a mental note to thank Kiraj and the pack later.

"We talked some more, and I spoke in your favor." A jolt of surprise ran down Ishik's spine. "I said that you weren't the strongest fighter. But you were still the strongest."

Ishik snorted. "I'm not the strongest, I lost to you remember?"

"You did lose," Zysk agreed. "And you aren't the strongest physically. But the injuries you received would be enough to immobilize a fellow werewolf, yet you stood and fought. You were banished from your tribe, yet you still want to save them."

"Humans are meant to hate werewolves, but you seek to free us. Manipulators are hated by humans, yet you Manipulate regardless. You faced a challenge that could have very well meant death; but you embraced it, hoping to win for the sake of others." Ishik wondered where Zysk was going with these statements.

"You have the strongest will of any being the tribe has ever encountered. You have the strongest determination, respect, and caring. So, in our eyes, you are the stronger one of us two. You proved that in our fight." Zysk concluded. There was more silence now; Ishik used the moment to take it all in.

"So, now what?" Ishik's question went out into the open air.

"The sons and daughters of Ragnok have agreed to assist you in your fight against Vrasta." Ishik's heart soared. "Only, on one condition." Zysk added. Ishik's heart plummeted. "You must take another name, one worthy of you."

Relief coursed into him. "Fine, I'll do it. Is there a certain one you have in mind?"

Zysk came forward, and Ishik felt a nick on his arm as a bone knife cut into his skin. "You shall be named Arthilc. After the last werewolf who managed to defeat the leader of the Ragnok tribe. Only your closest friends may call you Urbak."

Ishik could feel the blood running down his arm. *So now I have a third name,* he thought. *How many more am I going to have before this is all over?* He felt a large hand on his back push upward to help him sit up. Ishik complied and fought dizziness. He now saw Zysk's face, full of more humanity than most gazes he had ever witnessed.

A small, grizzled female werewolf was wiping the blood off the cut in his arm. It had clotted now and was a straight line. Zysk looked at him and bowed. "Today, Arthilc, you should do nothing. Tomorrow, you should be able to hunt with us. I would have you come today, but Inga," he gestured to the elderly female, "insists on you staying another day."

"Alright." All of his energy left him, taken by saying that single word. He laid back on his mat and slept.

He was awakened by Zysk gently shaking him. Ishik noted that his arm was bandaged over the cut Zysk had given him yesterday. When he was outside, Kiraj ran toward him and gave him a nearly suffocating hug.

"Urbak!" he said. The rest of the pack soon gathered around and joined him in a massive embrace. When they finally let go, Ishik was smiling. He then noticed there were some werewolves in their group that he hadn't seen before. Ishik went over to the small group and they seemed to shrink back from him a little.

"I don't recognize you. You mind telling me who you are?"

The werewolf bowed and answered. "Of course. I am Midin." He gestured to his silver fur-covered companion on his left. "This is Tourac." He then gestured to his silver friend on the right. "And this is Roci. We seek to accompany you, if you'll have us."

Ishik smiled and nodded. "Sure. The more we have the better." The three werewolves bowed and then walked away. Ishik turned around to see Kiraj staring at him, open-mouthed in shock.

"Urbak...are they to accompany us?" Ishik nodded warily.

"Yes. Is that a problem?" Kiraj shook his head.

"No...you wouldn't know who they are or how important it is. They are Children of the Moon. Chosen by the Moon herself to execute her will and assist her in praises."

"So, they're some kind of religious group?"

Kiraj nodded. "Yes. They are the priests of the tribes. They are the strongest werewolves from all of the tribes. For them to bow to you...I didn't think..."

"I'm glad they respect me." Ishik said. "It makes my life just a little bit easier."

Kiraj shook his head. "You don't understand. Bowing may mean respect in human customs, but in the tribes it means submission. The Children of the Moon bow only to the Moon herself. For them to bow to you means they believe you are a true Child."

"True child?" Ishik was now thoroughly confused.

"Yes. You see, the Children of the Moon believe that when chosen, the Moon adopts them into her family. They believe that you are not adopted, but her actual child." Ishik's mind was sent reeling when he heard these words.

So...am I...the son of a moon to them? How much stranger is this going to get before the end of this? Ishik quickly ate breakfast, checked on his arm and the rest of the pack. Ishik made sure his supplies were all in order before the pack headed out.

His Blade was lying there, as if waiting for him to pick it up. Ishik stared at it for a moment, and another thought hit him. *This Blade is ancient, hundreds of years old. And it chose me? Out of all of the people, most of whom would be more worthy than me... why?*

"I don't suppose you're going to give me any answers?" he said to the Blade. It remained motionless. He picked it up and looked at its plain grey patterns. For some reason, this Blade felt different now; more comfortable in his grasp. His mind now went to his biggest question about the weapon in his hand. All of the legends about the Blades said that the weapons could vanish when willed away, yet this one remained resolutely by his side. *Why?* he wondered again. A voice pierced his musings.

"Arthilc!" Ishik turned around to see Zysk holding a strange skin of some kind in a rough bundle. Zysk held out the bundle for Ishik. "This is for you." Ishik took it hesitantly.

"Thank you...What is it exactly?" Ishik unfurled the bundle and saw that it was an entire set of clothing made out of some sort of strange, overlapping material that was made of what looked like scales.

"This here is wurm skin. It can stand up to claws, swords, spears, and arrows. We thought, since you had practically lost your clothing, that you would appreciate a replacement."

Ishik quickly put on the wurm skin shirt. It fit fairly well. Soon, he found that there was a matching set of pants and boots. He put it all on and it felt slightly clammy against his skin. But he was covered and that was enough for now.

"Thank you," he said simply. "They fit wonderfully." Zysk held up a hand.

"But that is not the only gift we plan to give you." Zysk gestured to a nearby werewolf who stepped forward with a gleaming silver helmet. "Humans often wear helmets to protect themselves, but this one is different. Before the humans suffered the Great Collapse, their armor was like no other. This helmet is from that time. It has been our tribe's most treasured possession, given to us by Anazan himself. And it was decided that you will need it." Ishik was taken aback.

"Me?" Ishik took the helmet with a sense of reverence. He gently placed it on his head. It felt strangely light. "I...I... thank you." Once again he was at a loss for words. Ishik stepped forward did an unusual thing: He gave Zysk a hug. The werewolf seemed at a loss for what to do. Finally, Ishik stepped back.

"That's what humans do when they're sorry to say goodbye," he explained quietly. Zysk paused for a moment, then nodded and gave Ishik a nearly crushing embrace. When Zysk let go, Ishik took a few moments to take a few breaths and smiled. Zysk bared his fangs in the familiar grimace Ishik now knew was an attempt to grin.

Ishik now looked at the rest of the pack. Their numbers had swollen to over thirty. "Let's hunt!" Ishik declared. With a unified howl, the pack and Ishik charged south, toward Rhyth, into the wilderness, to save the tribes from enslavement and humans from slaughter. For the first time in a long time, Ishik felt he was heading to where he belonged.

Twenty-Four

Wiln was strongly against Emesos heading to the front lines so soon after his recovery from his latest experience. But after a few arguments and the Congregation's blessing, Emesos was finally allowed to visit the front lines. Emesos was unable to find any answers in the capital's library, so he figured he'd be more useful at the front to serve as a morale boost.

Wiln blatantly refused to let him travel alone though, so he gave Emesos a traveling companion and a company of guards. At the current moment, the companion was desperately trying to hold down a map without the breeze carrying it away.

Emesos had learned that the boy's name was Paolin, and that he was something of an unpopular child. People always seemed on edge when he was near, almost nervous. Emesos helped the young man flatten down the map and flashed him a smile. "Some wind," he said in a nonchalant voice.

"No kidding. Thank you for helping, great one." Paolin said, his voice unsure. "It's an honor for a Prophet to be helping me."

"You can just call me Emesos. I don't like being made a big deal out of." That statement made Paolin's hazel eyes widen in surprise. As Emesos turned around to talk with the rest of the soldiers, Paolin spoke.

"You didn't lie," he said. Emesos turned back around and gave Paolin's serious face an odd look.

"Of course I didn't lie. Why should I lie?" Paolin recoiled slightly. He then stared at the ground. He twisted a worn leather bracelet on his left wrist with his right hand. A single white piece of bone was on the bracelet with some kind of scratch on it.

"Sorry. I didn't mean to question you," Paolin mumbled. For a few moments, nothing was heard except birds and insects going about their daily businesses. The sun was setting over the horizon.

Emesos shrugged and gave him another smile, putting his hand on the young man's shoulder.

"Hey, don't take it too hard. You hardly know me. If you have any questions or curiosities about me, just ask."

With that, Emesos turned around and went to the head of his guard. The man seemed flustered. "Nothing's wrong, great...I mean, Emesos. All looks normal we should be at the wall in just a few more days." Emesos nodded. The captain put his hand on Emesos' shoulder.

"You handled that well, with Paolin, I mean. The boy has his heart in the right place, but... there's something about him. The other children in court don't like him much, you see."

"Court?" Emesos asked, shooting a glance at Paolin over his shoulder. The boy was staring at the map with incredible focus. He turned back to face the captain. "He's the son of a noble?" The captain shook his head.

"No, but that's only part of it. Paolin was the son of a cook and an unknown lady. Both of his parents vanished before he can remember. Their eloping was quite the talk of the castle. Hasin took him in for a little while and then discovered quickly that the boy is sharper than most."

"Sharp?" Emesos inquired, extremely confused.

The captain nodded. "Sharp as a sword edge. Smartest person I've ever met. He's memorized entire books before. But his intelligence has gotten him in trouble more than once. Hasin managed to repair some of the mistakes Paolin's made, but with King Wiln being busy and all..."

"It's safest to get Paolin away from court at the moment." Emesos concluded for him. The captain nodded. Emesos turned to look at the boy, who was still staring at the map, his entire attention consumed by the paper before him.

"Still... he's going to be useful, I'm sure. Why is everybody so nervous when he's around though?"

He looked at the captain's face and the captain looked somewhat embarrassed. "Well, the boy can be rather bluntly honest. He always seems to know when someone lies." Emesos nodded, storing away the information for later use.

The rest of their journey to the wall was rather quiet. Emesos tried to strike up conversation with Paolin, but was put off quickly. Then, on their final night before reaching the wall, Paolin spoke to Emesos rather suddenly after dinner. "So...you're honest after all." Emesos nodded, unsure of where the conversation was headed.

Paolin sat down next to him, his hands on his knees, his fingers twitching. "I'm sorry I haven't spoken to you very much, but I didn't know if I could trust you." Emesos nodded in understanding. "I am only thirteen," Paolin said randomly. Emesos noticed the young man was fiddling with his bracelet again.

"I'm only eighteen." Emesos replied Paolin paused and then nodded. "My poor family must be worried about me." Emesos said with a slight twinge of guilt. "I haven't seen them at all in a long time."

"That is unfortunate." Silence fell between them for a while. A chilling howl split the night. All the soldiers were instantly on alert.

Emesos summoned his Blade. Paolin drew a small dagger.

"Circle up! No backs exposed!" the captain cried. "Protect the Prophet and the boy!" The soldiers did so. Emesos could hear the growls. They came in a kind of twisted chant; too methodical to be a normal pack of wolves. The growls were getting closer. Soon, he could see their giant frames outlined in the light.

"Paolin." Emesos said quietly. "Stay close. A dagger won't do much to a werewolf." Paolin nodded, his hazel eyes glowing. The werewolves were now barking and growling. A single, mocking, deep voice came somewhere from the dark.

"Well...what do we have here? Vulnerable humans for easy pickings? I think we've found our food tonight." The werewolves gave loud, disjointed howls.

"Go die, mutts!" Paolin shouted. The howls were immediately silenced. The same voice spoke with venom.

"*Mutts*? You *dare* mock your killers?"

Emesos now drew himself to full height. "You will not kill us," he stated. "Go back to where you came from, or suffer the consequences."

The werewolves could take no more. They charged forward, fangs and claws unleashed. The soldiers fought off the first attacks, but the werewolves were quick, and slowly, soldiers began to fall. Emesos slashed and jabbed at the werewolves as much as he could. It was hard to see much though; his eyesight was limited by the dark.

For the first time, he saw how truly destructive a Blade could be in battle. Many werewolves he attacked were missing limbs.

Blood was everywhere. Those he stabbed were left on the ground whining. Soon, half of the attackers were killed. Only two soldiers, Paolin, and Emesos were still alive. Emesos kept slashing, attacking, yelling. No one else could exist.

If he hesitated for a moment, his life could have been lost.

He heard two cries of pain behind him as he slashed off a werewolf's foot. Emesos found himself slaying three werewolves at once. He heard a howl behind him. Emesos turned around and a werewolf collided into him.

Fangs descended toward his neck.

The werewolf stopped short and gave a yelp of pain. It let out more cries of agony. Emesos managed to look around the massive werewolf's frame to see Paolin stabbing brutally into the werewolf's back. The werewolf turned around with a roar. Emesos took the opportunity to shove his Blade deep into the werewolf's skull.

The creature died instantly. Emesos pulled out his Blade and found it was still clean, no blemish or blood was on it. Emesos heard another cry. The remaining werewolves had run away. Emesos got up off the ground and looked at the carnage before him.

Bodies and limbs were everywhere. Tents were knocked over, embers of a few dying fires sparked feebly. Blood covered the area in sickly red pools. Emesos looked over to Paolin. The young man's body was swathed in red. He was holding his dagger in his hand. He was swaying slightly from side to side and his eyes seemed unfocused. Emesos walked over to him.

"Paolin…" Paolin looked up, his hazel eyes watery. Yet the boy didn't cry. Emesos admired his strength. "Paolin, are you able to hear me? Are you able to speak?"

"Y-yes," Paolin managed to say, his voice quavering and ending with a choked sound. He gestured to the bodies before him. "T-they're all dead, aren't they?" Emesos nodded. The boy paused for a moment and then nodded. He looked at Emesos.

"W-what do we do now?" he asked. Emesos thought for a little bit before answering him.

"I think it's best if we get a fire going first." The two of them, unwilling to leave each other alone, gathered scrap wood together and built a small fire, away from the destroyed camp. The two of them gathered around it, rubbing their hands for warmth.

Paolin settled down slightly. Every now and then, he and Emesos made eye contact to make sure the other was still there and alive. "You realize what a werewolf group here means?" he asked Emesos. Emesos shook his head.

"The wall has fallen," Paolin said. "Rhyth's first line of defense is all but shattered. We have to go back and warn the king. That's what would make the most sense to me, anyway."

Emesos nodded. "That makes the most sense to me too. We should gather supplies before we leave though, and maybe two horses, if the werewolves didn't kill them."

"What do we do with the bodies?" Paolin asked. "We can't bury them all, can we?"

Emesos shook his head. "No, we can't. And burning them would let off a signal for other werewolves to follow. I guess we have to just let them be."

Paolin nodded, staring into the fire for a brief moment. "Logically, I know that this kind of thing happens in war. But... emotionally...it just seems so wrong." Paolin doubled over in silent tears. Emesos wanted to hug the young man, or show some gesture of support, but he was afraid that if he touched Paolin, he would feel the same inner agony.

Emesos nodded. He knelt down to Paolin's level. "It is different, isn't it? It's one thing to read or hear about war, but the experience of actually facing it..." Emesos let his words drift off as he stared at the fire. Silence and sorrow filled the air between them.

"But...we still have each other." Paolin looked at Emesos with a gaze that tore at his heart. It was something mixed between total trust and empathy.

"Right. We should gather supplies tomorrow, and then leave for the nearest town as fast as possible." Paolin stated. "I memorized the map, so I know what direction to take." Emesos smiled, despite his current state.

"You really are something else, aren't you?" he asked. Paolin shrugged, saying nothing. "You get some sleep; I'll keep an eye out." Paolin paused for a moment and then nodded, curled himself into a ball and drifted off to sleep.

Emesos looked at the stars and their sparkling. He didn't want to sleep right then anyway. He was afraid of the dreams that would come if he did.

He let Paolin sleep the rest of the night, and shook him awake in the morning. Paolin woke up, the dried blood cracking on his clothes as he sat up. Paolin knew immediately what had occurred.

"That's not fair! You deserve a chance at sleep too!" he protested. Emesos smiled and shrugged.

"Don't worry about it. I'll go gather supplies and see about our breakfast." Emesos went down to the ruins of the camp. The bodies smelled awful, but most of the blood had dried; giving the camp a dark brown color. He managed to find salted meat, a few canteens of water, and a roll of bandages. When he returned, he saw that Paolin had already started a fire and was chewing on something. "What do you have there?" He gestured to the plant Paolin had.

Paolin spat out a green wad and answered. "Just some weeds. I needed something to do...so I could keep my mind off...well...to keep it from drifting off." Emesos knew how Paolin wanted to complete that sentence, but he stopped himself, to keep a brave face. Once again, Emesos was surprised by Paolin's determination. They ate a small meal. After that, Paolin pointed in a southwestern direction.

"The nearest town is Arth, that way. On foot, we should reach it in just a few days. From there, we can get word out of the wall's defenses falling." Emesos nodded.

"Then let's go." They shouldered what little they had and set out with a fast walk to Arth. The day passed by without incident, although, they did have a few false alarms with the howls of normal wolves.

That night, Emesos tried to sleep, but nightmares kept him awake. Paolin had the same problem. So, to pass the time, the two of them talked.

"We should reach Arth tomorrow," Paolin stated. Emesos nodded. "Hopefully, we'll get there before anyone else." Emesos nodded.

"King Wiln didn't want me to go to the wall." Emesos said. "He thought it would be too dangerous. I guess he was right."

Paolin shook his head. "I'm glad you did though. I wouldn't have met you otherwise." Emesos marveled at the young man. It was amazing how close a near-death experience could make two people.

The two of them woke early and set out at a fast pace. It was around noon when they topped a large hill and finally saw Arth. Emesos smiled at Paolin. Paolin smiled back. They walked down to the city, where a guard stopped them at the gate.

"Where do you-" He saw that they were covered in dried blood. "Divine's creation! What happened to you two?"

"We were attacked, by werewolves," Paolin explained; his voice incredibly heavy. "We were on our way to the wall with a platoon of guards. We just barely made it away alive. The wall has fallen."

The guard looked at Emesos for a moment, and then his eyes widened. "You're the Prophet! No wonder you're alive, the Divine's chosen was with you!" He beckoned them into the guard house. "Wash up, I'll get you some food."

Emesos did the best he could to remove the dried blood from himself. Paolin did the same. The water from the barrel was cold, but at least it got them somewhat clean. Not long after they had finished, the guard returned with a plate of food for each of them. Emesos and Paolin ate eagerly. When they had finished, the guard seemed nervous.

"You...said the wall had fallen. Is that true?" Emesos nodded. The guard's eyes widened.

"We need to evacuate. I'll start the preparations at once!" The guard turned to leave.

"Wait." Paolin said with surprising command. The guard stopped. "You can't evacuate with werewolves on the loose. They'd tear you apart. No matter how skilled you are...you can't possibly protect an entire city outside a walled place with the limited number of men you have." Paolin fiddled with his bracelet for a while. He stared at his hand, speaking in a low voice.

"I've seen werewolves fight. It takes three normal soldiers with standard equipment to bring down a single werewolf. In other words, this entire population of people could die in a matter of days."

"What do we do then?" the guard asked, looking to Emesos for answers. Emesos thought for a moment. He closed his eyes, thinking back to the camp, to the soldiers that were slaughtered. His eyes snapped open and he clenched his fists.

"We stand our ground," he stated. The guard gasped. Emesos looked at him with conviction. "If we can't run, if we can't hide—we fight. The werewolves *will* attack this place. And even if we don't win...well...we buy the rest of Rhyth more time, right?"

"R-right. I'll tell the captain of the guard to get the town as battle-ready as possible." He bowed respectfully and dashed off. Paolin looked at Emesos. Emesos looked back. In Paolin's eyes was a strange glimmer; not tears, but something else. His face was set in a somewhat angry look, his eyes piercing into Emesos with a sharpness that had put so many people on edge before.

"Do we really stand a chance?" he asked.

Emesos' mind was suddenly elsewhere, he had a spear in hand. Another man was staring at him from across a table with a map full of marks. "Do we really stand a chance, Fellix?"

Emesos snapped back to the present. Paolin was still waiting for an answer. "Yes, we do. I may not know what to do, but between you and Fellix, I'm sure we'll do just fine."

Paolin smiled, his hazel eyes widening slightly. "So the rumors are true? You can see the past?"

Emesos laughed. "I can do more than that. But if there really is a Divine, he'll be kind enough to send me an experience or two...or any help really. Memories of a famous tactician or not... We'll need all the help we can get."

Twenty-Five

"**S**ome group was attacked here." Ishik said, looking at the decaying bodies. The pack had journeyed along, ambushing and killing any nearby enemy werewolves, until they stumbled on an abandoned camp that looked like it met an ugly and abrupt end.

Ishik was surprised to see so many dead werewolves along with the humans. Normally, even the best soldier was destroyed quickly when facing a werewolf. That, and many of the cuts on the werewolf dead were too clean, as if done with a single stroke. There was only one weapon that could cut like that.

"A person who has a Blade fought here," Ishik concluded. "And they aren't among the fallen, I bet." *Was it that knight? Or a King?* A thought came to him.

Only twelve werewolves were dead. Twelve more of the hunting pack was left according to Kiraj. "Where's the nearest town?" He whispered to himself. The answer hit him as he recalled the maps he had learned in the Congregation, so long ago: Arth. Werewolves were heading to Arth, their first major target in Rhyth.

"We head southwest!" he proclaimed. "An entire city is on the line!" Kiraj nodded and, without a howl, the pack began to run to Arth to face an opponent and their first real battle.

The first test, Ishik thought to himself. *We can't afford to lose this!*

Two days passed, and they reached Arth by midday. Werewolves had almost completely surrounded the northern wall. They were on the attack, trying to scale the wall. The humans were putting up a surprisingly organized resistance. But Ishik knew they could only last so long. Judging by the number of dead bodies lying at the foot of the wall, the humans were barely holding on.

Kiraj let out a massive roar. The rest of the pack followed suit. Ishik raised his Blade. "For the tribes!" he screamed. The pack charged forward.

The enemy werewolves were caught in a double-sided attack. *Now, if we could just have something to completely end it!* Ishik thought. The thirty or so members of the pack were crushing the enemy, and quickly killed twenty. But Ishik saw they were slowly being surrounded. Now they were in trouble. Ishik sent his Blade into the chest of a charging werewolf. He rejected the Force of gravity under a few to send them flying. *Divine...please...just a little more help,* he pleaded silently.

******

"They're helping us," Paolin whispered. "Now's the time we press the offensive." Emesos nodded. The werewolves that were attacking the wall had retreated to deal with the attackers. The soldiers looked at Emesos. Emesos felt himself grin.

"Let's help our saviors, boys!" The soldiers gave a cry and the remaining archers readied their bows. The soldiers burst out the front gates. A volley was sent flying by Paolin's signal from the wall above.

The enemy werewolves were caught completely off guard. The surrounded werewolves now surged forward. Emesos summoned his Blade and cleaved into the foe. The archers had stopped their volleys and were now charging forward to help, led by a fierce Paolin. Soon, almost the entire enemy was routed. Emesos found himself surrounded by a small cluster of the remaining assault force. He was back to back with another friendly werewolf that had suffered an injury to the arm.

"Ready to get out of this?" he asked. The werewolf gave a bark that sounded like a laugh.

"Always!" Together, the two of them launched into an attack that sent the enemy reeling. Emesos had no idea how to judge whether a werewolf was good in combat or not; but to him, his ally was clearly a fantastic fighter.

Soon, the enemy werewolves began to give ground. Some even started retreating. When Emesos fought his way clear, he saw Paolin was surrounded. His friend was standing over the body of a wounded soldier.

"Paolin!" Emesos cried, fighting his way through the chaos to reach his friend. The circle flew forward. Emesos let out another cry of concern. *I can't lose him! I can't!*

Suddenly, the circle was flung backward. Paolin was on the attack. He lunged forward, slitting the throat of one enemy, proceeding to fling himself off onto another foe, jabbing brutally at a werewolf's face. Another man was there in some kind of scaled clothes and a silver helm, a massive plain grey sword in hand. The two of them were a whirlwind, in almost perfect harmony. When Paolin finally halted, he let out a primal yell of challenge.

The attacking force, unable to cope, beat a hasty retreat numbers away from the city with their dwindled numbers. Arth had been saved.

The werewolves who had saved them now gathered in a huddle, looking at Emesos and the very few human soldiers who had managed to survive. The man in the helm was obscured from his view. Emesos looked at Paolin.

"I need you to see who can be saved and get them back to the city immediately for treatment. Can you do that?" Paolin stood there, covered in blood once more, his grayish blond hair twisted and matted. His hazel eyes widened and he nodded.

"Good, get these soldiers to help you. I have to talk with this group." Paolin nodded again and then ran off. Emesos kept his back to the werewolves, making sure the soldiers were doing their jobs.

The wounded werewolf Emesos had helped stepped forward. "Human...are you the leader here?"

Emesos nodded. "The old noble who used to lead this town died yesterday, so I'm in charge now. My name is Emesos. I am a Prophet of the Divine, chosen to save Daclynand's four Kingdoms from being destroyed." There was an awkward pause.

Emesos continued. "Thank you so much. We had been fighting for around three days. We wouldn't have survived if you hadn't shown up. Are you seeking to be a friend or foe?"

"Friends, hopefully." The werewolf responded.

Emesos smiled as he watched Paolin shout at a soldier who was cowering before him. "Excellent. Are you the leader of this...group?"

"No..." The werewolf said slowly.

"May I meet him? I want to thank him personally." Emesos turned around to face the werewolf. "Would that be all right?" The werewolf said nothing, but stared. His eyes were wide. The rest of the werewolves had the same reaction.

"What's the matter?" Emesos asked, concerned. "I didn't mean to offend. Have I asked for too much?"

The man in the silver helm now stepped forward. "No, you haven't. My name's..." The man's sentence drifted off. He stared at

Emesos and said nothing for a moment. The man ripped off his helmet and let it fall to the ground. Emesos gasped. They slowly walked toward each other, not daring to blink.

Brown eyes stared into brown eyes. Emesos raised his left hand. The stranger raised his right. They put their hands together.

They were the exact same size and shape. Both had brown hair, of the same shade. And their heights were so close together...

"Identical." Yeznia said. "They're identical." The revelation hit Emesos like a sword thrust through his stomach.

The man standing before him was his nearly identical twin.

Ryan Wilshusen

Part Five:

Exodus

Ryan Wilshusen

Twenty-Six

The two of them couldn't help but continue to stare. Emesos blinked a few times. The young man before him didn't disappear. He was real. *It's like looking into a mirror,* Emesos thought.

"My name is Emesos. W—what's your name?"

Ishik was going to say 'Arthillic', but shock and heightened emotions changed his answer. "My name is Ishik. I'm from a northern part of Rhyth. Where? Where did you come from?" Emesos knew that the question the young man was asking wanted more than a location as an answer.

"I...I come from Stryne, the capital of Stryne. I—I...wow... I didn't even think...is this even real? Did you even consider...?" Ishik shook his head.

Emesos was rocked to his core. This was the last thing he had expected to deal with. Werewolves, old prophecies, visions, death...he had prepared himself the best he could for all of them. But how could you prepare for this? *Does that mean...my family...isn't my real family?*

Emesos' mind flew back to what was only a few months ago. He had called Hane his brother...but...what if he wasn't? Did Hane know? Why didn't his mother or father tell him? *Mother...Father... can I even call them that?* The one solid fact in his life was now being swept out from under him. He felt like his mind was falling, drifting around without anything to hold onto. His eyes started to water. It took all of his self-control to hold his emotions back.

Ryan Wilshusen

Who is he? Ishik thought. *How could this even happen?* The cry of a wounded soldier pierced his imagination and brought him back to reality.

"We can worry about this later. Right now we both have people to take care of," Ishik stated. Emesos nodded, looking into Ishik's eyes intently.

"But we will talk later...right?" Ishik nodded.

The two of them turned around and went in opposite directions.

Emesos' mind was still spinning. *How could this happen? Why...how...how could they not tell me?!*

To rid his mind of the barrage of questions, he buried himself in helping to pick up the pieces of the city. It took nearly a week to treat all the injured. But at night, his mind would wander to that wild person, the one who looked just like him.

The opportunity to talk finally came on the eighth night. Emesos received a message in rough handwriting that he was to meet Ishik in secret in the back of the city, behind an old building being used as a medical ward. He was also told to bring his second in command.

The two of them slipped out of their living quarters when the moon was high enough to let them see. Sure enough, behind the building were Ishik and a larger werewolf. Ishik tilted his head to his large, hairy companion. "This is Kiraj. He's my right-hand man, I guess. Did you bring the young man?"

Emesos put a hand on Paolin's shoulder. "This is Paolin. He's the only survivor from my original group. He's sharp as a knife; couldn't ask for a better person." Paolin nodded respectfully to Kiraj and Ishik. Kiraj smelled the air briefly and snorted in surprise.

"The young one's scent...it's like...the tribes."

"We have been killing werewolves for the past few days." Paolin noted dryly. "Maybe you just smell those."

Kiraj shook his head, but didn't say anything. Ishik shrugged and turned his attention to Emesos.

"So... how'd a man from Stryne wind up in Rhyth?"

Emesos took a deep breath and took a seat. "It's going to take a while, so you might want to sit." They all sat down and Emesos, for the first time, told his entire story. There were quite a few questions asked and details elaborated on, but Emesos didn't halt his tale for anything.

Then, Ishik described his journey from just after he left the Congregation to the present. Paolin and Emesos said nothing, but marveled nonetheless at Ishik's determination and daring.

"So here we are," Ishik said, "Nearly identical people... with the same enemy, but with different methods. And somehow... we both have Blades. Anazan's involved in all of this, not to mention the Altherai thing...what in the three Hels have we gotten ourselves into?" The four of them sat in silence, pondering possible answers to that question.

"I think our next move should be to pull the people back toward the capital," Paolin suggested. "From there, we can work with King Wiln and figure out a better strategy from there." Ishik nodded.

"It's not like we actually have the resources to stay here much longer, anyway," Emesos said. "If we're going to move, we need to do it fast, before the rest of the werewolves come." Kiraj nodded.

"The young one speaks sense. I can sense them coming. They should be at the capital in just a few weeks."

Ishik now spoke. "How are you going to convince them that my group is trustworthy though? It's not like werewolves are the most loved beings in Rhyth."

"I'll speak to the people about it." Emesos answered. "As long as I keep reassuring them and no one does anything rash, we should be able to manage."

Ishik raised his eyebrows. "You're able to do that?" he asked skeptically. "How?"

"I've been proclaimed a Prophet by the Congregation, and have abilities supposedly given to me by the Divine."

"What kind of abilities?" Ishik challenged.

Emesos took a deep breath. "Hold out your hand." Ishik paused for a moment, then thrust out his calloused hand. Emesos gripped it.

******

An explosion of memories flew between their minds. Dinner with a family, a merchant caravan. Time, frozen. A young boy, whom Emesos guessed was Ishik, was peeking through a door, listening to a hushed conversation.

"The boy's no good, I tell you. Useless. We should have never taken him in," a man said.

A shrill woman's voice echoed through the crack. "And just what were we supposed to do? Let a baby die of the cold? His mother was nowhere to be seen." The words crashed over the young man. He slowly stepped back from the door. "I'm...not related to these people?" he whispered. "Then who are my parents?"

******

Emesos let go. Ishik was immobile, his face frozen in a wary look. "How did...wait...does that mean..."

"I could be your brother," Emesos whispered, voicing the thought plaguing his mind. "Your twin brother... My family could be..." Emesos' legs gave and Ishik quickly caught him, helping lower him to the ground. "Why didn't they tell me?!" Emesos cried. Tears were unstoppable at that point. He broke down, letting the tears fall freely. He lowered his head for a moment and then looked up at Ishik.

"We're the only real family we know of," Emesos said quietly. Ishik nodded.

"Looks that way...I've heard of twins in old stories before...I never guessed I would be one." He held out a hand and Emesos took it, hoisting himself off the ground. "I guess we better start learning how to be brothers..."

Emesos took a deep breath and smiled. He knew how lonely Ishik was from the moment he touched him. Ishik was constantly hoping, reaching for friends. And this...his most distant dream since that night of discovery about his parentage, had become a reality.

"Yeah, well, let's survive first, shall we? I think the four of us could do with some sleep, and some time to deal with our thoughts. See you... tomorrow then." With that, Paolin and Emesos walked off.

"What do you think of him, Urbak?" Kiraj asked quietly once the other duo was out of sight.

Ishik paused for a moment. "I think he's endured more than any human I've ever met. He took the news in stride and moved on. Either he's been through a lot, or we've met an extremely powerful person. I'm willing to bet it's a mix of both."

Kiraj let out the small growl that Ishik had come to associate with laughter. "It seems, Urbak, that you've finally met your equal."

Ishik couldn't help but smile. "Yeah, seems like I have. Make sure to tell the rest of the pack that we're moving out in a few days." With that, he turned around with Kiraj and they proceeded to leave the city to deal with wounds and food. In the soft moonlight and the rocky surroundings, Ishik's mind was focused on one thing.

He had a brother.

Twenty-Seven

The people of Arth deserved some credit, in Paolin's eyes at least. They had accepted that Emesos had a brother sent by the Divine to try and nobly convert savage werewolves, and to some extent; he had succeeded. Paolin had to admit Emesos had a flair for theatrics and public speaking. His lie was so convincing that if Paolin didn't hear about Ishik's real adventure from Ishik himself, he would not have believed Emesos.

He was having a hard time managing all of the people and the food, but there was one thing he was nearly at his wit's end about: the sniffing.

Constantly, over the past three days of travel, the werewolves had taken a keen interest in him. At least three would come up and take a deep smell in his presence. He didn't ask them to stop for fear of insulting them, but it was driving him to his wit's end.

Paolin felt like they were sizing him up for something. Ishik and Emesos were still talking, learning about each other. Paolin was trying to hold the people together the best he could, but migrating a large town wasn't easy.

On top of that, there were a large number of injured soldiers who had to be transported, slowing them down considerably. It made Paolin nervous. Werewolves traveled extremely fast and, at this rate, they could catch up.

Paolin had just finished making his normal rounds to check on all the injured and the food supply. The sun's rays did little to penetrate the autumn wind that blew upon them as they traveled across the hilly expanse that was Rhyth. Paolin looked at the sun and guessed it was close to noon, almost time to start breaking out the rations.

Paolin was on his way to Emesos and Ishik to make his report when he heard a sound that chilled him: the howl of a werewolf. Emesos and Ishik flew into action, making sure all of the citizens were in the center of the caravan and everyone was safe. The remaining soldiers gathered their gear and surrounded the people. The werewolf pack under Ishik's command quickly joined the circle of protection. Kiraj sniffed the air.

"I'd say around fifty," he told Emesos. Emesos merely nodded and summoned his Blade. Ishik drew his. Paolin looked around for a weapon, but all he could find that wasn't in use were two knives. He picked them up and put one in each hand. *Not much,* he thought, *but better than fighting barehanded.*

Sure enough, over the northwestern hills, came around fifty werewolves, bellowing a challenge that Ishik's group returned. The two groups of werewolves clashed, with humans helping out the best they could. Paolin himself was soon roped into the fray.

He managed to wound a few werewolves, but it was ultimately others who finished them off. The two newfound brothers were quickly decimating the opposing werewolf forces. Some were sent flying by a mysterious force. Paolin went to go back up some soldiers when a werewolf jumped in his way and began to go on the attack.

The creature kept lashing out, with Paolin just barely sidestepping in time. Finally, the werewolf found its mark. It scratched his face. With Paolin stunned the werewolf jumped on top of him and prepared for the kill. With his arms pinned by the werewolf's claws, there was only one option left for the boy.

Paolin turned his head and sank his teeth deep into the claws that were grasping him, kicking the werewolf in any place he could reach. The werewolf's hand slackened and Paolin brought up the dagger in his left hand, stabbing the werewolf in the elbow. The creature howled in pain. Its right hand slackened and Paolin shot his right hand upward, burying the other knife under the werewolf's jaw.

The werewolf gave an almost human-like scream of pain and then died, blood leaking from its wounds onto Paolin's face and arms. Paolin was just barely able to shove the werewolf's huge body off of his and got up off the ground to check at the immediate situation for threats.

There were none to be found. The enemy was retreating. Ishik and Emesos were back to back, covered in blood, muck, and ready for any other challenges. The other soldiers were looking around for any living comrades.

Ishik's pack had no eyes for fellow allies though. Their eyes were only fixed on him. "What?!" Paolin asked them. "Is something wrong?!" Emesos turned to the sound of Paolin's voice and came running as fast as he could.

"Paolin! Paolin! Thank the Divine." He scooped up Paolin into an embrace that knocked all the breath from his young companion. "When I saw the werewolf jump on top of you, I thought you were dead. Come on, let's get the people in order and get moving as fast as possible." He let go and started off to the people to get them calmed down.

Paolin was stunned. *Emesos...he was so...concerned...he...hugged me...* The moment had left him confused, and somewhat shaken. To settle his heart, he delved into the numbers of casualties, wounded, lost weapons, and how many days before they would reach the relative safety of the capital.

Still, whenever one of Ishik's pack members came close to Paolin, there was an almost electric feeling in the air. He took a deep breath and resumed his work, but his mind still kept drifting back to Emesos and his actions after the battle.

Finally at night, Paolin ate in his tent, accompanied by only his whirlwind of dancing thoughts. Someone coughed outside his tent. "May I come in?" It was Ishik.

"Sure," Paolin said. The well-muscled traveler came in and wearily pulled up a stool. He looked like Emesos for sure, but the deepness of his eyes and hardened face showed that it was a different person entirely.

"You okay?" Ishik asked. "I know Kiraj and the others are getting on your nerves. I told them to let up a little. I'm amazed you're still functioning at this point." Ishik laughed. "Hels, I'm amazed I'm still functioning at this point."

Paolin couldn't help a small smile. Ishik now got to what he really wanted to say. "I know that my brother's been asking a lot from you and so have I. Sorry about that." Paolin heard the pride in Ishik's voice when he said the word "brother."

Paolin shook his head. "I'm so useless," he said quietly, as if to himself. "All I do is crunch numbers and star gaze for directions. My entire life..." His sentence drifted off along with his mind.

Ishik shook his head. "You? Useless? Who told you that lie?"

"My instructors...other nobles...my parents who ran off without me."

Ishik looked shocked. "Ran off...without you?"

Paolin nodded twice. "When I was seven...when I woke up, they were gone. I never saw them again."

A kind of fire blazed in Ishik's eyes: his jaw set and his right fist tensed.

"Listen, Paolin..." Ishik said with quiet ferocity. "Don't you ever believe what they said about you, any of them. You are always worth something, and someday you'll prove to them all how wrong they were."

Ishik bid the young man goodnight and left the tent. He pondered over the words of advice he had spoken to Paolin. The more he thought, the more he was reassured. *Maybe we both learned something tonight*, Ishik thought.

Paolin stared at the ceiling of his tent and thought back to Emesos' reaction after the battle, and then his conversation with Ishik. Could it be, that maybe, for the first time in his life, he had a family?

Twenty-Eight

Cheers went up from the caravan as they saw the capital of Rhyth. Paces quickened. Emesos drew closer to his brother. They hadn't spoken in the two days that had passed since the werewolf attack. Ishik was always in deep conversations with his pack, so Emesos had kept his distance.

I can't believe we actually made it back safely. The thought had finally appeared in Emesos' mind. After so much killing and hardship, they had finally done it. Ishik seemed slightly on edge, as if he wasn't sure if he was going to like the city or not. Emesos spoke to his brother as quietly as he could.

"I think the werewolves should stay outside of the city. The people in the caravan are alright with them, but I don't think the people in the city will do as well," he suggested.

Ishik nodded. "That's fine. We actually planned to stay outside the walls anyway."

Emesos raised an eyebrow. "'We?' No, you have to come with me, to talk to Wiln." Ishik sighed.

"Damn. I don't have much of a choice, do I?" Emesos shrugged.

Emesos looked around a little and found Paolin. The boy was unusually pale. He was gripping something in his hand, tight as iron. It was the bracelet he fiddled with whenever he was lost in thought.

"Are you okay?" Emesos asked him, walking over to him. Paolin shook his head.

"No..." His voice was shaky. "I don't want to be back here. I hate it here." Emesos put a reassuring hand on his shoulder.

"You'll be fine. Ishik and I will take care of you."

"Promise?"

"Promise." The three of them walked carefully to the main gates of the city. The captain of the guard was certifiably flustered. It took around an hour of explanation, but the people were finally allowed to set up camp, as long as the werewolves kept a good distance away from the walls. Ishik, Emesos, and Paolin were all escorted up to the castle. They were led down twists of hallways, Emesos' heart beating faster every minute.

Finally, they arrived at the throne room doors. After being announced, Emesos and his companions walked through the doors to see a very tired looking Wiln's face brighten.

"Emesos!" He got off his throne and walked over to his friend, shaking his hand warmly. "When I heard the wall had fallen, I feared the worst." He now turned and shook Paolin's hand, but said nothing. He was introduced to Ishik and quickly took in the fact that Emesos had a twin brother.

"You'll be a great morale boost. It's been chaos here. It'll give people something to hope for," Wiln said with a beaming smile. "I've been busy here, and I'm glad you managed to save as many people as you did. They'll have plenty to do around here. The mobilization is now in full force thanks to some clever pen work from Lanita. Now...Paolin, if you don't mind, I have to talk with Emesos and Ishik in private."

Paolin bowed. "Of course, Your Majesty." He spun smartly on his heel and walked out the large doors. Inwardly, Emesos winced. The hard-working, strong-willed, kind boy he had traveled with had been replaced with one who was distant, polite, and tightly controlled.

Wiln now turned to Emesos and Ishik. The two of them launched into their respective tales. Wiln interrupted with the occasional question. When they had finished, Wiln took a moment to think and then said, "Well, we'd better let you three get a good night's rest before anything else. You've been through the Hels and back."

The two of them were being guided by a servant to their rooms when they saw Paolin, standing, head hung low, while several larger boys were surrounding him, saying something Emesos couldn't make out. Ishik could, his ears sharpened by living among werewolves for months.

"So...you're back, *pale alien*," one boy mocked. "How about you give us the maps that prophet handed you?" Paolin said nothing. "Or maybe that little bracelet you have in your hand there?"

Ishik and Emesos paused, watching the scene unfold. Emesos started forward to help, but Ishik held up a hand. "He's got to solve this by himself."

"Did you hear us, worthless?" a different boy challenged. "Give us your bracelet." The boy shoved Paolin hard. Paolin shifted his right foot and managed to stand upright.

"Take it and die," Paolin said quietly. It wasn't full of panic or venom, but Ishik could tell Paolin was holding his emotions under control.

"I'll take that challenge." The first boy sneered. He threw a fist toward Paolin's face. If Ishik hadn't seen it, he wouldn't have believed it. As the boy's hand struck Paolin, his wrist bent in a grotesque angle and snapped. The boy howled, clutching his wrist. That's when Ishik noticed that Paolin's left hand was near his face. He was wiping blood from the corner of his mouth now. Paolin's eyes dilated. He let out a growl that didn't sound human.

The other boys were backing away. Emesos now gripped Ishik's arm. "He has two glows."

"What?" Ishik asked.

Emesos now turned to face Ishik, eagerness in his eyes.

"I can see the glow of people's souls. It surrounds everyone."

"Soul?" Ishik said, with a tone of challenge.

"I've seen it wink out enough recently to prove my theory." Emesos snapped. "Everyone, even you, has a glow around him that shows their soul. Paolin has two glows. One of them is pulsing brighter than the other."

They turned back to look at Paolin. The boy who had hit him was clutching his hand, whimpering to himself. The other boys were beginning to close in, fists raised. Paolin flew into action. The first boy was down with a single swing. The second was humbled by a foot to the chest. The third was soon in Paolin's grasp. "Leave me alone." Paolin whispered, more to himself than the person in his clutches. "Forever." He let the boy go.

The four boys scrambled away from Paolin as fast as they could. Emesos noticed that the brighter glow was now merging with the other, becoming one again. Paolin turned his head and saw Emesos and Ishik. Paolin's expression was one of hurt, but he smiled at them anyway.

Just how much pain is he hiding? Ishik wondered. *I thought I had a rough time when I was younger, but Paolin is something else!* Paolin shrugged and walked over to them. Ishik stared at him with a new found appreciation.

"You ready to go to our rooms?" Emesos asked. Paolin nodded and the three of them were soon settled in the eastern wing of the castle. The three of them quickly fell asleep. Emesos felt a sudden pull on his mind. Not having the energy to resist, Emesos let himself be carried off.

******

He found himself in a court room. It was bright outside and plenty of light lit up the marble and oak that was used to make the room's fixtures, but the several men inside it were yelling at each other. In a cage were a young werewolf and a human boy that looked no older than five. The werewolf was covered in cuts and bleeding slightly from wounds that hadn't quite healed over. The boy was hardly any better off. He was covered in bruises and his hands looked as though they had been through a swamp. They clutched the bars of the cage. The werewolf and the boy both looked like they were on the verge of tears. Emesos now turned his attention to the men shouting at each other.

"This boy is a monstrosity! Not only is he a Manipulator, he's brought a beast with him!" An old man screamed. The boy now burst into tears. The werewolf put a comforting hand on the boy's shoulder.

"It will be okay, Orin, I promise." Emesos' mind was sent reeling. Orin?! Orin was a Manipulator?! And when did he befriend a werewolf?

He turned his attention back to the argument.

"The boy is not at fault. He has no control over it," another stated. "I believe we should just kill the werewolf and let the boy go with a warning. All those in favor?" The room was silent for a moment as the majority of the people in the court house raised their hands.

"No!" Orin screamed, his despair tearing at Emesos' heart. "No! Not Paolin! Please! He's not dangerous...no!" The name of the werewolf struck Emesos cold.

The werewolf's name is Paolin...just what in the three Hels is going on?!

Orin was ripped from the cage by two guards and then six more moved in, silver lances flashing. Trapped in the cage, the werewolf was powerless. The spears drove though his body, making him cough blood. The werewolf sank to the ground. Orin managed to wiggle free and knelt down next to the werewolf, his knees in a pool of blood.

"No! Paolin...don't leave me all alone..." The desperate sobs of Orin as he gripped vainly at the werewolf's fur was almost unbearable for Emesos to watch. "Paolin, don't go..."

The werewolf lifted a shaking hand, clutched in its bloody grasp was a ragged looking piece of material. "Where this...bracelet is... I am too..." Orin grabbed the hand and watched as it went limp, the bracelet falling from it into the blood of its former owner.

"No! Paolin! Wake up! Wake up! I need you! Paolin!" Emesos couldn't contain his sorrow any more. Tears fell uncontrolled down his face, Orin's pleas driving through him more than any weapon ever could.

The boy cried over his lost companion's body, his sobs and hiccups piercing the sudden silence of the court room. A soldier went to grab Orin's arm. Orin turned around and screamed in the soldier's face.

"I hate you!" The soldier paused for a brief moment. Orin's face was now contorted with rage. "You killed him, just because you didn't like him! I hate you! I hate you!" The soldier's face hardened as he picked Orin roughly off the ground. Orin tried hitting the solder, but it didn't faze the man. Orin was being forcibly removed from the court room. The boy turned around with a gasp, his eyes full of fear.

"No! The bracelet! Paolin! I can't leave him! Wait!" The soldier didn't stop. The court room doors opened ahead of him and closed behind him with a resounding thud. Emesos flew into action.

"Zane, what the hell are you doing?" Emesos ignored the question and went into the cage, picked up the bracelet and bolted for the door.

So the person I am now is Zane, *he thought, filing away the name for later. Right now, he needed to catch up with Orin. The soldier was still carrying a crying and struggling Orin away, ignoring all pleas.*

"Hey!" Emesos cried. "Wait, soldier!" The soldier turned around and hesitated long enough for him to reach the pair. Emesos held the bracelet out to Orin. "Orin, here." Orin's eyes went wide. He grasped the bracelet hard.

"Thank you," he whispered. "I won't forget you." As the soldier dragged Orin away, the little boy called out one last question:

"What's your name?"

"I am Zane." Emesos said, waving to the boy. "Don't lose that bracelet!" They vanished from sight. Emesos stood there for a moment, pondering how Orin's future would turn out. So little of Orin's early life before the war was known, it made Emesos extremely curious. A voice interrupted his thoughts.

"That was a very kind thing for you to do." A quiet voice noted behind him. Emesos turned around and saw an old man with violet eyes and silver hair. Strangely, no beard graced his face. The man was in a simple brown shawl with a hood that was down, gathering around his neck like a protective fold. The pants and shirt were just as plain. He carried a roughly cut piece of wood for a supportive staff. Something about the man seemed very familiar.

"Thank you." Emesos said. After a moment, he spoke again. "It wasn't right, what they did in that court house."

"No, it wasn't," the man agreed.

"I only wonder who will look after him now," Emesos said, his thoughts still on young Orin.

The old man smiled. "Well, I'm actually quite interested in the young lad. And considering he has no parents and I have no children, I figure I could use an assistant like him."

Emesos turned to the elderly figure. "You're going to adopt him? That's wonderful!" The old man nodded.

"Yes, love is a curious thing. It binds together family of blood, but more importantly, family of heart."

Emesos nodded and reached to shake the old man's hand. "Thank you so much. I'll be able to sleep easier tonight. By the way, what is your name?"

The old man laughed, his slightly yellow and crooked teeth flashing. He reached out and shook Emesos' hand. "My name? Of course, how foolish of me to speak to you of such serious matters and not properly introduce myself..." The old man straightened up right.

"My name is Anazan."

Twenty-Nine

Emesos gasped, awake and in shock. *Anazan?! That's what he looks like? How far back do those two know each other?*

Emesos turned to look at Paolin, human and next to him, his fist still clutching the ancient bracelet. *And how much does Paolin know? Is he the boy...or the werewolf?* Ishik's voice snapped him out of his thoughts.

"Hey, are you okay? You're sweating something awful." Emesos looked at his brother. Concern was clearly invisible in Ishik's face. Emesos kept his tone low to avoid disturbing Paolin.

"I had an experience, but I need to talk to you about it somewhere else," Emesos whispered. Ishik's eyes brightened in understanding. The two of them went outside the room and went about halfway down the hall before speaking in hushed tones. The sun had barely risen, so they didn't want to attract attention.

Emesos told Ishik about his vision. Ishik's face wasn't moving initially, but as the tale continued, his face slowly shifted to a look of shock. When he had finished, Ishik clutched his head, running his fingers through his hair.

"Divine bless us," he said, exasperated. "Just who did we manage to pick up? Orin was a Manipulator? Anazan knew him since childhood...Orin was friends with a werewolf...It's so much to take in at once. How do you manage?"

"I take it step by step, moment by moment. I have to." Emesos shook his head to focus it back on the matter at hand.

"I was a man named Zane, and I was from Stryne; so maybe we can find mention of him in the castle library?" Emesos suggested. Ishik nodded.

"Should we tell anyone about Orin or the werewolf?" The question was barely out of Ishik's mouth before Emesos responded.

"No. Not the king, not the historians, nobody."

"Not even Paolin?"

"Especially not Paolin... for now at least. Speaking of Paolin, what do you say we wake him up and grab breakfast? That way we can tackle this thousand-year-old mystery on a full stomach." The two of them laughed quietly and began walking back to their room. When they reach the door, they could plainly hear the sound of someone crying. The brothers exchanged looks of concern. Ishik hesitantly opened the door.

The two of them saw Paolin on his bed, his knees drawn to his chest, sobbing softly. Paolin's attention snapped to them immediately. He got off the bed and ran into them, tackling them, swinging his fists at them half-heartedly.

"Don't do that to me! I thought...I thought you had left...me...all alone. Don't go...I need you." The words brought chills down Emesos' spine. Ishik gave Paolin a hug.

"We would never leave you like that," he reassured the boy. "We like you too much. We just went to see if the kitchens had opened. Come on, let's go grab some food." The three of them managed to locate the kitchens after a bit of searching and had some warm bread and cheese. Paolin looked toward the two of them as they finished their meal.

"So, what's next?" he asked.

"Well, we were going to go to the castle library and search for a person called Zane. I heard he had something to do with Orin in the last War." Emesos said with ease. Ishik admired his elegance. He could mask the truth without telling a lie.

Paolin sighed. "You should have just asked me. I've read just about every book in the library. There was a king named Zanidius III. He was one of the best kings in Strynic history. He furthered Manipulator protection laws and even managed to make a law about werewolves, I think."

"We should check still; there are some other things I want to know." Emesos insisted. After getting lost for an unknown amount of time, they finally managed to reach the king's study. Wiln was there, at his desk, quill in hand and documents spread out before him.

Wiln looked up and smiled when he saw the three of them. Emesos quickly asked Wiln if they could browse and Wiln nodded, continuing his work. For the next three hours, they searched for anyone named Zane. Paolin found a few sources, so did Emesos. Nothing told them any more information than Paolin had told them. But it was Ishik who made a strange discovery.

As he went back to put a stack of books away, he discovered one that was extremely old and pressed flat against the shelf. Ishik picked it up and flipped it open. His eyes widened. "Emesos, I found something..." The other two crowded around him to peer at his new discovery. Paolin's eyes widened.

"No way...it can't be... it's..."

"A guide to Manipulating..." Paolin said softly, reading the faded letters on the pages. "I thought the Congregation burned all of those a few hundred years ago." He looked for the author's name, but couldn't find it. Ishik closed the book and quickly hid it inside his shirt. Paolin threw him a questioning look. Ishik shrugged, looking slightly uncomfortable.

"Emesos and I both have Blades. Since we have Blades, we should be able to Manipulate, right? So why not have some pointers ready, just in case?" Paolin took the explanation and accepted it. They continued their search, and after a little while, it was Emesos who found a curious tome.

The book wasn't quite as tattered and beaten as the Manipulator guide, but it had a definite quality of age in its look. Emesos grabbed it and flipped it open. The cloud of dust that shot into the air made all three of them cough. They examined it in detail when the dust dispersed. It looked to be some kind of journal. After skimming it and finding nothing interesting, he flipped to the end, about ready to give up the search.

This shall be my last entry. Notharil has fallen, and so the capital shall be next. What has become of my beloved Stryne? Vrasta has all but decimated the Kingdom. We're trying to evacuate, but we're running out of time. I know the end is near...I can feel the Divine on my shoulder, waiting to snatch my soul. But now...I wonder about the strangest things, memories from a long time ago. I had forgotten most of them, but it seems the closer I get to death, the more of them surface.

I cannot help but think of the boy with the bracelet. Orin, and his soon-to-be father, Anazan. I hadn't thought about them in years. But now, I hope they will not have to suffer the same way I have. Farewell, my faithful journal, and if anyone is reading this, I pray with all my might, that you will learn from my recounts.

Zane (King Zanidius III)

Emesos called over his two companions, handed them the book, and had them read the last entry. They both gave him puzzled looks. "It's the same person. Zane and Zanidius are the same person," Emesos elaborated. "But for some reason, his journal is here, even though he was the king of Stryne. Do you know anything about this, Paolin?"

Paolin nodded. "A little. In the fourth War, when Stryne fell, Zanidius retreated to Rhyth's capital. There he spent his last days with the king of Rhyth, Monocol, until they both died in the taking of the capital Vin a few weeks later."

There was a silence between the three of them. Ishik suggested they grab lunch, and they did. As they were eating, Paolin asked a question. "Why did you have a sudden interest in Zanidius?" he asked Emesos.

Emesos looked at Paolin and then answered. "Well, I learned he was alive in the same time period as Orin, so I figured he'd be worth investigating." Ishik noticed that once again, Emesos didn't tell all of the truth, but he didn't lie. Paolin seemed slightly skeptical of this notion, but said nothing.

Soon, they were all heading back to their rooms when Emesos felt dizzy. He staggered slightly. Ishik and Paolin turned around, their faces concerned.

"Emesos, are you alright?"

"Emesos, talk to me." Ishik commanded. It was the last thing Emesos heard before the room spun and went black.

******

Emesos was standing on a ridge, overlooking a burning city. Almost nothing was left standing. The smoke stung at his eyes and throat. He noticed someone in his peripheral vision. Emesos turned to get a better look and fought the urge to gasp. The figure next to him was none other than Sene, the Darkest Knight.

"And so another city falls," Sene said. "The only one between us and the capital." Emesos wasn't sure what to say.

"Lord Vrasta will be pleased," he said tentatively. Suddenly, Sene's orange and black blade was pointed between his eyes. Emesos' feet felt rooted to the ground.

"Know this, werewolf," Sene demanded, *his tone full of something Emesos couldn't quite identify. "It is not fortunate for these people to die. And Vrasta is not my Lord. My loyalty lies only to Altherai."*

"Altherai?" Emesos managed to say. "Why is Altherai so important to you?"

Sene now lifted Emesos off the ground with one hand. Emesos felt the air being choked out of him. "Altherai is all I am," Sene said quietly. "It's all I have left. Altherai's heirs have been chosen, and I will help them claim what is theirs!"

Emesos saw the Blade flash toward him, and everything went black.

******

Emesos woke up gasping. *I just died! I just died!* That was his only thought for a few moments. Once he had calmed down, he noticed that Ishik and Paolin were standing around him. He was staring up at a ceiling.

He told them immediately what he had seen. "It was in the present." He concluded. "That experience was from the present! He's coming...Sene's coming to attack the capital!"

Thirty

The three of them stood before Wiln looking at the king's shocked face. "How soon?" The question from Wiln was barely a whisper. Everyone's eyes were fixed on Emesos. Emesos lowered his head.

"I didn't find out. He killed me before I had the chance." Wiln raised his eyebrows.

"He killed you? Who is 'he?'?"

"Sene, the Darkest Knight." Wiln's face paled even further. "He's really on edge, though," Emesos elaborated. "He really doesn't want to kill people, but at the same time, he's willing to do anything to help a person named 'Altherai.' It's come up before, but I still have no idea what or who it is. Sene wants Altherai's heirs to be in power and will do anything to get them there. He was at a place called Northaril, if that gives you any estimate."

Wiln nodded. "We have around a week and a half then. We must prepare for any and everything. If the capital falls, so does Rhyth, and we can't afford to have that happen. Emesos, once again, Rhyth is in your debt...I don't know what we would have done without you."

Emesos shrugged. "Ishik would have taken care of things. He is my brother after all." The four of them smiled at that. "It's not every day you see a man beat a werewolf in a bare-handed fight."

Ishik blushed. "I told you I didn't win. It was a draw."

Wiln plunged immediately into tactics for preparing the city. "Ishik, I need you to ask the werewolves under you to perform patrols, if they don't mind."

Ishik laughed. "Are you joking with me? They'll be overjoyed. Having nothing to do has made them restless. I'll see what I can arrange." Wiln nodded and turned to Emesos.

"Emesos, I need you to talk to the people and use your influence to get them to evacuate." Emesos gave Wiln a hard look. The king sighed.

"I know you don't like your title as Prophet, but the Congregation has given you quite a bit of power. Now is the time to make the most of it, for the people's sake." Emesos looked into Wiln's eyes and saw the silent plea in them.

Emesos nodded; his face grim. Wiln turned to Paolin. "And Paolin, I need your help." The young man recoiled in shock.

"You want my help? What for, Majesty?"

Wiln answered without hesitation. "I need you to assess our defenses. I would use Emesos' memories from Fellix for that, but right now he has other things he needs to do and so does Ishik. Right now, you're the only other person who is able to look at our garrison from the perspective of an attacking werewolf force." Paolin let out a humorless laugh.

"Werewolves; do you think that's all that's heading our way? If I were Vrasta, I'd get a force of drakes as well, just in case. It'd make taking the city so much easier." Wiln cursed, making several of the guards at the throne room doors jump.

"We don't have much to defend against drakes; most of those forces were wiped out at the Northern Wall. What are we going to do?"

"I have a solution," Ishik said quietly. Emesos looked at Ishik, and for the first time since he had met his brother, Ishik looked lost in his own thoughts. "I have an answer to the drakes, just let me handle it."

Wiln's eyes widened, a look of surprise on his face. "Can you really do that? How?"

"I have my methods, but I won't say more than that."

Wiln held up his hands in a gesture of surrender. "You don't need to. When the enemy gets here, if there's a drake, your first priority is to take it down, understood?"

Ishik nodded. "Understood."

"Emesos," Wiln said, "get started on some kind of speech, and finish it fast. I'll have Lanita help you after she dispatches messengers to the more distant cities so they can evacuate now. Ishik, go meet with the werewolves. Paolin, you'll join the captain of the guard when he gets here and go with him." Emesos and Ishik bowed and left, letting Paolin stay behind to wait for the captain.

Ishik and Emesos went their separate ways as Emesos headed to the king's study and Ishik went to exit the castle through the main entrance. Emesos sat down with a quill, a few bottles of ink, and plenty of parchment. He worked for an hour before a very flustered-looking Lanita joined him. Together, they took another two hours to finish up the speech. When Lanita looked over the final draft, she was dismayed.

"You wrote the entire thing in Ancient!" She groaned. "Now I have no idea if you wrote it down correctly!"

Emesos picked up the sheet and read what was on it. Lanita nodded. "That sounds about right, but you need to be less monotonous. Put more emotion into it."

"How?" Emesos asked.

"Think about the people you care about and it will come to you." Emesos nodded. Lanita looked at the nine spent candles on the desk before them. "We should go to the square, where I told everybody to meet. The people should be there, or close to it."

Emesos raised an eyebrow. "An entire city? No one will be able to hear me!"

"I know," Lanita said. "But them seeing you alive and well is just as important to them as hearing you. You've become a beacon to them, and right now they need your light to guide them."

Emesos nodded. With his speech in hand, he and Lanita walked out of the castle and toward the city square. People had gathered there in massive numbers, but as soon as they saw him; they parted silently to make a pathway. When Emesos had finally reached the center, almost everyone was silent. It was eerie, seeing so many become so quiet.

Emesos cleared his throat and tried to think of his family when he spoke, but instead other images came: images of Ishik and Paolin, of the killed soldiers who tried to accompany them to the Wall. He looked away from his page and spoke as loudly and clearly as he could.

"People of this city! I stand before you today to bring you news you have already heard. The capital will be under attack soon and you must flee to safety! I implore you to cooperate with your leaders as much as possible." Those close enough to hear shifted uneasily. Emesos pointed at them, maintaining eye contact.

"I have seen the horrors that are done to people by the enemy we are about to face! I know your fears! I know you worry about your homes, livelihoods and futures! Even if this capital falls, a collection of buildings is all it is. But now you should worry about each other! What new friendships shall be formed if you unite, if you remain together!"

Emesos made a wide sweeping gesture, turning in a circle so everyone could see. "*You are Rhyth!* As long as you remain united, your country will never fall! Therefore, I ask you, Rhyth, to get to safety, so your legacy may be passed down into the epics of history and our descendants will know of your heroism!" The crowd was silent and still. Emesos was now completely immersed in his speech.

"Leave and live, for you, for friends, for Rhyth, for the four Kingdoms of Daclynand!" Emesos lowered his hands. Silence. Emesos swallowed, lowered his head and walked down the steps from the stand he was on. The crowd parted before him. Suddenly he heard one person clap, then another. The whole crowd exploded into applause. A chant soon spread through the entire group.

"Hail the Prophet! Hail the Prophet! Hail the Prophet!" Emesos continued walking, but with his head held high. When he had reached the castle, he told Wiln of the speech's success. Wiln smiled.

"Excellent," the king said. "Now all I need is for Paolin and Ishik to come back with news." His face looked ragged.

After waiting for another hour, Ishik was let into the throne room. Wiln became alert instantly. "What did the werewolves say? Will they do it?"

Ishik nodded. "They would be very happy to, but on one condition." Wiln's face grew serious.

"What condition would that be?"

"They want you to name Paolin as your heir in case you die."

Thirty-One

"What?" Wiln asked, recoiling in shock. "What did you say?"

"The pack wants you to name Paolin as your official heir in case you die," Ishik said. "They seem to have taken a rather large interest in him."

"Why?" asked Wiln. "Why would they?" Emesos and Ishik looked at each other and nodded.

"You have to make everyone but you leave before we explain," Emesos stated. Wiln impatiently made all of the guards leave and shut the doors behind them, giving them express orders not to let anyone in until he said so. After that was taken care of, he turned around to speak to the pair.

"I promise not to tell a soul. Why are the werewolves so interested in Paolin?" Emesos took a deep breath.

"Paolin has two souls inside him. One is his. The other is a werewolf's," Emesos said. Wiln looked dumbfounded.

"How...how did that happen?" Emesos kept his lips sealed tight.

"I can't say. You'll have to trust us." Wiln frowned slightly and then nodded.

"Fine, I understand. I won't force it out of you. I doubt I could anyway. So...if I name Paolin as my heir, the werewolves will patrol and fight for us?" Ishik nodded. Wiln shook his head

"I would...in a heartbeat. If only I didn't have this to worry about." Wiln raised his right hand and his Blade flashed to life in his hand. "The Blade would have to choose him. You know the law as well as I do, it's been set down since the Second War: The Blades shall appear to those proclaimed worthy by other people and the Blade itself. I can't influence that in anyway, and I doubt anyone would take Paolin seriously if he didn't have this Blade."

Ishik sighed. "I'll go try and make them understand that then... If you'll excuse me—" He bowed and left, letting the guards know it was okay to return to the throne room. Wiln willed away his Blade. It disappeared in a flash.

A short while later, Paolin reported in. His face looked grim. The king raised his eyebrows. Paolin bowed respectfully. "Well, Your Majesty...we are...a little underequipped, to put it lightly, but we should be fine if they attack with a force of a few thousand. As long as Ishik can make good on his promise, we should be able to hold. It would still be for the best for the people to evacuate though. The enemy commander may not want civilians harmed, but I can't guarantee his lackeys will want the same." Wiln breathed a sigh of relief.

"Good, now all we have to do is prepare and wait for Sene to come." Later that night, Ishik came and said that, after much negotiation, the werewolves agreed to fight for Wiln as long as Paolin was made a leader of high standing.

"They said they wanted 'one of their own and one that you trust' in command, so you'll have to think of something." Ishik explained apologetically. His massive Blade was strapped to his back by a worn leather piece that seemed to stem from the handle.

"Not a problem, inventing random titles is something kings do all the time for whiny nobles. This time, it'll actually mean something." Wiln laughed lightly.

"Get some rest and tell your friends to do the same; they've had a long day." Ishik bowed and left, returning to his room.

To his surprise, Paolin and Emesos were waiting for him, a small stack of biscuits on a stool before them. They were sitting on the ground. "You're just in time for our very fashionable dinner!" Emesos said with a beaming smile.

"We couldn't start a feast without you, after all," Paolin added, smiling. Ishik smiled back.

"Good, I'm starving," Ishik said, sitting down.

The three of them ate slowly, relishing the taste and each other's company. They fell asleep in the same room, unwilling to say goodnight to one another.

The next morning came and the three of them woke up, grabbed breakfast and received a message that they were to head to the throne room. They walked in to see Wiln, formally dressed and ready for something. "Hello! Good to see you again!" he greeted them with a smile. "Everybody in the city except for the soldiers is getting ready to leave. The entire city's been thrown into action, thanks to Emesos. They should start leaving today or tomorrow. According to Lanita, he was very convincing." Emesos blushed slightly.

"And now..." Wiln reached beside him and lifted up a scroll, handing it to Paolin. "This is for you." Paolin took it and opened it up.

He gasped. No words came out of his mouth. "What is it?" Ishik asked. Paolin just handed Ishik the parchment. Ishik read some part of it out loud.

"'I hereby state, as the King of Rhyth, that my subject, Paolin Hollowen, is appointed as Marshal of the Militia and Protector of the Blade.'" Ishik looked up at Wiln. "What's a Protector of the Blade?"

"The Protector of the Blade is an old position. Rhyth hasn't had one since the last War. What it means is that if I die, an unfortunately high possibility, my Blade will go to someone else; and it would be Paolin's job to protect them until it is peaceful enough for them to claim the throne properly."

Ishik raised both his eyebrows. "That's a very important position. The werewolves will definitely accept this. What is Marshal of the Militia though? I've never heard of that job either."

Wiln smiled slightly. "It's the Rhythian equivalent to Stryne's High Commander." Emesos gasped. Ishik turned to his brother for explanation.

"That means if Wiln dies, Paolin has full control over the military matters until the next king takes the throne." Ishik turned back around.

"You got as close to naming him your heir as possible, didn't you?" Wiln merely smiled and said nothing. Paolin bowed low to him.

"Your Majesty, I can think of no higher honor. I shall serve you the best I am able." Wiln nodded back, still smiling.

"Now, you three have some work to do..." Wiln sent Emesos to help the caravans of people, Ishik to go patrol, and made Paolin go to the barracks with him to do more preparations. By the time the four of them returned, they were exhausted. The next few days were similarly tiring.

Then, after three days of helping, Emesos awoke to see the sun rise over an almost completely abandoned city.

It was disturbing, the stillness. It filled the air with a sense of tension, sorrow, forgotten times... Emesos went to Ishik and Paolin's rooms, but discovered they had already left to do their various tasks. That was when the realization hit him.

For the first time in a very long time, I'm alone... For the rest of the day, Emesos wandered about looking for something to do. He really didn't have much, so it left him in the situation he feared most. He had nothing but his own thoughts to fill his mind.

Ishik and Paolin's return was a welcome sight. And after a simple dinner, they went to sleep, Emesos' mind at ease once more. The next morning when he awoke, he had a cold feeling in his stomach. The feeling of foreboding.

Something's going to happen, Emesos thought to himself. Finding himself alone, he went to the kitchens and had breakfast. It was then a messenger came saying he had to report to the throne room *immediately*. Emesos quickly reached the throne room and was let in. He entered to see a distraught Wiln on his throne, holding his head in one hand. Ishik was there as well his face grim.

Wiln looked up and nodded at Emesos. "The enemy was spotted," he said.

"Where? How far out?"

"They'll be here in around a day."

"How many are there?" Emesos asked.

Ishik looked at his brother, sorrow and worry in his eyes. "Around ten thousand."

Emesos recoiled. "Ten thousand?!"

"Plus drakes," Ishik added.

Emesos shook his head. This couldn't be happening. Not after all of the careful preparation he did. Vrasta wasn't going to hold back, and Emesos knew in his heart they would go into this battle losing.

"I suppose we'll just have to give them a fight to remember us by," Emesos said, his throat dry.

Ishik nodded. "They can count on it." The rest of the day, the two brothers wandered about the castle, not saying a word, taking in each moment they had with one another. When Paolin returned and received the news, he wasn't as sad.

"Don't worry so much," Paolin said. "I've had the soldiers building some things." With that, Paolin launched into explanations. Over the past week, all soldiers who weren't on duty were building engines of war. Catapults, oil barrels, things of mass destruction. It did little to bolster their confidence, however. When the three of them went to bed, Emesos felt a familiar tug on his mind. He surrendered to it.

******

Emesos was standing in a throne room that was bright. Sunshine gleamed through the stained glass windows. A blue and bronze banner with a golden sun was placed at the end of the hall. It was the throne room of Stryne's king. Emesos looked at the person on the throne and recognized him with a jolt. It was the king that had banished him from the castle. Beside him was Anazan in his plain clothing.

So I'm Fellix, *he thought.* What am I supposed to learn here? *A voice jolted him to the situation at hand.*

"Fellix, forgive me!" The king pleaded. "I was a fool! I should have done what you suggested! Now, we're facing impossible odds! How do we win?" Anazan let out a strangely chilling laugh that sent jolts up Emesos' spine.

"You don't win. You don't have a chance. Vrasta will tear you apart." The king held his head in his hands and did something Emesos never thought he would witness. The king cried, losing all composure.

For some reason, it felt unreal. Kings weren't normal people, kings weren't supposed to cry.

Emesos stepped forward and grabbed the king's arm. The king looked at him with watery green eyes. "We'll use what we have the best we can. The most we can do is buy the people some extra time while they reach safety."

The king straightened upright. "I may lose," he whispered, "But I won't die a coward." Emesos smiled. "That's my promise."

"That's the spirit; anything less than that and we'll all be dead by tomorrow.

******

The next day Wiln wouldn't stop pacing around. It was understandable, everyone was anxious. Wiln's major concern however, was the evacuating people. "Even with over a week's head start, they'll move slowly. We have to give them as much time as possible." He was in the throne room, a table before him containing a few maps. One was a layout of the city, another of the entire Kingdom of Rhyth.

Wiln pointed at the city map and gestured for Emesos and Ishik to come closer. The two brothers saw that Wiln had added hand-drawn markings all around the city, just behind the walls. From an overhead view, the capital was set on a slight hill. Its walls had a square shape.

"All of these marks are war engines. Most will be concentrated on the eastern and northern walls, since the enemy is approaching from there. Ishik, I need you to be there for the inevitable drake attack. Paolin will be with you, directing the war engines the best he can. Emesos, you and I will take the northern wall."

"Isn't that far away from the enemy?" Emesos asked.

Wiln shook his head. "No. Since a majority of the engines are on the eastern wall, they'll want to take the northern wall, to sweep into the western wall. That way, they can trap the eastern wall between two fronts. We'll put Ishik's pack on the eastern wall as well, just in case." Emesos nodded, following his reasoning.

Wiln went over the plans one more time with each of them, before suggesting they suit up for battle.

At the armory, each of them had his turn getting the equipment he needed. Ishik's wurmskin clothes and silver provided more than enough protection, but the master armorer wouldn't hear it. So, after some arguing, Ishik consented to wearing bracers and leather gloves, along with a hardened-leather undershirt that was to go under the wurmskin.

Emesos was given more protection. He opted for a padded leather shirt and, over that, chainmail. Greaves were put on his shins, and bracers on his arms. A good helmet and pair of gloves completed his preparations. Emesos was a bit unaccustomed to the weight, but it wasn't unmanageable.

The most difficult to outfit was Paolin as he was only thirteen and not fully grown. The armorer managed to find a set of bracers that covered up Paolin's forearms and a set of practice chainmail that was only half the length of normal chainmail. It didn't cover everything, but it would have to do. After some experimenting, they managed to make a helmet fit by putting extra layers of leather in it. Despite these shortcomings, Paolin still looked like a commander, his two trusty daggers at his side.

They parted ways, unwilling to say goodbye. A goodbye now could mean goodbye forever. Emesos quickly found Wiln. The king was dressed similarly to him. Wiln merely nodded. Emesos nodded back.

Together, the entire city waited. The anticipation was almost stifling. Ishik's werewolves returned and after what felt like a century of dread, or even an eternity, the signal horn sounded.

Everybody readied his weapon. Emesos and Wiln summoned their Blades.

The fight for Rhyth was about to begin.

Thirty-Two

Paolin raised his arm. The engines prepared to fire their projectiles. Some were full of wood that was bound together with rope, others were simply piled with rocks. The ten thousand werewolves drew closer and closer. Within a few moments, they were in range. Paolin threw his arm forward, screaming. "Fire!"

He heard all the siege engines groan as they sprang into action. Soon, lumps of stone and wood were in his vision, flying toward the enemy. The stones quickly smashed into the pack, some rolling along the ground and killing even more.

The lumps of wood hit the ground. They exploded into thousands of pieces, spraying the attackers with deadly shards. Paolin smiled grimly. His invention of splintering projectiles was working.

He waited patiently for the men to reload. The werewolves got even closer. It seemed like an eternity, but a signaler finally waved to him and Paolin gave another signal. Another volley flew, and more of the enemy were eliminated. Now, there arose a new problem. The werewolves started to pull apart, some of them shifting right to scale the northern wall while the remainder tackled the continued the assault on the eastern wall.

Paolin signaled for another reload, but as they prepared a third volley, a multitude of cries pierced the air on the wall around them. Some werewolves had actually gotten close enough to scale the walls using their claws and they started decimating the lines around them. At the same time, Paolin heard the cries of drakes in the distance. Ishik was already helping the soldiers on the walls, but numbers were against them.

Paolin was forced to leave the war engines in the hands of a signal officer as he was fighting one on one with werewolves and trying to save as many soldiers on the walls as he could. For some strange reason, whenever werewolves tried to approach Ishik, they were sent flying backwards. Paolin didn't ask, and at the moment he didn't care. The drakes were getting close and would be there within minutes.

Paolin stabbed viciously into a werewolf's throat, blood seeping out of the wound. Paolin withdrew the dagger and shifted focus to his next opponent. A few swipes were avoided and Paolin stabbed once, twice, three times. The werewolf fell. For some reason, everything seemed to be slowing down. He was amazed at his own reflexes. It was like someone else was in his body and he was merely a spectator.

A pile of bodies mounted around Paolin and Ishik, but the opponents just kept coming. After a while, Paolin started to wear down, receiving several cuts and bruises. Suddenly, the werewolves drew back, and a black and orange blur shot through the air and landed on the wall with a ground shaking crash. The Darkest Knight stood before Paolin, a wicked black and orange sword in his fist, armor of the same colors covering his massive frame.

"Step aside, boy." The words were a command.

Paolin put his two daggers in front of him. "Not a chance!" he shouted. The knight sighed.

"Then I will make you." The knight threw up his arm. It did nothing. Paolin flew into action. Dodging past the sword that flashed in front of him, he stabbed at the knight's neck, but the man's sharp reflexes allowed him to dodge, the knives grazing his helmet. The knight's arm flashed out, grabbing Paolin by the throat. Paolin gasped as he felt his throat slowly closing. Paolin's feet left the ground as he was picked up.

"Paolin!" The knight turned and saw Ishik fighting his way toward them. The knight thrust his arm forward, throwing Paolin away from him and off the ledge of the wall.

"No!" Ishik rejected gravity under his feet, flying toward the knight, Blade ready. The knight blocked his opponent's onslaught and spoke calmly.

"We will fight a later day. For now, I recommend you stop those drakes, otherwise your men will suffer."

"What do you want from us?!" Ishik shouted, swinging his Blade and being stopped with ease. It filled him with more rage than he had ever experienced.

"I seek your so-called *king*. This is farewell for now, son of Altherai." The knight rejected gravity and was sent flying away, toward the northern wall.

"Get back here, bastard!" Ishik yelled. He saw a drake starting to swoop down on his men. With a curse he realized the knight was right. This fight would have to wait. Right now, he had to deal with the drakes.

Making himself reject gravity once more, he planted himself firmly on a drake's back and increased the gravity. The drake plummeted down onto a large group of werewolves, crushing them and snapping its own neck. Ishik rejected himself back onto the wall and continued onto his next target, propelled by grief for his friend and concern for his brother and his king.

******

Emesos and Wiln watched from the north wall as a drake picked up a war engine and dropped it onto their soldiers. A small figure kept jumping to extraordinary heights and crushing them.

Emesos saw a large, black figure crash down on the northern wall and start cutting through swaths of their men with the help of werewolves

"He's here," Emesos said.

"Who's here?" Wiln asked.

"Sene, the man who killed your father; he's looking for you."

Wiln gripped his Blade tight, his eyes flashing. "Well, he's going to find me and, when he does; I'm going to kill him." After much fighting, the knight reached the western wall. Fighting their way through a multitude of werewolves, Emesos and Wiln were soon within shouting distance.

"Sene! I'm here! Call off your dogs and we'll have a proper fight!" Wiln's face was contorted with fury.

The Darkest Knight looked up and held up a hand. All of the werewolves disengaged and moved behind Sene, a good distance away. All of the healthy soldiers took the chance to drag away wounded comrades or dead bodies. Soon, a large gap between the two forces formed, both sides not daring to move. The soldiers cleared a path for Emesos and Wiln. Wiln started to step forward and Emesos put a hand on his shoulder. The king's emotions were a mixture of rage and determination; a dangerous combination.

"Wiln, don't do this. If you fight him alone, you'll lose," Emesos said. "Let's fight him together, we might have a chance!"

Wiln shook off Emesos' hand. "I can fight him myself. I will win. This is my fight, and if you don't stay out of it, I will never forgive you." Wiln stepped forward and brandished his Blade toward the Knight.

Sene seemed to sigh. "It brings me joy to see you care so deeply for a son of Altherai. Shall we begin, *king*?" He said Wiln's title like it was an insult. The man could take no more.

Wiln charged forward with a cry, slashing at the Knight's shoulder. He seemed to slide into the Knight, as though he were on ice. Emesos was confused and then it hit him.

His Blade's Manipulation ability is the Force of friction! One of the four Forces that could be Manipulated was under Wiln's control, and the king was using it to his full advantage; sliding and side stepping all about to try and land a jab or cut on the Knight.

His foe was untouchable. Wherever Wiln went, the Knight's Blade was also. The fight went on for what seemed an eternity. Wiln jumped back and dashed forward, manipulating the Force of friction to give him extra momentum, almost becoming a blur. The knight held up one hand and Wiln suddenly froze, as if he was stuck to the ground. The knight stabbed forward. The Blade plunged into Wiln's heart. Emesos saw the glow around Wiln suddenly stop.

"No!" Emesos shouted, charging in. He blinked once and it was as though the scene of the battle had changed completely. He was in a throne room; the man on Sene's Blade was different. Emesos felt his heart almost overflowing with some kind of energy that he could hardly contain. He threw himself into a flurry of strikes that Sene stopped without pause. Emesos jumped back, out of Sene's range, and felt something strange.

You're holding your Blade wrong, a small, instinctive voice inside his brain said. *Try another way.* Emesos looked down at his Blade and noticed the Blade was in his hand the way any sword would go. He relaxed his grip on the Blade and let it fall slightly before he caught it. The Blade was now facing away from Sene, backwards in his hand.

This is right, The voice said. Emesos had to agree. The Blade felt much more comfortable in his hand now. *Now, unleash your emotions!* Emesos took a deep breath and charged at Sene. He let that feeling wash over him as he attacked. He felt as though it was pulling him apart...

Suddenly, he was in two places at once, with two pairs of eyes. He was striking from the left...no, the right. Direction soon lost all meaning for him in this dual sight. He only knew one thing. He was attacking Sene.

Sene was on the defensive. The Darkest Knight jumped backward. In his dual vision, Emesos saw an opening. He raised his arm and charged forward in a massive diagonal slash...

Suddenly, he was no longer seeing double. He was back in one place, Wiln's body near him, with Sene down on one knee, his Bladeless fist on the ground, the other clutching the Blade for support. "So...you've finally started to unlock that Blade's cursed power. How I pity you..." Sene said. "Nevertheless, you managed to land a strike strong enough to wound me. I am proud of you, son of Altherai. I will make you a deal."

"I'm listening," Emesos said with hatred in his voice.

"I will give you and all of your men a four day head start to head to Stryne, for your growth here today."

Emesos' mind reeled. Part of him wanted to say no, but then he thought about how many more would die if he did. *Is he really offering us a chance to escape? Will he keep his word?*

Yes, said the small voice inside his head. Emesos gave the Knight a short nod.

"Fine, but you have to give us one day for medical treatment, and keep your werewolves two miles from us."

Sene nodded. "Agreed. Farewell, son of Altherai." With that the Knight and all the werewolves before him jumped off the wall, landing safely and heading away from the capital. A howling signal of four notes was given and soon, all of the enemy werewolves were retreating. There were no drakes left to follow suit. Whatever Ishik's method was, it was very effective.

Emesos watched them go. Emesos willed his Blade away, fell to his knees, and started to cry; Wiln's lifeless body only a few feet from his.

After all his tears were spent, Emesos commanded all of the soldiers to take their wounded to the nearest medic. The king's body was reverently lifted away and brought down from the walls. Emesos' thoughts now turned to Ishik and Paolin, praying silently that they survived the battle. He headed over to the western wall and saw Ishik running toward him, covered in black blood that wasn't his own.

The two brothers collided in an embrace. "Thank the Divine you're still alive!" Ishik said. "Come on, we need to check on Paolin. The knight threw him off the wall!" The two brothers ran among the walking soldiers and the moaning wounded, looking for their friend. When he wasn't there, Ishik and Emesos' hearts fell.

He can't be. Emesos thought. *Not him too...no...*

"There you are!" Emesos and Ishik wheeled around to see Paolin walking toward them, bandages around his head. "I've been looking all over for you!" The two brothers embraced the young man, each relieved the other was still in one piece. "Where's Wiln?" Paolin asked Emesos. Emesos looked down and somehow made the words come out.

"He's dead. The Darkest Knight killed him." Paolin gasped and Ishik lowered his head. They had a moment of silence, in remembrance of their king. Emesos quickly told the two of them how it happened, and how he managed to somehow fight to a draw with Sene and buy them four days so they could run.

Ishik shook his head. "That's amazing. Your Blade's powers...I've never heard of anything like it."

"You Manipulated gravity, didn't you?" Emesos asked. Ishik nodded.

"My Blade gives me two kinds of abilities." Ishik said. "To Manipulate gravity and heat. Wiln's was friction."

Paolin sighed. "I guess I'm leader...now," he said with a slight choke in his voice, "At least, until I find the person worthy of Wiln's Blade."

Emesos put his hand on Paolin's shoulder. "Don't worry; we'll be there to help." Paolin nodded.

"I know..." Paolin's voice drifted off into silence. "We should probably patch up and gather all our forces." Emesos and Ishik agreed, and soon, they were running about the city, gathering all of the wounded in one place, taking in numbers and checking on equipment. It took the rest of the day.

When they had finished, Paolin didn't like the results. "Half our force has been killed or wounded. The enemy lost around a fifth of their force. Most of the equipment is in good order though. We should be able to head out tomorrow." The three of them sat down to a humble meal of cold bread and cheese; letting the soldiers have the fires to warm their food and sanitize what little medical equipment they had.

"The men are telling incredible stories about your fight with the Knight, Emesos," Paolin said. "What really happened?"

Emesos explained the strange, double vision. Paolin exhaled sharply, impressed.

"According to the soldiers, you glowed and then split into two people. One of you was you; the other was like a white, shimmering figure of you. Apparently, you and the mist version of you took on Sene and defeated him."

Two of me?! Emesos thought. *That would explain the double vision.* "I really don't care how I beat him," Emesos said, "I'm just glad I did. If I hadn't, we probably wouldn't be standing here right now." Ishik nodded.

"We should host a funeral for the king tonight," Ishik said suddenly. Thinking quietly about it, Emesos and Paolin agreed. Wiln deserved a proper sendoff.

That night, all of the soldiers who weren't treating wounded or actually wounded to immobility stood in the town square, where Wiln's body lay on top of a large stack of wood that had been assembled from the leftover ammunition from Paolin's war engines.

After everyone had gathered and enough torches had been lit, Emesos got up to speak. "My fellow soldiers, let us all pay our respects to one of the finest rulers Rhyth has ever produced. And let us pay our respects to the finest warriors Rhyth has ever produced. Your king and comrades nobly sacrificed themselves to make sure you lived. And until such time as the Blade has found one worthy of its wielding, as declared by our late king, Paolin shall lead you." The soldiers gave a murmur of agreement. Most of them had gotten to know Paolin well in the past week and trusted him.

"May we pray for the Divine to accept the souls of the fallen here tonight." A torch was brought forward and thrown onto the wooden altar. It shot up in flames, Wiln's body hidden in the blaze. Emesos turned back around to face the crowd. Ishik stepped next to him, as did Paolin.

"And may the Blade of Rhyth recognize its new wielder," Emesos declared. Emesos summoned his Blade. Ishik drew his. The two brothers pointed them at the stars. Every soldier slowly raised their weapon to the sky. The only sounds to break the silence were the drawing of swords from scabbards and the crackling of the fire behind them. Tomorrow, they would be running for their lives. But tonight, tonight was for reflection, a night for remembrance, a night for sorrow.

A night to never forget.

Thirty-Three

Ishik looked back over his shoulder at the abandoned capital of Rhyth. He and what remained of Rhyth's Militia had gone far enough that it was now just barely visible. Despite having so many wounded, they had made very good progress that morning. If they kept it up and were unopposed, they would be able to come close to the border of Stryne. Paolin was immersed in his role, checking on all the troops of the caravan, making sure everyone got an equal amount of food, and looking after the wounded.

Emesos mostly spent his time with the wounded, talking with them, keeping them company and notifying the medics when someone passed on. Ishik was now back in the company of his pack, and his group was glad to have him. Only a few of them had fallen in the battle, but it still bothered Ishik deeply.

Right then, his attention was fixed on Kiraj, as his friend lumbered into view. "What's the matter, Kiraj?"

"The pack wishes for your friend Paolin to take a second name, Urbak."

"Really?" Ishik said, surprised. "Why?"

"The Children of the Moon said that Paolin has the spirit of one of our kind in him. Is that true?"

Ishik thought for a moment and then decided to answer truthfully. "Yes."

Kiraj nodded. "Then we consider him one of our own. And because of his bravery for facing the Darkest Knight without a

Blade and without hesitation, we thought it only fit for him to acquire a second name."

Ishik shrugged. "As long as he doesn't object, I don't think there would be any major problems." Kiraj nodded and then walked away, going to talk with the other werewolves. At the time night fell, the capital was well out of sight and far away.

The second day, they managed to travel about the same distance with no incident at all, other than a few more casualties among the wounded. But with two thousand people to feed, Paolin realized that food would be running low soon.

It was the third day of travel that was strange. They came upon the town of Fofra and it was completely abandoned. There was no food, no blood, no bodies, nothing. A town without even ghosts. It was there they decided to make camp that night when the sun fell. In just a few more days, they would reach the relative safety of Stryne's border.

Finally done with his rounds, Paolin was heading toward his tent when he saw Kiraj standing in front of it. "Is there something wrong, Kiraj?" Kiraj shook his head.

"No, would you follow me?" Paolin nodded, uncertain. He followed Kiraj down a series of alleys, until he came to an open area where all the werewolves had gathered, along with Ishik.

"Is something wrong? Have I done something to offend you?" Paolin asked. Ishik laughed.

"Nothing's wrong. The werewolves have a request: They want to give you a second name." Paolin nodded, still uncertain.

"It's a big honor." Ishik said. "I'll explain later." Paolin smiled hesitantly and turned to face Kiraj.

"Human who is called Paolin," Kiraj started, "you have proven your bravery multiple times. You dared to face the Knight, without a Blade, without armor, without hope. Yet you found the strength to oppose him and fight back. Do you say this claim is true?"

"Yes," Paolin said slowly, still not sure where this was heading.

Kiraj continued. "You have shown us kindness beyond measure. You have treated us not as something below you, not as something to be feared, but as equals. Do you say this claim is true?"

"Yes," Paolin said with more conviction in his voice. "A person is a person. We are equal in the eyes of death."

The werewolves gave growls of agreement, making the hair stand up on the back of Paolin's neck. There was something in the atmosphere. Paolin felt as though part of him was rising to the surface. Scents were coming alive, the smoke from nearby fires sharp, the wind carrying the smell of approaching rain, the smell of oil for weapons, and the smell of werewolves.

The scents of war, life and death, mixed together in his mind.

Kiraj spoke again. "You fight not for just humankind, but for the tribes as well, carrying the spirit of one of our ancestors. Do you say this claim is true?"

"Yes," Paolin said. The rising feeling seemed to settle, content to stay where it was. Paolin felt himself smiling, but he wasn't sure why. It just felt right. Kiraj now reached the climax of the ceremony

"Then accept this name: From now on in the tribes, your name shall be Caslon." Some werewolves gave yips of surprise. "You have proven yourself worthy of this name, the name of a warrior willing to lay down his life for those he cares about. Do you accept this name?"

"I do." The werewolves gave out a unified howl, a strange sound. Paolin raised his head to the sky and smiled. Later that night, Paolin went to sleep, with a new name, his bracelet clutched in his fist.

When he woke in the morning, Paolin made sure everyone was ready to go. Today was the last day of their head start. They had to make it count. They soon were out of the city and making good progress. Paolin found himself next to Emesos. The two of them hadn't talked much recently.

"So...I heard you got a second name," Emesos said. Paolin nodded. Emesos beamed at him. "That's wonderful! It's a real honor, right?" Paolin nodded again.

"How are things with you?" Paolin asked. Emesos' smile fell and he shrugged.

"I'm alright, but I keep asking myself the same questions over and over. Who is Anazan really? Who is Altherai? Sene called me a 'son of Altherai'...does that mean Altherai is my actual father or mother? Why did Sene let us run? If he was really following Vrasta's orders, I'd be dead by now, and so would you. So why is he giving us the chance to escape? And why is Altherai so important to him?" Emesos shook his head. "It's like a puzzle when the pieces don't come together because you're missing one."

"And without that piece, you don't know what to put together," Paolin finished for him. Emesos nodded. "Well, whatever happens, I'm sure the piece will come to you, and when it does, Ishik and I will be there with you."

"I know." The two of them rode together until nightfall. When night had fallen, Ishik, Paolin, and Emesos all got together. They were almost out of food. They had to reach the border to Stryne and fast.

They sat around their fire thinking on this for a moment. Ishik broke the silence with a random thought. "You know...we've saved each other's lives, fought major battles together, and traveled across a Kingdom, but we still don't know each other's favorite colors?"

"Well... mine is green," Paolin said, laughing. "It is kind of strange we've been through so much and know so little about one another."

Emesos shrugged and smiled. "Well, we'll have plenty of time to learn. My favorite color is kind of a muted violet; reminds me of the setting sun."

Ishik smiled. "My favorite is blue. I remember I used to stare at the sky and figure out what clouds looked like all the time." The three of them fell silent and drifted off to sleep, exhausted.

The trio woke up early and the caravan got a head start, everyone moving faster and keeping watch for signs of attack. The four days had ended and they needed to reach Stryne's border fast. Everyone moved at double the speed without being ordered. They knew what could happen to them if they didn't.

Fortunately, as the sun was going down that day, a small line appeared in the distance. The men cheered and increased their pace. Emesos and his friends did too. Just as the sun dipped below the horizon, they reached the gate. Emesos waved a white flag.

The guards at the wall that protected the Strynic border came down, weapons ready. Emesos explained the best he could, all that had befallen Rhyth. The captain seemed unsurprised. "We let in a massive group of villagers around a week ago. We assumed that the worst had happened," the captain of the group said. "Is this all that's left of your fighting force?" Emesos nodded. "Who's in command? Where is King Wiln?"

Emesos felt a hole open up in his heart. "The king fell in battle." He handed the captain the document that Wiln had signed appointing Paolin Protector of the Blade and Marshal of the Militia.

The captain read it and nodded. "And you're Paolin Hollowen, then?"

"Actually my name is Emesos." The captain's eyes widened.

"*The* Emesos? The Prophet of the Divine?"

Emesos held out his hand and willed for his Blade to appear. It did so in a flash, ready for combat, in his hand backwards, the way he fought Sene. "That would be me. Also, the werewolves with us are allies, don't harm them."

"Of course." The captain saluted and barked orders for his men to open the gates. Slowly, the two massive doors of iron and wood creaked open, creating a pathway into Stryne. "I wish you the best of luck, Prophet." He handed back the papers, which Emesos handed back to Paolin, who tucked them away safely.

The entire caravan slowly marched forward. When they crossed under the gate, Emesos couldn't help himself. He smiled.

For the first time in a long while, he was home.

Thirty-Four

"Welcome to Stryne," Emesos said to everyone. The soldiers near enough to hear him laughed, relieved to finally not have to look over their shoulders when they made camp. It had been two days since they crossed the border into Stryne from Rhyth. It would be another seven until they reached the capital. Now, they just had to make steady progress. The guards at the wall were willing to give them food, and the men marched with renewed vigor in their steps.

Emesos, Paolin, and Ishik all gathered around the fire again that night, this time smiling. "Looks like we made good use of those four days Sene provided," Emesos observed. Ishik snorted.

"Got that right, now we're safely inside Stryne and ready for just about anything," Ishik said. After a slight pause, Ishik spoke again. "And I finally get to meet your family."

The words made Emesos' stomach flip. He had forgotten, in all of the chaos, about his parents not telling him he was adopted. Now that he thought about it, it cut at his heart.

"I can't wait," Emesos said. Ishik nodded. He knew his brother was only partially telling the truth.

"And then we get to meet King Gonra again and figure out what we're going to do from here." Paolin laughed. "You know, I always have had a plan, but for once...I don't know what to do next."

"That makes two of us," Ishik said.

"Three of us," Emesos commented dryly. The fire crackled slightly in the silence, broken by the shuffling of soldiers' feet or bodies as they rolled around in their sleep.

"Want to hear something funny?" Paolin offered. Ishik and Emesos shared a look and then nodded. "When I first got the paper saying I was Marshal of the Militia, I was worried about paying the soldiers."

Emesos and Ishik burst out laughing. Paolin allowed himself a sheepish grin. "Here I was, wondering how much their salary was, when they just wanted to survive." After a little while, they calmed down and bade each other good night.

The next day, Emesos felt a buzz of excitement. "We'll be reaching Leac soon!" Ishik raised his eyebrows.

"Is that a good thing?" he asked.

Emesos nodded. "Definitely," he said with a smile. "It's the first major city in Stryne with a river. And it means we're that much closer to the capital." Sure enough, after a few hours of traveling, Leac came into view.

It was a bustling place, full of so many carts and merchant stalls that having a horse was more of a hindrance than help. The sun was shining brightly, piercing the sky and winter air. The soldiers all seemed heartened to see other people after passing through Rhyth without a sign of human life.

When they made camp, Emesos was greeted by the city mayor, who looked out of place without a uniform or weapon.

"Greetings, Prophet," he said formally. "I trust you will only be here temporarily?" Emesos shook the man's hand. The mayor's gaze was one of ice. Emesos could feel all the emotions from the touch in the mayor's hand. He was rather unhappy that roughly two thousand people showed up suddenly, scaring his townspeople.

"Sorry to unexpectedly come here like this," Emesos apologized. "We're only here for a night; we'll be gone by tomorrow morning."

"And where will you be heading?"

"To Rei, the capital." The mayor nodded.

"I see. I hope your stay is safe." The man let go of Emesos' hand and walked away, bumping into Paolin, shoving him aside. "Out of the way, boy!" he snapped. Paolin grabbed the mayor with both hands and hoisted him upwards. The mayor yelled in shock. "Put me down at once! I demand you put me down!"

"As you wish." Paolin let go and the mayor fell, stumbling onto his feet. "Remember to show respect to everyone," Paolin said in passable Strynic. "The next person might not be as nice as me." The mayor hurried away, an outraged look on his face.

Emesos walked over to Paolin. He had just now noticed how much stronger Paolin had gotten. "Are you alright?" he asked. Paolin nodded.

"I'm fine. That mayor just needed to be put in his place." Emesos couldn't help but smile. Paolin didn't mention his position to the mayor to show him he was wrong. He used a direct method.

"We'll be gone tomorrow, so I wouldn't worry about him too much." They made camp that night, eager for darkness to pass so they could be on their way. Everybody went to sleep.

Emesos woke to the sounds of shouting. "Fire! Fire!" someone cried. Emesos rocketed out of his tent, staring in horror at what he saw. The camp was being set ablaze by an angry mob. They were burning the tents, heading to one place:

The werewolves' sleeping location.

Emesos cursed, running toward the area. He noticed that Paolin and Ishik were right behind him. Soon, they were directly in front of the mob. The mob halted.

"If you don't stop and go home now, people may be hurt," Emesos said loudly. "These werewolves are under our control. You don't have to worry about them!"

"They're an evil to the land!" one man called. "The Congregation says they're a spawn of evil! Do you dare reject their teachings, Prophet?"

Emesos summoned his Blade and slammed it into the ground with so much force that the mob backed away slightly.

"I never wanted to be a Prophet! I didn't want to be a religious figure! Your *Congregation* made me one! The Divine blessed us with werewolves who saw reason to fight for us! Are you really complaining about us getting more help when there are *thousands* of werewolves that are charging in?! We haven't done anything to you! These men have lost their king, their homes, and their Kingdom, do you really want to make their life harder?"

The people in the mob murmured doubtfully, unsure of their actions now. Emesos spoke again. "I'll say this only once more: Go home, otherwise, some of you could be hurt." Slowly, gradually, the mob filtered away, heading back up to the city. Emesos took a deep breath. He turned around to see Ishik and Paolin, wide-eyed.

"What?" he asked. The two of them looked at each other and then spoke.

"You were glowing." Paolin said. Emesos shrugged.

"So? We all glow. I see it all the time."

Ishik coughed once before speaking. "We could all see it, though. It was like some sort of white mantle settled on your body."

Emesos picked his Blade up out of the ground. "We should check our damages," he said quietly. Inwardly, his mind was spinning. *A white mantle,* he thought, *and a glow...* Emesos summoned his Blade and looked at it again. *Just what Force does my Blade control?*

He shook his head to clear it and made his Blade vanish. Now was not the time to add yet another question to his growing list. Right now, he had to check on the people around him. All in all, the soldiers had come through relatively unharmed, other than a few minor burns. The real damage was to their supplies. A great deal of food and many tents had been scorched beyond salvaging.

"This is going to make our march to the capital a lot harder." Ishik reported as everyone settled back down. Emesos nodded, looking at Paolin. The boy had gotten little sleep within the past few weeks, and yet he still kept going. It reminded Emesos a lot of when he first received his visions: Paolin was stretched and strained. But unlike himself, Paolin didn't give.

He never did, Emesos thought, going to help other soldiers repack for the day. *And he probably never will.* Ishik noticed Emesos' actions and moved over to help. When they had finished that night, the three of them fell asleep, exhausted and outside of their tents, too tired to move from their nightly fire.

The next morning, the Rhythian force moved out, leaving behind blackened spots where the tents had burned. Emesos and Ishik helped out the best they could, but the Rhythian soldiers seemed rather grim as they continued the long journey.

Taking a lesson from the incident at Leac, the group avoided major cities, instead going through the small towns like Heda a few days later. Though the population was nervous, they believed Emesos' intentions and allowed them to camp outside of the town.

Most of the soldiers used what little money they had to go to the local tavern and enjoy their first pint in over a month, as all the tavern owners had evacuated with the rest of the civilians from the capital back in Rhyth. Emesos apologized for the strain he caused the owner, but he just laughed.

"Are you kidding me? This is the best business I've had in years!" Emesos couldn't help but smile. He turned around to see Lanita and he jolted with surprise and guilt. Over all of the chaos and constant managing of the soldiers, he had completely forgotten she was there. She said nothing, but raised a pint at him and winked. Emesos laughed and walked over to her table.

"Mind if I join you?" he asked. Lanita gestured for him to take a seat. Emesos did so. "How are you managing?"

Lanita shrugged. "I'm doing alright, feeling slightly useless though." Emesos smiled.

"Don't worry, when you reach the capital, there'll be plenty for you to do." She groaned.

"I know; the legal documents are going to be awful."

"When are legal documents not awful?"

Lanita smiled. "Good point. Say, how are things with you? I bet your girl back home is worried sick about you. Glad you finally get a chance to see her?"

"No, I don't have a girl waiting for me."

"Really? A nice young man like you without a girl? That's just wrong."

"It's just the way life works I suppose. No one said life had to be correct all the time."

"Who knows, with all the fame you've gotten, girls just might flock to you!" The statement made Emesos slightly uncomfortable.

"I hope not. I think I'd rather be with a girl I've known for a while."

"That's interesting to know...Well, is Paolin alright?" Lanita asked

"He's doing fine, but he's under a massive amount of stress, just like the rest of us."

Lanita finished her beer in silence. "Well, I suppose I better go to bed then."

"Right, see you around then."

After bidding Lanita good night, Emesos returned to his tent and fell asleep, happy to have a moment's peace. He relished it while he had the chance.

The soldiers left Heda with reluctance and continued onward toward a goal that once seemed so far away, now so close within their grasp. Two days of travel passed. One more day until they reached the capital. Emesos' heart kept plunging with each passing day.

One less day until he had to talk to his adoptive parents. Ishik and Paolin seemed to be aware of Emesos' stress and did the best they could to cheer him up. But Emesos noticed he wasn't the only one who was under strain.

Paolin's stress of managing the troops, the journey, the prospect of facing King Gonra as a near equal, combined with lack of sleep had made him rather jittery. He jumped at everything and drifted off at random moments. Something had to be done. Emesos and Ishik concocted a plan and decided to put it into action.

Emesos walked up beside Paolin. "Hey, how are you?"

"Fine."

Ishik now walked up beside Paolin. "Fine? You don't look like it to me. Tell you what, you either get some sleep, or we knock you unconscious and make you get some."

"You wouldn't." Paolin said, sounding scandalized. Ishik gave him a look that told him that told him he would. "Fine, I'll get some, but how do you expect me to get sleep when we need to travel?" Emesos smiled.

"Like this." Emesos took one end of the tent cloth Ishik had hidden behind his back and Ishik took the other. They scooped Paolin up, enfolding him in a make-shift hammock.

"Let me down!" Paolin yelled.

"If you don't settle down, I *will* knock you out." Ishik warned him. Paolin grumbled, but did as he was told. Emesos smiled as he and his brother each carried one end of the hammock for the rest of the day's march. At the end of the night, they carefully lowered Paolin to the ground. The young man slept on, oblivious. Emesos and Ishik rolled their sore shoulders and smiled at each other.

"All in a good day's work, right, brother?" Ishik asked with a mischievous grin. Emesos returned the look.

"Certainly, brother." The two of them fell asleep outside, near Paolin, exhausted and pleased with their work.

The three of them woke the next morning, feeling a tingling atmosphere about the camp. They would reach the capital today. They marched at double pace, eager to see the castle come over the horizon.

And sure enough, toward the end of the day, Rei came into sight. The cheer from the men was extremely loud. They rushed toward the city. One of their men actually found a signal horn among the supplies and let out three high notes; a greeting for allies.

After a brief moment, the signaler repeated the call, over and over, until the capital's guards heard and responded similarly. When they reached the main gate, Emesos was beaming. Everyone was cheering. After a long, hard journey, they had survived. They had made it to Rei.

As the main doors opened, Emesos saw a familiar taut face with slate-grey eyes, dressed in in chainmail with a look of shock. "Emesos," he whispered. "Is that you?" The men went silent. Emesos smiled at the figure.

"Hello Erk, good to see you again. I'm back from Rhyth..." Emesos said with a sheepish grin.

"I might have picked up a friend or two along the way, though."

Ryan Wilshusen

Part Six:

Revelations

Ryan Wilshusen

Thirty-Five

"We thought you might have died," Erk said. It had taken two days to get all of the Rhythian soldiers settled in and everybody settled down. Now, Emesos, Ishik, Paolin, and Kiraj were all in King Gonra's study, joined by Erk and Velenry. Gonra was busy at the moment, talking to advisors and trying to figure out where to place all of the Rhythians who had fled in the wake of the War. "When we heard the Wall had fallen, we feared you were dead."

"We came close to being dead," Paolin said. "A little too close." Emesos was grateful that both Erk and Velenry were fluent in Rhythian; it saved quite a bit of time. Emesos had just finished explaining the situation that had driven them to flee to Stryne.

Velenry was still shaking her head. "To go to the werewolves, ally with them, evacuate an entire country, *and* defend a capital...what a crazy situation you four found yourselves in." Emesos was glad that Velenry and Erk had gotten over their initial hesitation to involve Kiraj. They had loosened up a little when Kiraj spoke politely to them.

"So now...we have thousands of werewolves and possibly drakes heading this way?" Erk asked for clarification. Emesos nodded.

Erk sighed. "You have the worst luck of any human I've ever met."

Emesos shook his head. "Actually, I consider myself pretty lucky. I managed to avoid death several times, plus I met a brother I never knew I had, so it wasn't a total loss." Erk smiled and then his face became serious.

"On to business. I'm assuming Rhyth' forces will want to pool with ours to fight off Vrasta?" Emesos nodded. Erk gave a sigh of relief. "Well, that makes things quite a bit easier. Ollou doesn't want to help, and Gyllithia wants to maintain neutrality as far as sending men, but they are willing to provide supplies and places for refugees to go. King Gonra's finishing the agreement now. So...where's this Paolin Hollowen who's in charge?"

Paolin raised his hand. "That would be me." Erk's eyes widened with surprise.

"You...you're in charge of the Rhythian militia? You're Paolin Hollowen?" Paolin produced the document Wiln and he had signed and wrote down his signature on a spare piece of parchment. Sure enough, the signatures matched.

"I am." Paolin said. Erk rubbed his temples with his fingertips.

"Gonra's not going to like this."

"And I don't suppose he'll enjoy me being Protector of the Blade, either," Paolin observed. Erk looked up, his eyes suggesting the panic he felt.

"You're the Protector of the Blade too? Oh, Divine! This is going to make the king *so* happy. We have our Prophet, who found an identical twin brother who leads werewolves and has a Blade, and a twelve-year-old who's in charge of an entire Kingdom's military!"

"He's thirteen," Ishik commented dryly. Erk threw him a withering look. Velenry patted Erk affectionately on the shoulder.

"The king has had Erk working like mad lately," Velenry explained. "And this only makes thing worse."

"If the king has a problem with Paolin, he'll have to take it up with me," Ishik said fiercely.

"The both of us," Emesos added, his voice just as strong. "He's been a commander and inspiration beyond belief to the soldiers of Rhyth. They are completely loyal to him. Paolin is one of the few reasons all four of us are standing in front of you. Without him, I would have died."

Paolin smiled at the both of them. It was nice, having friends on his side.

Erk sighed again. "I need some air," he muttered. He stood and walked out of the study, Velenry following him. Ishik turned to Emesos.

"Poor guy; is he always like that?" Ishik asked. Emesos nodded.

"Yes, all the time."

"I'm sure we'll get along just fine," Paolin said, his voice laden with sarcasm. Silence enveloped the group. After a while, Erk returned, his face pale.

"The king wishes to see Emesos and Paolin alone," he said quietly. Emesos threw a questioning glance at Ishik. Ishik held up a hand.

"Don't worry about Kiraj and I, we'll be fine. Best that you don't keep His Majesty waiting." Emesos nodded. The two of them walked down hallways that Emesos felt like he hadn't seen for centuries. *It's only been a few months...* he thought to himself. *It seems almost impossible that so much has happened in so little time.*

When they reach the doors, they were quickly let inside. Gonra sat on his throne, his face paler than when Emesos had last seen him, and a great deal thinner.

"Emesos," he said. "It is good to see you again." Emesos and Paolin bowed.

"It is good to see you alive, Your Majesty," Emesos said. Gonra now turned his attention toward Paolin.

"And this is who?" the king asked. Paolin bowed slightly.

"I am Paolin Hollowen," he said in Strynic. Color rushed to Gonra's face. Emesos took it as a bad sign.

"You are Paolin Hollowen? The Marshal of the Militia of the Rhythian Army?" Paolin nodded.

"And Protector of the Blade as well, Majesty," he added. Gonra's face flushed more at this. Emesos knew what was coming.

"What was Wiln thinking? Putting a boy in command of his men and as a *Marshal of the Militia*? He must be mad!"

"King Wiln no longer lives, Sire," Emesos said quietly. The king's face remained unchanged.

"I'm sorry to hear that, he was a good lad. But why would he place so much power in someone so immature?"

Paolin's face colored slightly. Emesos came to his defense. "He's not as immature as you think he is, Sire. He led over two thousand men to safety. And he helped defend the capital of Rhyth."

Gonra snorted. "Could it be that the capital fell due to Wiln's lack of judgment? Rhyth had plenty of fine officers in the capital, yet he chose to let this boy have control?"

Paolin now spoke quietly, in a voice Emesos knew was extremely dangerous. "I will not have you speak ill of my king, sir. It is impolite to mock the dead, no matter their errors." Tension was filling the room, Emesos could feel it. Paolin's temper was stretched thin.

Gonra laughed slightly. "I'm fairly certain he doesn't care. Regardless, I will not work with you. If I want to speak of military matters with someone, I will speak to an actual officer with training. Until then, I will not negotiate with Rhyth."

Emesos saw it in Paolin's eyes. The same ferocity that arose when he took on those boys when he returned to Rhyth was rising in him now. He saw Paolin's glow split into two different shapes: One around his body, one in the shape of a werewolf. Paolin raised his head.

"You let pride cloud your judgment," he said with venom. "I was chosen by the late king. If you wish to stand a *slight* chance against Vrasta, I recommend you negotiate."

Gonra shook his head. "I do not listen to over-confident children from foreign Kingdoms."

"*You will listen!*" Paolin shouted, pointing his index finger at the king. "You *will* give Rhyth the respect it deserves!" Gonra acted slightly amused.

"On whose authority?" he challenged. Emesos knew he had to rein the situation in before it got even more out of control. Paolin raised a hand.

A flash; a metallic, other-worldly clang as it pierced the floor. Wiln's Blade was there, stabbing through the throne room floor, Paolin's hand upon it.

Silence filled the throne room. Emesos stood there in shock. Gonra's eyes were full of disbelief. Paolin's face lost all color.

"On a king's authority," Erk answered. "It seems the Blade of Rhyth has chosen."

Thirty-Six

No one said anything for what seemed an eternity. All of their attention was focused on the Blade in Paolin's hand.

"Me?" Paolin finally said weakly. "I'm...it picked me?" He pulled the Blade out of the floor and stared at it, his eyes wide. "Why?"

Gonra tried to form words but seemed unable. All the aggression in the throne room had melted away. Now instead, silence filled the void.

Erk stared at the Blade. Emesos looked at Paolin, trying to read the young man's face. He gripped Paolin's shoulder and felt an explosion of mixed emotions. He winced and jerked his hand back.

Erk was the first one to recover. "May I suggest that Emesos and Paolin be taken to their rooms, and we all think about this overnight?" Hearing no protests, Erk carefully guided Emesos and a shocked Paolin, who was still holding his Blade, to their rooms. Erk put both of them in one room. "I'll be back in a moment with Ishik and Kiraj. Don't move from here." He left.

Paolin sat on his bed, with the Blade across his lap. "This shouldn't be mine," he said quietly. "I don't deserve it. So why do I have it? Why did it pick *me*?" His face was a mix of fury and pain.

"I'm sure it's for a good reason," Emesos reassured him.

"I'm not supposed to have this," Paolin said. "I didn't need it again." Emesos' mind was sent reeling.

"Wait, you've had it before?" Paolin looked up.

"Yes." His answer was laden with misery. "Just once...when...when..." Paolin started weeping; it broke into hacking sobs, then uncontrolled tears.

"I killed them! I killed them!"

Emesos sat down on the bed next to him. "Killed who?" He was careful not to touch him. He didn't want whatever awful feelings Paolin was experiencing to rush into his mind.

"I told Ishik that when I woke up one day, my parents had abandoned me." More sobs came from his shaking body. "I-I lied to him. I killed them! I killed them both; with this!" He slammed a fist on the handle of the Blade in his lap.

Emesos sat next to him, stunned. "Why? How?"

When Paolin had calmed himself sufficiently, he haltingly spoke. "When I was younger, around seven, my parents were a maid and a cook. My father-my father used to...hit me, when he was angry. My mother...she didn't care. And one time, my father hit me, and I wished with all my heart, to just once, to be able to hit back. The Blade appeared in my hand. I threw it at my dad and he..." Paolin shuddered. "It went through him, and my mother behind him. Then it vanished."

"Oh, Paolin..."

"It took me a few moments to realize what I had done. I did the only thing I could think of: run. I ran and ran...away from my parents, away from that place. Hasin found me abandoned and when he heard about my parents' death, he took me in, feeling sorry for me. He didn't know he was sheltering a murderer. Even after all of that, it decides to come back...why...why did it have to come back?!" he cried.

"It came back because it chose you," Emesos said. "It's always chosen you; it just had to wait a little longer before you were ready to take it. It saw you weren't ready when you were younger, so it just waited till it was able to come back to you."

"But I'm not ready... I'm not ready to use this..."

Emesos nodded in understanding. "I wasn't ready to experience the past and present through other people, but I had to. I guess things like this don't wait for you to feel ready. They decide when you're ready."

"Where did you pick up that piece of wisdom?" Paolin asked.

"I made it up to make you feel better."

"But it doesn't feel like a lie..." Paolin said quietly. "Not to me...that means its true..." Paolin sighed. "Thanks Emesos...I guess it means I'm stuck with this thing." He threw a grim look at the Blade in his hands.

"Looks that way," Emesos said with a grin. Underneath all his intelligence, it seemed Paolin was still a regular person. Paolin looked at Emesos with that same look he gave him in Rhyth, so long ago, after the attack on their trip to the wall. Utter trust; it tore at Emesos' heart just like it did back then.

But something still didn't quite make sense in Emesos' mind. *How would Paolin be able to have the Blade back when he was around seven? Hasin would have had it then...* Emesos turned slowly to Paolin. "Why do you think the Blade appeared to you?" he asked.

Paolin spoke, seeming to carefully measure his words. "When it came...it was when King Hasin had yet to name Wiln as a successor to his throne. Hasin said he would let the Blade decide. The Blade vanished and disappeared for two weeks." Paolin took a breath and continued his tale.

"I had it during those two weeks. Then, the Blade appeared in Wiln's grasp and he was chosen as the heir, and I haven't touched the Blade until now." A sudden thought occurred to Paolin.

"Please don't tell Ishik or the others," he pleaded.

"I won't," promised Emesos. Together, the two of them walked out of the room, wandering into the king's study. He found Ishik and Kiraj waiting there. Kiraj was holding a book in his massive claws, looking very confused.

"All these little scribbles mean something? How in the world do humans manage to use these?" Ishik was trying not to laugh. The two of them turned to see Emesos and Paolin enter. Paolin was still clutching the Blade in a vice-like grip, as though he were afraid it would run away.

"Gonra's in a right fit with himself," Ishik said. "You should have heard him insulting himself as he went down the hallway. That king has the most explosive temper I've ever seen." Emesos nodded. Paolin said nothing.

Ishik now looked at Paolin with sympathy. "I know this was a big shock to you. If you need any help, the three of us will be here, won't we?"

"On the honor of the tribes," Kiraj said with a sense of finality.

"Of course," Emesos stated. Ishik smiled at Paolin. Paolin couldn't help but smile back.

"Thanks," Paolin said, fingering the ancient bracelet around his wrist. For a moment Emesos' mind went back to little Orin, his hands grasping the bracelet like it was a priceless treasure.

Erk came walking into the room. "I thought I told you to not move, Emesos...oh...well, I was going to bring Ishik and Kiraj to you...but what's really important is that everyone is here. I had to go and calm King Gonra down. He's beside himself that he let his temper get the best of him. And he asked me to profusely apologize to Paolin in his place, he said the 'shame was too great to face him in person.'"

Paolin shrugged. "He shouldn't worry about it. Of course I accept his apology; I would have thought the exact same thing if it was me." Erk breathed a sigh of relief.

"In fact, am I allowed to invite him to dinner at the Rhythian camp?" Paolin asked. Erk's face brightened.

"Certainly. His Majesty would jump at the chance, I'd think. I'll go ask him now. In the meantime, I suggest that you go to your camp and show them their new king," he said to Emesos. The brothers nodded, and Paolin paled. After being escorted out of the castle, they made their way out of the city and back to camp. Paolin had willed the Blade to vanish before leaving the castle. After a few frustrating attempts, he managed to make it disappear. Ishik and Kiraj had separated from Emesos and Paolin to go start gathering all of the men. Sure enough, in the center of camp, a large crowd had gathered. Paolin was guided to the center of them and the crowd fell silent.

"I have an announcement to make," Paolin said loudly, his voice cracking slightly. He held up his hand and willed the Blade to appear. It flashed into his hand. The crowd gave a large, nearly unified gasp.

"The Blade chose me to wield it. So I guess I'm king now." Paolin said lamely.

The reaction was almost instantaneous. The men sent up a massive roar of approval. Many clapped their hands, a few banged their spears and shields together. Paolin turned to Emesos.

Emesos shook his head in mock disappointment. "You're a king now. Surely you could have given a better speech than that."

Paolin smiled. "Well, let's hope I'll have time to practice."

Thirty-Seven

Emesos had been dreading the moment his parents were mentioned. That moment came when Erk and Paolin returned from the second day of negotiations with Gonra. Now that Paolin had a Blade, Gonra was extremely polite, and seemingly more willing to get to know Paolin. That didn't stop him from shrewdly negotiating terms with the boy. They were in the king's study winding down from a day of complex political talk. Emesos was just back from a day of religious talk with the local Congregation. Ishik had spent the day checking on the Pack and making sure they were all content.

"You think it would be simple," Paolin groaned. "But no, instead we have to talk about every little detail. And Sene's already heading this way..."

Erk nodded to him in sympathy. Then, his face grew grave. "Speaking of which, all civilians should be starting emergency evacuation preparations. You should go see your family while you still have the chance, Emesos. This could be the last time you get an opportunity to see them in a long time."

Emesos' heart plummeted. *I don't want to face them...* he thought. *I don't want to tell them...I don't want to admit...* He shook his head and steeled himself. *I have to do this...I'll regret it if I don't.* "Alright, I think I will...would you like to go too, Ishik?" Ishik gave Emesos a look of surprise.

"You think I'd be welcome?" Ishik asked. Emesos nodded.

"Well, you are my brother, so that would make you family." Emesos was praying desperately that his brother would say yes.

He didn't think he'd be able to handle the reunion alone. Ishik slowly nodded. Emesos felt relief course through him.

"I guess we should then," he said.

The two of them said goodbye to Paolin and Erk and left the castle. Emesos kept getting stopped on the streets by commoners who either wanted to say hello or ask for a blessing.

Each delay to their destination increased the panic in him. The familiar streets let him know he was getting closer...and closer... Emesos was sweating now.

Finally, he was there, in front of his home, where he lived only a few months ago. Those times seemed so far away, like a different past that belonged to someone else.

Emesos drew his hand up to knock and then lowered it. He repeated the motion several times. Suddenly, he felt a hand on his shoulder. It was Ishik.

"I'm here," he said. That's all he needed to say. Emesos knocked once... twice.

The door opened and before him stood his father. His eyes widened. His mouth moved, but no sound came out. He had to grip the doorway for support so his legs didn't give out from under him.

"Emesos..." his father whispered. "Emesos...is that you? Why are there two of you? I must be going mad..." Emesos stepped forward and hugged his surrogate father, his eyes filled with tears.

"You're not mad. I'm here. I'm real."

His father didn't let go for a long time. Finally, they ended their embrace. Con wheeled around. "Merra! Merra! You have to see this!" Footsteps.

"What is it? I'm in the middle of making-" Merra came into view, holding a heavy pot. Her eyes darted to Emesos. The pot hit the floor as Merra slammed into her child, winding him. "Emesos! Emesos, you're back! Oh thank the Divine, we were so worried!"

"Did you say 'Emesos?'?" a familiar voice asked. "He'll be fine, but it'd be nice to hear from..." Hane's sentence drifted off as he spotted his brother; another hug that winded him. Hane's grip was so tight, he nearly suffocated his brother before letting go.

"You're back...you came back...we thought you had died." Hane whispered. Emesos felt a pang of guilt.

"Sorry, I'll explain everything later, but first, I'd like you to meet someone." Ishik stepped into full view. His family's eyes widened. "This is Ishik. He's my twin brother."

As the two brothers crossed the threshold into the house, Emesos realized the dread was still there.

It was time to confront the truth.

Thirty-Eight

"So...now you know what's happened to me," Emesos concluded. Hane shook his head.

"That's incredible...to think all of this happened to you in just a few months. How did you stay sane?"

Emesos smiled and gestured to Ishik. "That would partially be his doing." Ishik smiled, but said nothing. Emesos was used to overcoming the barrier of language with ease, but this was the first time he realized the challenges it represented.

"You're not mad we never told you?" Con asked, concern in his voice. Emesos could tell even without touching him that the question was heavy on his mind.

Emesos stared at his plate. "Part of me wants to scream and shout at you. The other part of me is just happy to see you again. I really don't know what to make of it. Whoever left me with you had their reasons. I'm curious to know who my actual parents are...but at the same time...aren't you my real family members? You raised me. I suppose I'm more curious than I am angry. I'm not even sure if I want to know the answer. But how do twins wind up in separate Kingdoms?"

Ishik gave Emesos a questioning look, so Emesos re-spoke what he said in Rhythian unconsciously. Ishik nodded in agreement.

"I wonder that too; all the time, in fact," he said. "I also wonder what Anazan, Sene, this Altherai person and the Blades have to do with us. They all seem connected, but how?"

"I wonder too. I keep looking for answers and every time I get one, two more questions appear. It's so annoying." Emesos looked at his family and realized that they had no idea what the two of them were saying.

"Sorry," Emesos apologized. "We had a bit of a lapse. Now, how are things here?"

"Not much has changed, actually," Hane said. "Although you vanishing has made quite a few stories appear. We weren't sure what to believe. And when we heard a new Prophet had been declared by the Congregation, we didn't ever think it would be you."

Emesos laughed slightly. "Really? I didn't want to be a Prophet, they made me into one. I don't even see the future, and half the things I see don't make much sense."

"What about you, Ishik?" Merra asked, trying to include him in the conversation. "Were you declared as a sacred hero or something similar in Rhyth?"

Ishik smiled. "Not exactly," he said, using Emesos as a translator. "I actually wasn't too popular in Rhyth, you see. Emesos doesn't know this either, but I'm a Manipulator; even without my Blade." Emesos looked at Ishik.

"Why didn't you tell me?" Emesos asked, his voice showing hurt.

"I couldn't. There were too many Rhythians around." Emesos went back to translating for his brother so he could elaborate. "Here in Stryne, Manipulators aren't liked by the Congregation, but they're under protection of the king's law, so they can't be harmed. In Rhyth, Manipulators can be legally killed." Merra gasped.

"How can the Congregation get away with murder?" Con asked, his tone biting.

289

"The Congregation has quite a bit more power in Rhyth than in Stryne, or at least it did before Vrasta invaded. A bribe here or there and blind eyes would happen at convenient times. It's part of the reason I left the Congregation. I discovered my powers while I was an acolyte, so I had to run away before I was killed. I accidentally killed a poor monk and was exiled from the monastery. From there, Emesos told you what I've told him."

Emesos nodded, beginning to understand. Ishik and his attitude suddenly made more sense. After a few more hours of discussion, laughter and food, Emesos and Ishik had to leave to return to the camp. As they were heading out the door, Hane grabbed Emesos' arm. Emesos turned around.

"Come back again." It left no room for debate. Emesos smiled.

"I'll see you again...I promise." The two brothers walked away; the door closed behind them. When they arrived back at camp, Paolin was there, waiting for them.

"How'd it go?" he asked. The twins just shrugged and went to bed.

The next morning was rough. Nobody was entirely awake. Paolin had to borrow some cold water to get Ishik up. Both of them were awake after Ishik chased the new king of Rhyth clear through the camp with a stick, much to all of the soldiers' laughter. Emesos was awakened by the hilarity.

They arrived back at the castle to finalize the agreement for alliance between Rhyth and Stryne. Paolin was shaking. "Relax," Ishik said. "Everything will go fine." The young man said nothing.

On their way to the throne room, a rolling feeling had planted itself firmly in Emesos' stomach. *Why does this situation feel so familiar?* He thought of the time he walked down the same hallway to be inducted into King Gonra's military, but this feeling was different.

The feeling increased as they got closer. The room flickered and spun between two images, too fast to distinguish. Emesos shook his head to try and clear away the images. It didn't work. In fact, they increased; a faint sound from beside him, then black.

******

Emesos was walking down a hallway and Sene was beside him; his black hair and orange eyes glowing.

I must be Anazan, then, *he thought.*

"I never thought father would be so interested in my project! I guess I have you to thank, for helping me like you promised," Sene said enthusiastically.

The doors opened to reveal a man on a throne. He was large, with silver hair and orange eyes. His expression was serious. "Sene, Anazan...it is good to see you again." His voice was deep.

Is this Altherai? *Emesos wondered.*

Emesos bowed slightly. Sene did the same. "It is good to see you as well, father. You wished to see us?" Sene asked.

"Yes," the man said, "it concerns that project of yours...those Blades. Do you have the prototype with you?" Sene nodded.

"Of course." Sene held out his hand and a Blade flashed into it. It was grey and plain, with brown leather of some kind wrapped around its hilt.

Ishik's Blade...it's a prototype? *Emesos made a mental note to report that. This was the first time they had gotten solid historical events to tie in with the Blade.*

"Good." The man said. "Now...it needs to be destroyed." Sene gave his father a shocked look. Emesos was very confused.

"What? But...it would allow good people to run the Empire! Why...why would you want it destroyed?"

The father sighed. "Son...as much as I admire your dedication, the Blade must be disposed of. No one should have that kind of power."

"But—"

"I grow weary of this conversation. You have heard my decision, now leave my sight."

Sene threw his father a hard look, bowed and stormed out the door. Emesos followed quickly behind him after giving the man on the throne a quick bow.

When Emesos caught up with Sene, he could tell the young man was fuming.

"He wants me to destroy it. I thought the Blade would be the perfect way of choosing the next ruler of the Empire; but no, he doesn't see it that way. And even if I actually wanted to destroy the Blade-"

"You couldn't," Emesos finished for him. Sene gave him a wary look.

"Right...but how did you know that?"

"Intuition," Emesos lied smoothly. "I figured my brother wouldn't want his prize project to be broken so easily." Sene nodded and then shook his head.

"Mark my words," Sene said darkly, "if father doesn't accept the Blade, the Empire will fall." Emesos saw his chance to finally ask the question that had been bothering him for a long time.

"What Empire are you talking about?"

Sene shot him a look of frustration. "Are you alright, Anazan? I'm talking about the Altherain Empire, of course. You need to get your head out of the clouds."

******

"Altherai wasn't a person!" Emesos shouted, shooting up. "It was an empire!" He was in the medical wing of the castle, Ishik, Paolin, and Erk were standing over him.

"Really? An empire?" Paolin said. "I've never heard of one before in any of the history books."

Ishik shook his head. "Sounds a little strange to me. Maybe you should actually explain to us what in the three Hels you're talking about." Emesos quickly explained everything he had witnessed in the experience. When he was done, everyone's face was serious, lost in thought.

"So, Altherai was an empire, most likely an ancient one. So where did it go?" Paolin asked. Erk straightened up.

"Well, Sene said it himself. His father didn't accept the prototype Blade or the Blades made after it, so they went to the people who ruled the Kingdoms instead," Erk guessed.

"You think the Kingdoms and this empire are connected?" Paolin asked Emesos. Emesos nodded.

"They have to be. And Anazan was somebody important to the empire, just like Sene. Now if only I could find out what Vrasta had to do with it, I might have this whole mess half-way solved." Emesos said cheerfully. He jolted in remembrance.

"Oh, the agreement! How did it go, Paolin?" Paolin looked at Erk and they both laughed, hard.

When they were finally able to calm down, Erk elaborated between chuckles. "King Gonra was so worried about you that he and Paolin signed the agreement in five minutes and left to make sure you were taken care of in the medical wing. It had to have been the fastest ceremony in the history of the Kingdoms!"

Emesos went back to camp after being cleared by the medic. The next few days were uneventful for him and Ishik. Paolin was busy giving everybody new orders and assigning posts for people. But then the message came. A horseman came in looking exhausted, clutching a letter in his fist.

"I seek the Prophet Emesos." He declared. Emesos stepped forward and the messenger handed him the letter. "This was found near the wall by a patrolman in front of a guard house. It's addressed to you and it says that you would be able to understand it. The rest is just one line of random marks. We thought it might be Rhythian."

Emesos took the letter and opened it. He recognized it immediately as Ancient. It was only one line.

I'm coming. Prepare for him. Hail Altherai.

Emesos' heart skipped a beat and the temperature seemed to rapidly decrease. He went over to Ishik's tent, only to find his brother wasn't there. He went to where the werewolves made their quarters and found him there, playing chess with Kiraj.

"Checkmate," Kiraj declared. "That is what you say when the king is trapped, correct?" Ishik groaned and put his head in his hands.

"You are the last werewolf I face in chess...*ever.*" He looked over and smiled at Emesos. "Hey, how are you?" His smile fell as he saw Emesos' face. "What's wrong?"

"We have a problem. Vrasta's forces are coming and Sene sent us a warning."

Thirty-Nine

The throne room was silent. Gonra sat there, utterly serious. Paolin had been found and informed quickly. The three of them were before the king, their faces equally somber. "Are you sure it was Sene?" Gonra asked.

Emesos nodded. "Positive. No one else but Sene would be able to write Ancient except maybe Vrasta, and Vrasta would never warn me that my home Kingdom's about to be invaded." The king shook his head.

"Why warn us if he was an enemy?"

Emesos sighed. "I'm not entirely sure if he's an enemy anymore. At least, he doesn't seem to want to harm Ishik or me because we're important to Altherai; but I don't know why or how we're important."

Gonra spoke. "While you try to find those answers, I think we should speed up the evacuation of the citizens, while it's still safe to do so." Paolin nodded in agreement.

"And I'll see if I can use my troops to bolster yours wherever you need it," he said. Gonra summoned his Blade. Paolin did the same. The twin brothers followed suit.

"From this day forth, we four Blade wielders will do whatever it takes, for the sake of the Kingdoms, to stop Vrasta," Gonra declared.

It was a simple promise that would be hard to keep.

The next five days went by in a flurry of activity. Troops and messengers were everywhere. Citizens were gathering up their things and evacuating. Emesos and Ishik were doing everything they could to help. Paolin was busy assigning the Rhythian troops into squads and platoons. Kiraj and the other werewolves kept their noses and ears directed north and west, searching for any sign of invaders. Long distance werewolf patrol quickly became commonplace.

Soon, it came time for Emesos' family to leave. Merra was in tears. Con was close to it.

"We'll miss you..." Merra said, in between sobs. Emesos finished hugging her. He gave his dad a brief hug. Con didn't say anything. Then, Hane gave him a hug and let go, smiling.

"You better find us when this is all over, ya hear?" Hane said, wiping his eyes. Emesos nodded, tears in his eyes as well.

"I will." Emesos grabbed Ishik's shoulder. "We both will." His family got in a cart and was soon out of sight, waving as they disappeared.

"Now you have to live," Ishik commented. "They're a family I want to go back to, too. And since you dragged me in on your promise..." Ishik tousled his brother's hair, "you don't have a choice." In spite of everything that had happened...and everything that was to come...

The two of them laughed.

Two more days passed. Emesos was busy helping a civilian family load the last of their flour on another cart when the messenger came and got him.

"Prophet, you have been ordered to report to the throne room of the Strynic castle at once by His Majesty King Gonra." Emesos said his goodbyes to the family he was helping and quickly walked to the castle. He was rushed in and almost forced to sprint to the throne room.

Everyone was there. Velenry and Erk stood before beside the king, their expressions grave. Paolin and Ishik's faces were equally grim. Gonra sat there with another letter in his hand.

This one was splattered with a brown, dried substance. "Vrasta is at the border," he said heavily. "The War has now officially just reached Stryne and almost a fourth of our force there is already dead...I can't help but feel this might be the end of the Kingdoms."

Paolin let out a chilling laugh. "You think this will be the end of our problems? Anazan...Sene...Vrasta...Altherai... this War, and everything in between them are all connected. The fighting isn't the end of our problems...it's just the beginning."

Emesos looked out a window that led to the north where, far away, soldiers were fighting for their lives. He couldn't help but agree.

This fight isn't over and neither is this damn mystery of the past. After that his mind went blank for a moment and then one thought settled on his brain with the weight of Manipulated gravity.

We have to find an answer to Vrasta now, *before the Kingdoms give out.* Emesos looked at Paolin and Ishik. The three of them nodded in unison.

The parts they had to play in the War weren't over.

Not even close.

Ryan Wilshusen

ABOUT THE AUTHOR

Ryan is a high school senior who lives in Springfield, Virginia. When he is not busy concocting new plot lines for book projects, he can be found cheering on his friends on the Lancers baseball team; annoying his favorite chocolate Labrador, Jessie; or raiding leftover pizza from the downstairs refrigerator. He is currently working on the sequel to *Darkest Siege* while plotting his escape to college.

www.ingramcontent.com/pod-product-compliance
Lightning Source LLC
Chambersburg PA
CBHW020725210626
46807CB00016B/90